Cozy Girl Fall

www.penguin.co.uk

Cozy Girl Fall

Magnolia Springs Series, Book 1

WILLOW HURST

PENGUIN BOOKS

TRANSWORLD PUBLISHERS

UK | USA | Canada | Ireland | Australia
India | New Zealand | South Africa

Transworld is part of the Penguin Random House group of companies whose addresses can be found at global.penguinrandomhouse.com.

Penguin Random House UK, One Embassy Gardens,
8 Viaduct Gardens, London SW11 7BW

penguin.co.uk

First published in Great Britain in 2025 by Penguin Books
an imprint of Transworld Publishers

001

Copyright © Willow Hurst 2025

The moral right of the author has been asserted

This book is a work of fiction and, except in the case of historical fact, any resemblance to actual persons, living or dead, is purely coincidental.

Every effort has been made to obtain the necessary permissions with reference to copyright material, both illustrative and quoted. We apologize for any omissions in this respect and will be pleased to make the appropriate acknowledgements in any future edition.

As of the time of initial publication, the URLs displayed in this book link or refer to existing websites on the internet. Transworld Publishers is not responsible for, and should not be deemed to endorse or recommend, any website other than its own or any content available on the internet (including without limitation at any website, blog page, information page) that is not created by Transworld Publishers.

No part of this book may be used or reproduced in any manner for the purpose of training artificial intelligence technologies or systems. In accordance with Article 4(3) of the DSM Directive 2019/790, Penguin Random House expressly reserves this work from the text and data mining exception.

Typeset in 11.25/15.25pt Sabon by Six Red Marbles UK, Thetford, Norfolk
Printed and bound in Great Britain by Clays Ltd, Elcograf S.p.A.

The authorized representative in the EEA is Penguin Random House Ireland,
Morrison Chambers, 32 Nassau Street, Dublin D02 YH68.

A CIP catalogue record for this book is available from the British Library

ISBN
9781804997956

Penguin Random House is committed to a sustainable future for our business, our readers and our planet. This book is made from Forest Stewardship Council® certified paper.

Playlist

Two Ghosts
Harry Styles

invisible string
Taylor Swift

About You
The 1975

Fool
Frankie Cosmos

Would That I
Hozier

we fell in love in october
girl in red

Sweet
Cigarettes After Sex

All Too Well (10 Minute Version)
Taylor Swift

Apple Pie
Lizzy McAlpine

Willow
Taylor Swift

Spooky
Dusty Springfield

Last Request
Paolo Nutini

Till It Happens To You
Corinne Bailey Rae

golden hour
JVKE

Kiss Me
Sixpence None The Richer

To anyone who's ever needed a second chance

1

It had never occurred to Penny Larkin that there might be something more embarrassing than having to return to her hometown after crashing and burning at her dream job in the city. And yet, here she was, in said hometown, being set up on a blind date by her mother.

When Penny had shown up on her parents' doorstep out of the blue less than forty-eight hours earlier, her meagre belongings packed into a singular suitcase, her mom had just smiled and asked if Penny wanted breakfast. Clearly, her mom had been more concerned than she'd let on if *this* was her solution to Penny's problems.

Being the good daughter that she was, Penny had agreed to drive into town that morning to take care of a meeting with a vendor her mom had said was giving her trouble negotiating prices.

Point one to Angie Larkin, because the man waiting in Coffee Affair was not, in fact, a vendor playing hardball. Of course, Penny didn't immediately realize this.

Jake Hopman was two years her senior, with a warm

smile and a twinkle in his eye that had spelled trouble when he'd been seventeen and captain of the football team, and hadn't dimmed one bit in the twelve years since Penny had last seen him. There wasn't a girl at Magnolia High who hadn't known his name. Being back in Magnolia Springs and seeing Jake made her feel like she was in some kind of strange time warp, because in no world would fifteen-year-old Penny have been sitting across from Jake in the town coffee shop—though that was mostly because she'd only ever had eyes for one guy in high school.

Maybe if her mom had told her this 'meeting' was a date, Penny might have been a little less . . . aggressive.

Instead, she'd stormed into the coffee shop, thumped a wad of folders on the table so hard it made the surface shake, and leant on the tabletop as she stared Hopman down.

"Jake," she said, trying for a cool, unaffected tone even as her brain struggled to wrap itself around the idea that she was standing in front of *the* Jake Hopman. She'd expected some hostility, maybe some hardball, based on what her mom had told her, so she was surprised when he stood and awkwardly wrapped an arm around her shoulders before kissing her on the cheek.

That had been the first clue that something was amiss.

Instead of seeing the move for the warning sign that it was, Penny shrugged it off and assumed Jake was just friendly. Maybe he was trying to soften her up so she'd go easy on him.

Penny narrowed her eyes but sat down in the hard metal chair Jake pulled out for her. The coffee shop was busy, absent-minded chatter in the air that put her at ease even as she speared Jake with her best *don't mess with me* look which she'd perfected while working in San Francisco.

"It's great to see you again, Penny," he said and the corner of her mouth curled, smug that he'd broken their silence first.

"The pleasure is all yours," she said and he frowned slightly, blinking his doe eyes slowly. A tray of coffee slid onto their table and Jake smiled at the barista, thanking her, before he gestured to the spare mug on the tray.

"I wasn't sure what you'd like, so I just grabbed a latte. I hope that's OK. It's just so busy in here with the lunch crowd, so I didn't want you to have to wait—"

Jake Hopman was rambling. That was odd. Not for the first time since returning to Magnolia Springs, Penny found herself wondering if the past week had been a bad dream, that she would wake up at any second still in her bed in the city, still employed in the restaurant where she'd worked her way up the ranks . . .

Hopman was waiting for a response to whatever he'd been saying while she was lost in her own thoughts, an earnest smile on his (admittedly very handsome) face. Penny sighed, reaching for the mug of coffee and taking a sip. It wasn't as sweet as she'd have liked it, but it would do.

"Thanks for the coffee," she said eventually and Jake looked relieved. "Now, tell me, do you *like* preying on the elderly?"

Hopman, mid-sip, spluttered, choking on his coffee, and the man at the table behind them turned to thump Jake on the back. "W-What?"

"You can't just raise your prices by fifty per cent and expect us not to look into it," she insisted and Jake seemed lost for words as he tugged at the sleeve of his red sweater. Penny leant in across the table, fixing him with a glare. "I'm not going to let you take advantage of my parents."

Jake leant back until he was half-leaning out of his seat. "Penny, I think there's been a mistake—"

"No," she said sharply and flipped open her folder before spinning it around for him to see. Jake jumped at the speed of Penny's movements, one large shoulder knocking into the passing barista and her full tray of coffee. Penny watched with wide eyes as the whole thing tumbled toward her in slow motion.

Luckily for the shop, none of it hit the floor.

Unluckily for Penny, it gushed over her white jeans in a hot flood that made her curse. Loudly.

"Oh shit, I'm so sorry. I just didn't expect—with the folders—" Jake said, visibly flustered.

Around them, the coffee shop had gone completely silent as every head turned toward their table, watching the disaster that was unfolding. Penny was desperately trying to keep her cool, taking deep, steadying breaths, determined not to make a scene so soon after returning to town. Meanwhile, Jake was frantically grabbing napkins from the table beside them and throwing them in her direction in lieu of patting her crotch. Unfortunately, it only succeeded in attaching wet napkins to the spreading disaster of her jeans.

"Worst date ever, I guess. I'm sorry, Penny."

Date.

Oh God.

She was going to kill her mother.

At the mention of the D-word, she'd given up on maintaining any integrity and instead hobbled toward the door with the eyes of the entire cafe heavy on her retreating back. She hadn't even bothered to pick up the folder full of research she'd put together to show what the typical price of apple crates was versus the quote her mom had received. She'd clearly been gone for too long if she'd forgotten just how much her mother loved to meddle.

"Excuse me," Penny muttered as she pushed past a startled barista and made a beeline for the paint-faded door. "Had to be wearing white." She groaned as the door jingled cheerfully behind her and she emerged onto the sidewalk. But her white jeans were cute when she paired them with her favorite mossy green sweater and knock-off Uggs, perfect for the hint of fall in the early September air. Admittedly, they were less cute now that a brown stain covered her crotch and ran half-way down her thighs.

She'd hoped she might have hit her embarrassment quota for the day but, in true small-town style, of course she would run into one of the last people she'd want to see while covered in coffee and visibly flustered. She couldn't say she'd have been particularly pleased to run into *anyone* she knew in that moment, but Shelby Patterson was definitely one of the worst. They'd gone to high school together, and even though it had been ten years since they'd last seen each other, Penny *really* didn't want to run into the popular girl from school looking anything but her best—and this *definitely* wasn't Penny's best.

The familiar blonde hair had appeared ahead of Penny as Shelby walked out of the local movie theater, head down as she focused on whatever was on her phone.

Gotta love small towns, Penny thought to herself as her eyes darted left and right, checking for anyone else she knew. If she was quick and careful, she might just be able to avoid having to actually speak to—

"Penny Larkin?" Shelby's high-pitched drawl was unmistakable across the small square, and Penny sent a stream of curses skyward as she turned, plastering a smile onto her face. "Gosh, it really is you. What's it been? Ten years? Figured you'd forgotten where our small town was at this point."

"Shelby, hi! How are you?" Penny tried her hardest to sound sincere but there was no hiding the grimace behind her words.

"I'm fine . . . Better than you, by the looks of things,"

Shelby responded with the hint of a smirk pulling at the corner of her lips as her eyes traveled down to the enormous coffee stain covering both of Penny's thighs.

"Yep, well, you know me, clumsy as ever!" Penny garbled her words, desperate to escape to the safety of her car. "Anyway, sorry, Shelby, I've gotta run but it was *so* good seeing you."

"Mhmm," Shelby barely responded, eyes already returning to her phone as she lost interest in torturing Penny any further.

What a bitch, Penny thought to herself as she hurried away, trying not to think about how uncomfortably cold her damp legs were becoming in the fall breeze. How had Shelby even recognized Penny anyway? They'd moved in *very* different circles in high school and several long years had passed since then. Penny pushed the thoughts from her mind, focusing instead on avoiding any other awkward run-ins with ghosts from her past.

Her luck held and by the time Penny reached her trusty old Volkswagen Beetle, parked just opposite the old church, her racing heart had begun to find its normal rhythm. Luckily, she was pretty sure she had a spare grocery bag in the backseat of her Volkswagon Beetle that she could sit on to try and protect her fabric upholstery.

She knew better than most how difficult it could be to stay on your toes amid all the crap life threw at you, but she couldn't quite believe how awful this first trip into town had been. It was just a relief that she'd made it through this latest shit show without any critical casualties.

Well, mostly, she thought, glancing balefully down at the stained white jeans as she turned the ignition in her car. She was pretty sure it was going to take multiple washes to rescue those.

The roads were largely clear, what with it being the middle of the day. Most of Magnolia Springs' residents were at school, work, or eating lunch around this time. Though a handful of retired older ladies could usually be found in the park doing tai chi on most weekday lunchtimes and, sure enough, she drove past them stretching under the shade of the magnolia trees on her way out of the old town, toward the bridge that would take her out to the sticks.

Also known as her parents' place, along with the adjacent apple orchard they ran.

The only other thing that was just as far out of town were the stables across the way from the orchard which old man Colton had owned since she was little. When she was a kid, she'd often strolled across the field and fed the horses any apples they'd picked that were a little too bruised to sell. During her childhood, fall was always filled with the scent of sweet apples, grass and horses, and the occasional vanilla milkshake at Cathy's Diner in town, which had been like a second home when she was a teenager.

It was funny how quickly time passed.

The trees outside of the window were familiar as

she drove by, the leaves still largely green even as a few edged toward turning yellow. San Francisco was an altogether different kind of beast to the small town she'd grown up in; she'd always felt an edge of unfamiliarity to the city, even after she'd lived there for ten years. In comparison, she hadn't realized just how much of Magnolia Springs was ingrained on her heart and memories until she was driving past old haunts, able to recognize familiar turnings by the shape of tree branches alone as they flanked either side of the bridge up ahead.

In truth, she hadn't expected that returning to Magnolia Springs would feel quite so nostalgic. Familiar, but not. Small and subtle changes made the town feel slightly off-kilter, like looking in the mirror the morning after you dye your hair and being slightly surprised by what you find—same, but different.

Penny could probably categorize herself that way too.

She knew she'd changed in the ten years she'd been gone, but being back here . . . it was hard not to fall into familiar patterns. Waking up early for a cup of coffee with her dad, taking extra-long showers now she didn't have to worry about her water bill, suddenly wanting to rewatch old TV shows that she'd been obsessed with as a kid but had hardly thought about since then (*Gilmore Girls* was, unsurprisingly, top of the list at this time of year). Clearly her mom was having the same problem, given that she was already sniffing around Penny's love life.

The car jolted as she made her way up and onto the bridge over the river, the space only big enough for one vehicle at a time. A groan from her car made her wince, the suspension having forgotten the country roads around here after its time in the city. The sound unexpectedly shoved her into a not-so-fond memory of her first driving lesson once she'd got her permit. It had been late summer; the heat was starting to ease off in favor of the cool evenings that marked the approach of fall, so they'd had the windows rolled down. The sound of the water beneath the bridge had been soothing. So soothing, she must have relaxed a little too much. She'd nearly driven off the bridge after applying the gas a little too heavily. The car had lurched forward, her instructor had shrieked and that had made Penny shriek too until they crossed the small bridge and came off the other side, still screaming.

Now, the drive was so familiar it felt like she was on autopilot, like at any moment she'd be turning into her high-school best friend Tasha's drive to go to the movies or out to the springs at the top of town. Lost in the memory, the rest of the drive back to the orchard passed quickly until she was turning into the narrow dirt lane that led to her parents' cottage and parking on the pebbles by the side door.

"That was fast," her mom called out of the kitchen window as Penny slammed the car door closed. "Did you get what—" Her eyes widened and suds flew through the air, splattering against the window as her hands flew up to cover her mouth. She choked on the soapy water as she took in the state of Penny's pants. "What happened to you?"

Penny raised one eyebrow as she ducked under the low-hanging frame and pushed the door closed behind her. Angie Larkin looked a great deal like her daughter, their hair the same shade of chocolate brown, and the heart shape of their faces matching one another. But where her mom's eyes were brown, Penny's were a green-gray that changed depending on the light.

Water dripped from her mom's hands, a puddle quickly forming on the wooden floor as suds continued to slip down the pane of glass that overlooked the garden and makeshift carport.

"I wore white and God laughed," she muttered and her mom clucked sympathetically as she reached for a cloth to dry her hands and mop up the mess. "And *we* need to have words."

"Oh dear, well, go ahead and get changed, honey. Then I want to hear all about your date with Jake."

Penny bit back her groan and instead nudged off her Uggs before heading for the stairs to her left. The creak under her feet was as familiar to her as the freckle on the back of her hand and she didn't even wobble when she neared the top and the second-to-last step bent and gave under her foot—the warped wood had been that way ever since she could remember.

The route to her old room was the same, but the contents had changed a lot since she'd left town at eighteen without looking back. It was the second, and smaller, of the two bedrooms in the cottage and her parents had redecorated it about five years ago. Instead of the hot-pink walls and jewel-toned drapes she'd favored as a teen, the room was now bright and airy. Her mom had called it *modern farmhouse,* whatever that meant.

But it was refreshing and she was glad to have a break from the constant déjà vu being in town gave her.

She peeled off her ruined jeans and sighed as she crumpled them into a ball. They would probably have to be trashed, which was seriously annoying because they didn't even make this style any more. And even if they did, she couldn't afford to splurge on them. Not having a job was irritating that way. She had some savings, but she couldn't justify spending money on jeans when she was back living with her parents again.

After a quick shower and a change into some comfier clothes, Penny knew she couldn't avoid her mother any longer. Not if she wanted to maintain a semblance of privacy anyway, because her mom could and would come charging into Penny's bedroom at any given moment that the fancy took her. Plus, they needed to talk about the surprise blind date she had conned Penny into going on.

2

"So what did you think of Jake?"

Penny choked on her tea and her dad thumped her on the back in between turning the pages of his newspaper. "Well, mostly I thought that I was meant to be taking a very important business meeting and that surely my mother would have told me if she was trying to fix me up with someone."

Her mom turned, hands on her hips above her frilly-edged apron, her hair starting to curl around her temples from the heat of the stove.

"Then I was mostly thinking that I wouldn't be able to replace the jeans that were a casualty of my mother's meddling."

A quiet chuckle emerged from behind the paper and Angie Larkin speared her husband with an equally sharp look as the one she'd just leveled on her daughter.

"Jake is such a nice boy," she mused, as if Penny had said nothing at all. "You could do a lot worse, honey."

Penny rolled her eyes and opted not to respond. If she gave her mom an inch, she'd take a mile. Instead, she placed a palm into the center of her dad's paper and pressed lightly so he lowered it. "Did you know about her scheming?"

Philip Larkin was a kind man, but he was not a strong-willed man. At least, not when the whims of his wife were involved.

His green eyes, a reflection of Penny's own, crinkled at the corners as he gulped his own steaming-hot tea and Penny couldn't help the twitch of her lips at the sight of his large hands cradling the delicate teacup. "I plead the fifth."

"Of course you do." She snorted, her stomach grumbling when she forcefully inhaled a large whiff of the spiced apples her mom was prodding on the stove. Her mom may have her flaws, but there wasn't much Penny couldn't forgive in exchange for a slice or two of her mom's famed apple pie—freshly made with apples from their orchard.

It was nice being back in her parents' cottage; it felt more comforting than nostalgic, unlike the rest of the town. Maybe that was because it had looked pretty much the same for her whole life ... barring the fiery drape incident of '05 that had prompted a swap to blinds in the kitchen windows.

Her parents were the one constant in her life, like rocks the waves of life parted around, and their cottage felt the same, too. Like a place out of time. The floor was the same aged wood it had always been, though the ornately patterned mint-and-pink rug that sat in the middle of the kitchen floor was new, as was the matching rug in gray that sat under the large coffee table in the living room. Sunlight streamed in through the open blinds, touching the cream and wooden cabinets and countertops. The beams of light caught in the crystals of the suncatcher that hung from the open shelves near the fridge, sending a pastel rainbow over the white walls and wooden ceiling beams. Her dad had actually built and fitted all of the cabinets himself before Penny had even been born. In fact, he'd done most of the decorating in the cottage—under her mom's strict direction and oversight, of course.

But, as much as Penny might wish it, her parents weren't invincible. In fact, part of the reason she'd felt a little better about coming back to Magnolia Springs was that she could help with the apple boom that this time of year presented. Her parents couldn't manage it by themselves any more, and they couldn't afford to hire more help than they already had, so Penny had come to the rescue.

Well, that was how she preferred to think about it anyway.

The alternative was admitting that she'd crashed and burned at her job in the city after finally snapping and screaming at her pig of a boss, which had left her no choice but to come running back to mommy with her tail tucked between her legs.

Oh yeah, Penny to the rescue, she thought, eyes twitching as she fought the urge to roll them. It was one of her mom's biggest pet peeves and if she caught

Penny doing it there'd be no peace at the kitchen table. And Penny *really* wanted some of the pie her mom was making.

Besides, with everything that had happened to her recently, she *deserved* pie. She'd been trying hard to focus on the positives, to keep busy helping her parents, since she'd been back in her hometown, but whenever she sat still for longer than a minute the doubts came creeping in. Being back here would mean being judged by people she'd known for most of her life, and she couldn't help but feel like they would be disappointed. Or worse, pitying, that she'd failed in the city and had to come back to the place she'd been so desperate to leave. If she was being realistic, she knew that people probably weren't thinking about her one way or the other. Still, though, she couldn't help feeling like returning to Magnolia Springs was a massive step backwards, especially after she'd worked so hard to leave and pursue her dreams in San Francisco.

"You ready for your big day tomorrow?" Philip folded his paper and grinned at her, his smile making him look ten years younger than his graying hair would have you believe. "Been a while since we had you out there pickin'. Pretty sure the last time you were at the orchard you dragged along that boyfriend of yours. It'll be just like old times."

She laughed. It was true, the last time she'd been out on the orchard she'd been seventeen and her biggest problem had been worrying whether her high-school boyfriend, Ethan Blake, was going to ask her to prom. *Spoiler alert: he did.*

At the same time, though, Penny couldn't help a little pang of guilt at the reminder that she'd left her parents on their own for so long to run everything. Even though there'd been no reproach in her dad's words and her parents had never complained, she felt shitty about it nonetheless.

"I'm excited for it," she said and her dad nodded while Angie stirred the apples and added in cinnamon and other spices. "It'll be good to be out in the fresh air, using my muscles. Like you say, it'll be just like old times."

"You'll be a pro in no time," he said, standing from the table and pressing a hand to her shoulder as he passed her chair on his way to the fridge. "By next year's season, it'll be like you never left." With his back to her, he didn't see how her face dropped.

She was happy to help out, but she'd promised herself when she came back to Magnolia Springs that it was *temporary*. She'd help her parents during their busy period and figure out what she wanted to do with the rest of her life after that. One thing was certain—staying in Magnolia Springs wasn't on the cards. Not if she wanted to follow her dreams of being a chef for a big restaurant in the city. Although, technically she had done that already. It just hadn't worked out like she'd imagined—and she definitely hadn't predicted she'd be back sleeping in her childhood bedroom, even if it did look different now.

"If you start flagging out there tomorrow, you can always ask Ethan—"

Penny shushed her dad. "That definitely won't be happening." With any luck, she wouldn't bump into Ethan at all while she was home for the next few months. Especially after the way she'd left things—she couldn't imagine he'd be happy to see her. Better to steer clear of him as much as possible.

"Honey, quick, taste this for me." Angie didn't wait for an answer, just shoved a wooden spoon at Penny until she was forced to open her mouth or end up with apple-pie filling all over her face.

It was tart and tangy, with the right balance of sweetness that made her mouth water. It was the flavor of her childhood and fall, of warm summer evenings spent in the garden with her parents or her friends. It tasted like her first kiss with Ethan Blake and hope and regret all wrapped up in a complicated swirl of sticky sauce.

"It's perfect," she said, voice tight with emotion, and her mom beamed.

"Good enough to outsell Ellen's lemon loaf at the Halloween Orchard Fest?"

Penny smiled to herself at the thought of the festival. She'd missed a lot of the small-town events that ran every year in Magnolia Springs, particularly because there was no real equivalent in the city. The Halloween Orchard Fest was Penny's favorite, had been since her parents started it up when she was seven and she'd discovered the joy of candied apples, but the bonfire in mid-October and the Christmas markets were a close second and third in her book. There was just something about being out in the cold evening air with a warm drink in hand, surrounded by people she knew, that made her feel at ease. The pace of the city didn't leave much room for languid evenings sipping cider by the bonfire.

"Your apple pie eats Ellen's lemon loaf for breakfast," she reassured her mom and then frowned. *Try saying that three times fast.* "Or doesn't eat it for breakfast? I don't know. Basically, Ellen's lemon loaf sucks."

Angie waved Penny off, a pleased gleam in her eye even as she said, "Oh, honey, let's not be cruel. Ellen tries her best, I'm sure."

Only Angie Larkin could make a compliment sound like the opposite.

Fresh cup of tea in hand, Philip sat back down and glanced between the two of them before shaking his head. "I had no idea the competition was so intense. I'd have thought it would be a piece of cake. Get it? Piece of cake?"

Penny shared a look with her mom before forcing out a weak laugh. She'd been home for just over forty-eight hours and the dad jokes had already started.

Though, if she was being honest, she'd missed hearing them when she'd been living on her own in San Fran. Not that she'd ever tell her dad that.

"Oh! You'll never guess who I ran into at the grocery store." When Penny waited in silence her mom sighed before continuing, "Tasha! You remember Tasha, don't you, Phil? Such a nice girl. You should call her. Let her know you're back."

Penny hid her grimace behind a gulp of her tea and bit her tongue so she wouldn't yell out *I'm not back! This is temporary*.

Instead, she nodded vaguely and tried to remember the last time she'd seen Tasha. Ethan wasn't the only one she'd left behind when she'd rushed out of Magnolia Springs like her hair was on fire. Tasha had been a good friend and they'd been virtually inseparable during high school; Penny had often found herself thinking about her former best friend and what she might have made of her life while Penny had been gone. But, much like Ethan, she wasn't sure Tasha would want to see her after all this time. It was one of the biggest regrets she had, leaving the way she did ten years ago, but there wasn't anything she could do about it now. Besides, the last thing she wanted was to reopen old wounds.

Now, Penny wasn't sure she even had Tasha's number. Or what she'd say even if she could call. Would Tasha want to talk to her? Ten years was a long time to go between phone calls and, where girlfriends were involved, Penny was out of practice. Sure, she'd had work friends that she sometimes went for drinks or food with, but with the way she'd left things in the city she couldn't see any of them picking up her calls either. It seemed like she had a gift for poor departures. She could only hope that when it came to leaving Magnolia Springs this time around, she would do it right.

Maybe it was the distance she'd now gained after leaving San Fran, but, in retrospect, she couldn't help thinking the life she'd built for herself sounded awfully lonely, with work eating up all her time and leaving little room for friends. At the very least, if there was one thing you could count on in Magnolia Springs, it was that you were never alone—whether you wanted to be or not.

3

"Gloves," Mrs. Ashley reprimanded as Penny walked past and dipped to grab a bendy plastic bucket.

She winced but pulled the gloves out of her jeans pocket and waved them at the older lady. "Got them." Though it wasn't Penny's first time helping with the harvest, it seemed like old Mrs. Ashley had somehow forgotten this, if the way she kept berating Penny was anything to go by. But Penny hadn't forgotten everything about apple picking. For one thing, she'd remembered to wear layers, knowing she'd quickly warm up while picking. So she'd opted for her stretchiest jeans, a tank top, knitted sweater, and a coat as a top layer. By the time the afternoon rolled around it would likely be a little warmer too, and this way she could strip as needed and not worry about that horribly cold but sweaty feeling she'd get if she went the whole day in just her sweater.

Mrs. Ashley nodded stiffly, brown eyes narrowing. "You'll be thanking me for the reminder when you get caught on a particularly stubborn branch."

Penny smiled and hurried away before the other woman could say anything more. It had been this way ever since Penny had arrived at the orchard for her first shift that morning. Sure, she hadn't done this in a few years now, but it was apple picking—not rocket science. Plus, the longer she stood in the orchard, the more it all came flooding back to her.

The orchard was a sea of browns, greens, and orange leaves against the pale sky. She'd arrived earlier than her parents, wanting to make the most of the dry weather. Apple picking in the rain was not her idea of a good time, so the more she could do now the better. Her parents would be in later, working in the shop that was located at the very front of the orchard in a small barn-like building. A large gate sat behind and to the left of the shop, supposedly for keeping out trespassers but Penny wasn't sure she'd ever seen it closed. Her parents had always said that if someone was desperate enough for food that they came to the orchard then they'd rather they have the fruit than go hungry. It was a lesson Penny had taken with her to the city too, inspiring her to sometimes volunteer as a cook at a homeless shelter downtown. It was probably the only thing about San Francisco that she missed.

Gloves firmly in place and the wind trying to blow her hair in all directions, Penny walked through the central row that split the orchard into two sides for the different types of apples they grew. Penny had often thought that the long walkway between the trees would make a fantastic wedding aisle, but her parents felt it was too much work to open the orchard up as that kind of venue. Now, of course, Penny realized that they most likely didn't have the time to take anything else on.

Guilt stabbed at her with the thought. If she'd stuck around after she'd graduated then maybe they could have had more chances to experiment and push the business.

I'm here now.

They'd been assigned different corners of the orchard to work and her hopes of some peace and quiet were short lived when Mrs. Ashley walked to the far end of Penny's segment, the purple of her bodywarmer catching Penny's eye.

"Thought I'd stay close in case you needed help on your first day," she said and Penny wasn't sure if her grimace could pass for a smile.

"Oh, that's very kind but not necessary. It's not really my first day."

Mrs. Ashley's brows drew together. "It's not?"

Who did she think Penny was?

"Mrs. Ashley, you do realize I'm Penny? Phil and Angie's Penny?"

The plastic bucket in Mrs. Ashley's arms hit the ground as she gaped and an expletive fell from her mouth, making Penny's eyes widen. "I didn't realize! Little Penny Larkin, all grown up. I thought you were away in the city?"

San Fran was the last thing she wanted to talk about, but she forced a smile anyway, relieved that

Mrs. Ashley wasn't being rude on purpose. To be fair, despite the fact that she'd known Mrs. Ashley for half her life and had grown up spending a lot of time in her husband's now-closed candy shop, it had been a long time since they'd seen each other. "Oh, well, I just wanted to help Mom and Dad out in the busy season."

The smile that the other woman gave Penny was a little tight, and Penny wondered if Mrs. Ashley was judging her long absence and clear desire to get away as soon as she could. No doubt the rest of the town would be judging her for it soon enough. If they hadn't known she was back yet, they would by the end of the day. The devil worked hard, but the small-town gossip mill worked harder.

"Well, I'll leave this quarter in your capable hands."

Penny nodded, tugging awkwardly at her gloves as Mrs. Ashley retreated between the trees. One thing she'd loved about apple picking as a kid was the peace and quiet, the simplicity of the task keeping her mind calm as her thoughts roamed aimlessly.

It was chilly that morning, a sweet freshness in the air that was soothing. The grass was dewy and slippery beneath her boots and her cheeks stung from the cold, but the thick black gloves she'd borrowed from her mom kept her fingers warm and free from scratches.

She worked on the bottom branches first, inspecting the pink apples and discarding any that had been munched on by caterpillars and other bugs, or that had ripened too quickly and were now a little mushy on one side. Most of them were in good condition though and she'd been out there an hour before she knew it, just clearing the lower-hanging branches.

She had a stepping stool for the higher branches, though thankfully they drooped lower than usual with the weight of their fruit, so she didn't have to climb to the top step that often. After about another half an hour, she pulled off her coat, and after two she shucked off her sweater too.

The bright light made the apples gleam, their glossy red skin more than a little tempting as Penny's stomach rumbled the longer she worked.

The sun peeked through the leaves as she navigated the branches, arms aching as she reached above her head for the last apples on the right hand side of the tree, and nearly took a branch to the face when it pinged back at her after she pulled free a particularly stubborn apple.

Her wet soles squeaked on the metal of the ladder as she descended, placing her apple haul into the larger bucket she'd left on the ground half-full. The time on her phone told her it was nearly twelve, so she figured this was as good a point as any to stop and take a break.

Leaving the stool and bucket where it was so she could find where she'd left off, Penny peeled off her gloves, freeing her sweaty hands as she stretched her fingers gingerly. She'd forgotten how much apple picking made her ache—it hadn't even been a full day and she was already feeling the burn in her arms and shoulders. It made sense that it was harder on her now than when she'd been a kid, filled with boundless energy. But now there was only one thing that was going to help her power through to the end of her shift.

"Coffee," she muttered, following the straight path that led out of the rows of trees toward the small store where her mom stocked jams, pies, and apples that could be bought by the bagful. Penny's green bug waited exactly where she'd left her in front of the small building, now accompanied by a truck so large that its wheel came up to her hip.

Somebody's overcompensating. She smirked, climbing into her car and pulling out of the orchard parking lot with the ease that came with habit.

The roads were quiet, much like usual, and it surprised her how quickly she was able to fall back into the routine of *usual* when it came to being back in her hometown versus the city. She'd thought it might irritate her, that even having left Magnolia Springs her roots there had been so firmly embedded that she could slip back into life in her hometown like there'd been no interruption. But in reality she felt relieved. Like at least here she belonged, that a small space had been carved out of the town just for her and had waited patiently for her to come back. Whereas San Fran had always felt like she was desperately clawing at the door, demanding that the city let her in and show her its soul, yet all she got in return was pain, not acceptance.

Her favorite coffee shop, Coffee Affair, wasn't far past the row of boutiques that she'd loved to shop in when she was sixteen—she'd even bought her prom dress from one of them. The walk into the old town from where she'd parked by the church was short but felt more nostalgic than usual. Maybe it was working on the orchard again, but she could almost see the ghost of her younger self giggling on the sidewalk eating frozen yogurt and gossiping with Tasha.

It seemed like forever ago and the thought sent an unexpected pang of longing through her, though she wasn't exactly sure what for. For simpler times, maybe.

Not for small-town life though.

The thought was only amplified when the few customers inside the coffee shop all turned to stare at her as she walked in. Penny wasn't sure what was worse, the thought of being recognized from her exit the previous day and people trying to start awkward conversations with her, or people judging her like she was over from the new town that had been built up past the church.

Neither appealed.

Thankfully, conversation had resumed by the time she stepped up to the counter and smiled at the unfamiliar barista.

"Hi, I'll take a pumpkin spice latte please. Biggest size you have." She was going to need the caffeine to get through to the end of the day, before her arms stiffened up too much to move.

"Sure thing." The girl behind the counter smiled and

Penny handed over five dollars, waving off the change as she waited at the other end of the counter for the coffee.

The bell rang over the door and Penny looked up. She smiled automatically as she caught the familiar brown eyes beneath bangs that were new, but above a grin that was just the same as when they were young.

"Penny?"

Her smile wavered, suddenly unsure what kind of reaction she could expect from Tasha. If the roles were reversed, Penny would ... Well, she wasn't sure what she'd do, and maybe Tasha didn't know yet either as they both stood frozen, staring at one another. At least Tasha had recognized her at first glance, unlike Mrs. Ashley, but Penny wasn't sure if it was a good thing to be spotted yet. If Tasha started swinging then Penny would have her answer.

All of a sudden, Tasha came charging forward, purse rocking from side to side, nearly sending a coffee on a nearby table flying as she did so. Tasha's arms closed around Penny and a light laugh escaped her when Tasha squeezed her tightly before breaking away, two pink spots standing stark against her pale skin.

"Hey, Tash."

Natasha Blake was taller than Penny by about an inch, so when Tasha pulled back to look into Penny's eyes, there was no avoiding her gaze.

"It's been forever and all you can say is *hey*?" Tasha teased, the slight frown on her face letting Penny know there was some truth to the words. "If I wasn't so happy to see you I might be pissed."

Penny winced but couldn't blame her former best friend for being angry. Leaving without much of a goodbye was a shitty thing to have done, and if she could take it back she would. In all honesty, Penny had just been excited for the new life she'd been imagining—and she hated goodbyes. Plus, if she had stopped to tell her friends she was leaving . . . Well, she wasn't sure she'd have been able to go at all.

"I hope you had a better greeting for my brother," Tasha continued, the words somewhat pointed, and Penny stopped breathing for a second as she glanced around, unsure if she felt excitement or dread at seeing the only other person she'd been sad to leave behind. "He's not here," Tasha said helpfully and Penny relaxed. "Oh God, that means you haven't seen him yet."

Penny half nodded and half shrugged. "I've only been back in town for a few days. I've not seen much of anyone except my parents."

The silence that followed felt awkward, for Penny at least as the guilt of how she'd left Magnolia Springs reared its ugly head. Tasha had a piercing way of looking at people that had been amusing to watch as a kid, but was less fun for Penny now that she was on the receiving end of it.

A shrill sound pierced the air as the milk for her latte was frothed and the barista handed over Penny's coffee a few moments later, breaking the tension. Penny thanked her, rooted in place while Tasha gave her order and paid and then turned back to Penny like the moment of awkwardness hadn't fazed her.

"How long are you in town for?"

Penny cleared her throat as Tasha flipped her light-blonde hair, a few shades lighter than Ethan's, over her shoulder. "I'm not sure yet. A few months at least."

"Good," Tasha said, accepting her own coffee and walking toward the door with Penny at her heels. "Then we have some time to catch up."

"That would be great." She meant it too. If Tasha was willing to give her a second chance, she wouldn't screw it up this time.

"Great, well, my number's still the same. Text me and we'll get drinks or something."

"Sure." Penny smiled a little hesitantly and her shoulders relaxed as Tasha nodded. "We can get the gang back together." The words made Tasha's face drop, bringing all of Penny's anxieties rushing back at once.

"Do me a favor?" Tasha said after a moment, slow and considered as if she was still turning the words over in her head. "Steer clear of Ethan while you're here. You already broke his heart once. We should avoid an encore."

Penny swallowed hard and nodded to show she understood, only slightly unnerved by the fact that she was once again on the receiving end of Tasha's piercing stare. Tasha wasn't trying to be cruel with her words, she was just *very* protective of her brother. Penny knew that better than most.

In a moment, the warning look on Tasha's face was replaced with a smile as she waved goodbye, leaving Penny with an acrid taste in her mouth that was uncannily guilt-flavored as she walked through the town square in the opposite direction to Tasha.

The fountain was on, the seats at its rim empty, and Penny walked over and sat down heavily in the shade of the magnolia tree that overhung the stone monument. Water trickled lazily behind her as late-flowering magnolia petals and orange leaves skittered across the ground and clung to the dew on her boots. The fountain had been here since the town was founded and had been one of her favorite spots to sit and think when she'd been growing up.

Her coffee burnt her tongue at the first sip but she ignored the pain and swallowed, running her fingers over the mostly smooth plaque next to her that proclaimed this fountain to be Magnolia Springs' very own *Fountain of Wishes*. She couldn't say whether the claim held any truth. She'd never bothered to make any wishes of her own, despite coming to the fountain so frequently she might as well have had her own seat reserved. But before she'd left, she'd had everything she could have wanted: a best friend who'd genuinely cared about her, a boyfriend who'd been the literal guy of her teenage dreams, and parents who'd loved her enough to let her leave for the city. Plus, back then, throwing a coin for a wish had seemed like a waste of perfectly good candy and make-up money.

She could use a little magic right then, though. It would be nice to fix things with Tasha, especially since facing her again after so long hadn't been as awkward as Penny had thought it might be. But even if she did make amends with Tasha, it wouldn't change her mind about how she felt at the possibility of seeing Ethan—even without Tasha's threat. Up until Tasha had mentioned him, Penny had been doing well not thinking about Ethan, though it had been harder than she'd expected when everywhere in Magnolia Springs was filled with memories of them together.

She definitely had no intention of seeking him out, but now Tasha's words kept running in circles through her head, making her dizzy. *You already broke his heart once.* Did she owe him an apology? Or would that be dredging up the past unnecessarily out of the blue? Penny couldn't make up her mind.

Something shone on the ground and Penny leant down, picking up the quarter by her boot. As she cupped it in her hand, she wished she could change the way she'd left things. She sighed and threw the quarter over her shoulder, hearing the soft *plop* as it landed in the fountain.

Penny knew that there was no way she could fix the past. She'd made her choice all those years ago and now she had to live with the consequences—things between her and Tasha, and her and Ethan, would never be the same. All she could do now was try to figure out a way to help her parents while she was here and hope she could continue helping them once she got the hell out of Magnolia Springs again.

4

By the time Penny had cleared the last of the apples from the tree and started on another it was late in the afternoon. Her legs were shaking from the repetitive bending and reaching and her nose was sore from the cold wind that had kicked up as she neared the end of her shift.

It was no surprise that her parents couldn't manage the harvest themselves any more. It was hard work—she'd forgotten just how hard in all the years she'd been gone. Guilt stabbed at her as she imagined her parents out here, struggling in the cold, forced to leave some of the apples to fall and rot because they couldn't get through them all.

She hadn't realized it while she'd been in San Fran chasing her dreams, but she'd been a shitty daughter up until now. Her parents had always come to visit her, rather than her coming to them, and she'd always thought they'd wanted it that way, to have the chance to escape this suffocating small town. Except now, looking back, she wondered if maybe they'd come to her because the alternative was not seeing her.

Well, she was here now. Maybe she did have a habit of selfishness that extended past her abrupt departure from Magnolia Springs ten years ago, but she could change that. Starting now, she resolved, she would do her best to be a better friend, a better daughter.

Penny left the apples where they were—someone else would be along to gather up the day's harvest to weigh and catalog the haul—and made her way back to the entrance of the orchard where she'd parked.

Mrs. Ashley had left hours ago, waving cheerfully, but the owner of the big truck parked next to hers had to still be out there picking apples. At least one other car had pulled in too, its owner starting later in the day than Penny—she preferred to get there early and leave before the sun could quite set.

As Penny walked through the gate that marked the entrance to the orchard, she decided to stop in on her mom in the shop, to see if there was anything else she could help with before she headed home. The door to the shop opened without a creak and Penny unconsciously relaxed as the familiar scent of apples and cinnamon washed over her.

"Hey, Mom."

Angie looked up and smiled at her daughter, the corners of her eyes crinkling as she peered over the top of her reading glasses. The space was warm and cozy, the lights casting an orange glow over the wood interior, and by the time Penny reached the counter her mom was working at her eyes felt heavy.

"Good first day?"

Penny nodded. "It was, actually. I'm beat now, though, I forgot how hard the harvest is."

Angie hummed, her eyes already back on the ledger spread open in front of her. "It's good to have you here, helping out."

Penny swallowed, picking up a pen from the counter and fiddling with it nervously. "I'm sorry I wasn't here before."

Her mom rescued the pen from Penny's tight grip and patted her hand. "You're here now, that's what matters. Go on home, I've got a little more to do before I leave."

"Are you sure? I can help—"

Angie was already shaking her head before Penny could finish her words. "I'll see you at home, honey."

Penny nodded, pressing a quick kiss to her mom's warm cheek before turning for the door. A hot meal and a bath sounded like heaven at that moment. She'd probably fall asleep by eight at this rate.

She slipped her keys out of her pocket as she exited the small shop and her bug chirped cheerfully as it unlocked. The sound was loud in the quiet air and she smirked again at the enormous vehicle to her left when she walked past it.

The horses in the next field over were barely audible, and she'd nearly made it to the driver's-side door when footsteps sounded and Ethan Blake rounded the corner from behind the building.

Her eyes flew wide, mouth running dry, suddenly she was feeling a *lot* more awake. He hadn't seen her yet and she took the opportunity to drink him in, familiar and yet not. His hair was the same dark blonde it had always been, but longer, and he was tall now—even more so than he'd been when they were teens. Ethan had had a good few inches on her back then, and he had a hell of a lot more than that now. The stubble on his jaw looked surprisingly good, covering the strong angles of his face and highlighting the softness of his mouth.

There was a confidence in the way he moved, in the lines of his body, that made her shiver as she wondered what else had changed since she'd seen him last. Back then, he'd only been a boy, more cocky than confident. But now? He was all man.

He glanced up and she didn't think, just dropped down into a crouch as her pulse raced. Worse than how good her ex looked was the fact that his sister's words were whirling round and round inside Penny's head as she stayed stooped by her car door, waiting for Ethan to leave.

You already broke his heart once. You already broke his heart once. You already broke his heart once. You already broke his heart once. You already broke his heart once.

Penny huffed out an irritated breath and then fell completely still when she caught movement out of the corner of her eye.

Brown boots, sturdy and well worn. Denim-clad calves leading to thighs thicker than both of her legs put together. Navy Henley, flannel shirt, and full lips curled in amusement as Ethan Blake looked down at where she crouched on the ground.

"Here they are!" Her voice was pitchy, too high and squeaky, as she lifted her keys triumphantly like she'd been looking for them rather than hiding from him. "Oh, hi, Ethan. I didn't see you there. What are you doing at the orchard?"

His cool eyes ran over her and she could have sworn she heard a chuckle before he stepped closer, the pleasant smell of sandalwood drifting over her. Her chin lifted, head craning back slightly so she could look up at him.

"I work here."

Her mouth dropped open, mind flashing back as she remembered what her dad had said the previous evening. *Pretty sure the last time you were at the orchard you dragged along that boyfriend of yours. It'll be just like old times.* Cursing herself, she wondered how she hadn't put two and two together. She had failed to realize that he'd meant she'd be working alongside Ethan *now*, too.

Standing in front of him, there was a definite edge of panic to her thoughts. Her past and present were colliding, this new version of Ethan re-writing the image of the one she'd held in her brain all these years. Her heart raced too fast to be comfortable and her mouth was too dry. At the same time, her palms were sweaty, a riot of butterflies were taking off in her stomach, and the combination of it all made her feel dizzy.

"Do you mind?" he said, and there was definite amusement in his voice that transformed into a lazy grin when she balked.

He was standing close, too close to be casual, and she opened and shut her mouth incredulously as he leant in. Surely . . . he didn't think they were going to pick right up where they'd left off?

Another step closer. Ethan's tongue wet his bottom lip as he raised a brow at her and a mixture of irritation and desire made her suck in a sharp breath. A lot had changed, but those eyes on hers were the same. It was like she was a teenager all over again.

The air crackled between them and Penny pinched her thigh to snap herself out of whatever this was. "Yes, actually, I *do* mind. Even if your sister wouldn't have my head over it, why would you think you could just waltz right up to me and—and look at me like *that*. It's been ten years! I don't know you any more, certainly not well enough to kiss you and—"

A large hand fell over her mouth and she snapped her jaw shut before she could taste Ethan's skin, his sweet scent overwhelming her senses.

He slowly let go and her lips tingled at his brief touch. God, it had been a long time since she'd got laid. Enough that, for a second, she reconsidered her words. Maybe she *did* want him to kiss her? But before she could say anything more, Ethan reached out and grabbed her by the shoulders, lifting her up and—

Moving her to one side?

She blinked, more than a little taken aback as Ethan smirked at her and opened the door to the large truck parked next to her. The door she'd been blocking with her body.

Oh God.

Heat flared in her cheeks and she knew she had to be the same shade as a tomato when Ethan backed up out of the space and lifted his hand in farewell, the growl of the engine growing fainter the further away he drove back into town.

The only thing more irritating than her absolute mortification was that, on top of everything else, she was also wrong about the truck and its owner. Ethan Blake wasn't compensating for *anything*.

"Stupid," she reprimanded herself as she finally climbed into her car and caught a glimpse of her still-flushed face in the rearview mirror.

Well, as far as avoiding Ethan Blake went, Penny was off to a *stellar* start.

5

Penny's second shift at the orchard had proved much less eventful than her first—a lot less embarrassing too. She wished her parents had provided a little more warning that Ethan was working for them before she'd found out by bumping into him unexpectedly. She'd managed to avoid him during her shift today, and most of her was relieved because it meant she wouldn't have to face an awkward confrontation any time soon. The smaller, more traitorous, part of her was a little disappointed not to have caught another glimpse of her ex.

Back when they were younger, things with Ethan had always been comfortable, easy as breathing, so it felt strange now to be so torn in two about his presence at the orchard. Inevitably, she would come face to face with him again and while on the surface that didn't seem so bad, the truth was that she was scared of what he might say to her. The accusations he might level. Or worse, maybe he'd moved on completely and hadn't thought about her at all in the ten years she'd been gone. For some reason, the last possibility stung more than any other.

She'd had a lot of time to think while working in the orchard today—a little *too* much time, really, because now her thoughts were a swirling mass so heavy they sat on top of her like a perpetual rain cloud. So much for enjoying the peace and quiet that came with picking.

Her mom had dinner waiting when she got home, and Penny was grateful. The second shift had been even more tiring than the first, especially when her thoughts had been running in circles all day and her body had been on edge, jumping at every small noise in case it proved to be an approaching Ethan. He'd never appeared, saving her from any further embarrassment but not the stiff muscles her constant tension and hypervigilance had caused.

Though, naturally, the universe made up for her lack of humiliation that day by instead forcing her to endure an interrogation by her mother.

"How did you find it today, honey?"

Swallowing a too-large mouthful of lasagna, Penny nodded. "Fine." Her parents exchanged a look and Penny braced herself.

"Only fine?"

Penny sighed and set down her cutlery. "What do you want to know?"

Angie lit up, eyes taking on a feverish gleam that indicated only one thing: gossip. "I heard that you had coffee with Tasha the other day."

"And I heard you bumped into Ethan," her dad added and Penny nodded calmly even as she fought the urge to scream. Goddamn the gossip mill of small towns and perpetually nosy parents.

"Yes to both," she said and her parents eyed each other again in a way they probably thought was subtle. It wasn't. At all. "I'm actually getting drinks with Tasha this Friday," she offered and her mom beamed, happy for the new information. Or maybe that Penny was getting out of the house for something other than apple picking.

"Oh, that's wonderful. Where are you girls going?"

"I don't know, I think Tasha said it was called Cocktail Club?"

Angie sipped her red wine and nodded. "Yes, I hear that's where all the youngsters hang out these days. Of course, when your father and I were young the Last Call was the hopping place to be. It's a shame it closed down."

Penny's eyes twitched from the effort of not rolling them skyward. *Hopping, really?* "Where are you hearing all this?"

A wave of the hand was the only answer Penny got. "Tell us what happened with Ethan." In sync, her parents leant forward, piercing her with their eyes from across the small table, like her life was the latest episode of her mom's favorite reality show.

"Nothing," she replied honestly. And she was lucky that was really what had happened. He would have been perfectly entitled to be mad at her, instead he'd acted like seeing her was no big deal. She wished she could say the same, but Ethan Blake had always had a way of getting under her skin.

Their shoulders slumped, but Angie soon recovered. "Well, I hear that he's very in demand these days."

What was that supposed to mean? In demand how?

As if she could see the questions brewing in Penny's mind, her mom continued, "He works in design, or architecture, right, Phil?" She didn't wait for an answer before plowing on. "Of course, the poor boy can't seem to sit still for more than a second. That's why we took him on at the orchard—"

Penny grimaced, the lasagna turning to paste in her mouth as she washed it down with a large gulp of her wine and tuned out her mom's mooning over Penny's ex-boyfriend. Hiring him at the orchard was one thing, they'd needed the help and of course they shouldn't have turned it down just because it was coming from her ex. But still, Penny thought, the adoration was a bit much. Then again, Ethan was the only boyfriend of Penny's that they'd met, and they'd been together for nearly four years, so she couldn't blame them for being attached to him. Even if it did make things harder for her.

Her dad nodded along, murmuring his agreement with a glazed look in his eyes, and Penny was right there with him until something Angie said caught her attention.

"—terrible business, we were all so sad when the news broke."

"Sorry, what was that?" Penny blinked her mom back into focus and pushed her plate away, appetite gone.

Angie huffed but repeated herself. "His engagement. It's been a little while since the town had a local wedding, so we—"

"Wait, what do you mean engagement? Engagement to *who*?" An uncomfortable silence grew and Penny forced herself to smile, to ease the scrunched-up tension in her shoulders. "I just hadn't heard about it before," she added lightly and her mom nodded, unconvinced.

"You remember Shelby Patterson, don't you? Oh, they made such a lovely couple. They would have had beautiful babies," Angie said wistfully, swirling the red wine in her glass and shrugging when Penny and Philip stared at her. "What? Oh, well, you know I always liked you two together, honey, but it was good that he moved on after you left. And anyway, things didn't work out for Ethan and Shelby, so what does it matter?"

"Who broke it off?" Honestly, she wasn't sure why she cared. It was none of her business who Ethan had dated—or nearly married—since they broke up. It wasn't like Penny had been celibate while she'd been in San Fran. And Ethan was nice. Tall. Funny. And had clearly been channeling his singledom into working out, judging by the size of his muscled thighs. Anyone would be lucky to date him. She shook her head free of the reminder of those legs in her direct line of sight while she'd been on her knees in front of him.

But Shelby Patterson? No wonder she'd been sizing Penny up the other day as though they were in competition with one another. The thought made Penny shudder. It felt a little like falling into an alternate dimension, it just seemed so *wrong*. They'd never hung out in high school, and Shelby had always been . . . particular. She wouldn't be caught dead in an off-brand outfit, and she had been appalled by the pie-eating contest they'd held at the Halloween Orchard Fest one year—and even more disgusted that Tasha and Penny had taken part. Penny just couldn't imagine Shelby being Ethan's type—then again, she didn't know this new version of him, the one who'd grown up. Not really, anyway. Maybe designer brands were now his go-to and he'd cringe if he saw the way she could put away an apple-and-pecan pie.

Angie pursed her lips. "I'm not sure. I mean, there are rumors, of course."

"Of course," Penny muttered, pushing up and away from the table and then gathering the dirty plates and silverware together.

"Maybe you could ask Tasha," Angie said thoughtfully. "Report back."

"Definitely not." Tasha had been clear enough on where she stood when it came to Penny and Ethan. If Penny showed up with a bunch of questions about him it would raise one too many red flags.

. . . Even if she *was* curious.

Hot water poured into the butler sink and Penny

added soap before dumping the plates into the near-scalding water and scrubbing at them with an intensity that made her parents give each other another one of those unsubtle looks.

"What?" she barked and they looked away.

"Nothing," her dad said, eyes a little too wide to be honest and Penny sighed, washing the plates a little more gently.

"Sorry, I shouldn't have snapped. It's just weird being back here, talking about Tasha and Ethan like no time's passed and I'm still in high school."

Angie picked up a dish towel and began to dry the plates as Penny stacked them before pressing a quick kiss to her cheek. "You're handling it well, sweetie."

Penny wasn't sure if she'd agree, but smiled anyway. "So, what else have I missed since I've been gone?"

Her mom chatted on as they worked together until the tableware was clean and dried and Penny's eyes were heavy. It had been a long time since she'd done physical labor quite like apple picking and she couldn't say it wasn't affecting her.

"Why don't you go on up?" Her mom said softly, wrapping her in a quick but warm hug and squeezing briefly. "Have yourself a hot bath to ease your muscles."

"That actually sounds perfect," she admitted. "Night."

"Goodnight, pumpkin," her dad called after her and she blew him a kiss as she headed up the stairs and set the bath running with a healthy dollop of bubble bath.

The bathroom was one of the more modern rooms in the cottage, with a large claw-foot tub that was freestanding against the wall opposite the doorway and a walk-in shower to her right. The sink and toilet were hidden behind a paisley blue screen in the far left corner that matched the blue tiles in the shower and the feet of the tub. The small pops of color made Penny smile as she locked the door and stripped off before turning on the heated towel-rail so that her fluffy towel would be toasty when she got out of the bath.

Warmth cascaded over her body as she submerged herself amidst the bubbles and reached up to turn off the faucets before the bath could overflow. She could practically feel her muscles unknotting as the heat soothed her overworked arms and shoulders.

She was used to being on her feet for long periods of time from working in a restaurant kitchen in San Fran, but picking apples for five-plus hours was a little more intense. It wasn't just the repetitive motions of reaching and plucking and then hauling her load down from the tree into the bigger bucket, it was the way the cold weather made her muscles tense and brace against the wind, and climbing the steps of the stool several times like it was a StairMaster.

At least she'd be in great shape in time to overindulge at Thanksgiving and Christmas.

The manual labor was nice, though. Something different, yet easy as breathing from her time working at the orchard as a teenager. The only downside so far was seeing Ethan and her embarrassing reaction to him.

It had been a long time since she'd seen him, and it felt like almost as long since she'd had a boyfriend or even a casual hook-up. It was the only reason she could think of for her body's reaction to him in that moment, and even a day later her cheeks still pinked at the memory of his large hands on her shoulders, lifting her like she weighed nothing. If she wanted to keep her cool around her high-school sweetheart, then she definitely needed to get that itch scratched.

Note to self: get laid before you see Ethan again.

Not by Ethan, she quickly amended to herself and grimaced.

Not by anyone in this town. Unless she wanted her parents, and the rest of Magnolia Springs, to know exactly what she was doing and with whom, then a trip out of town to the closest city might be in order. Ideally before she ran into Ethan again and was forced to be faced with his strong jaw and stubbled cheeks and the large palms with gentle calluses that had pressed against her mouth and—

Penny shut her eyes and shook her head. *Off limits.*

You already broke his heart once, Tasha's voice reminded her and Penny blew out a long breath, annoyed that her vanilla-musk bubble bath reminded her of Ethan's sweet sandalwood scent against her lips.

If she made it to Friday without seeing Ethan again, then she would be able to look Tasha in the eye over their cocktails, knowing she hadn't broken her promise to stay away from Tasha's brother. But if not ... Maybe it was best to keep both of the Blake siblings out of her mind, to try to stop it from wandering.

Fuck, she thought and then, as if the universe had heard her thoughts, her phone buzzed on the side of the bath, lighting up with Tasha's name and starting her spiral all over again. "Fuck."

6

Penny was grateful for a break from working on the orchard on Wednesday; her muscles ached after two days of manual labor and her head was a little fuzzy from exhaustion. The town was only a short drive away, so she decided coffee would be a good way to get out of the house without being too exercise-intensive. Plus, she enjoyed driving. Her little green bug had been a trooper on the long drive from the city and she knew she'd be bummed when the time came to replace it.

Pulling out of her parents' drive, tiredness sweeping through her limbs, she was reminded all too clearly of the day she'd left Magnolia Springs. She'd been exhausted that day too, but her excitement for her dream job in the city, working under the head chef of one of the most highly rated restaurants in San Francisco, had kept her going. It had been a conscious decision not to say goodbye, one she'd thought made sense at the time but that she could now see had been a mistake.

She'd loved Ethan, and Tasha, and her parents too—but she hadn't thought they would understand wanting to get out of this little town, to find something bigger. None of them had ever wanted to leave, making her the outsider, and whenever she'd tried to talk to them about it before she'd gone, she'd been unsuccessful. And then she'd realized that if she was going to leave, she needed to just go, otherwise she'd do the comfortable, easy thing and stay with her friends instead of following her dreams. Still, she could have handled the whole thing a lot better. But she'd been young and stupid, brash in her overconfidence. Qualities she hoped she'd grown out of ten years later.

Penny parked the bug by the church and enjoyed the cool breeze as she walked into town. She'd layered a thick, cozy pink sweater over the top of some denim overalls and was glad she'd opted to wear her sturdy black boots given the deceptively deep puddles along the sidewalk. Her sneakers were more comfortable to drive in but had a tendency to let in water and with the way the gray clouds had been looming, she hadn't wanted to take any chances. There was nothing she hated more than wet socks.

Coffee Affair was busy, with a long line of customers winding its way past the register and along the cake counter. But they did serve the best coffee in town, so Penny joined the back of the line and breathed in the coffee-scented air, her mouth already watering at the thought of her pumpkin spice latte.

"Good to know some things don't change," a quiet voice murmured behind her and Penny jumped, glancing over her shoulder and then whipping around to face straight ahead again with wide eyes once she saw who was behind her. The warmth at her back should have been the first giveaway really. Ethan always had run hot.

"You know me," she said, injecting false cheer into her voice and wincing when it cracked. "Need my fix."

He didn't reply and the silence made her all too aware of her pulse pounding in her ears and the lack of space between their bodies. It had always been this way with him, ever since they were kids. There was some draw between them, pulling them closer even when they hadn't known what it meant. More than that, they had thrived in each other's company—Ethan Blake wasn't only her first love, he'd been her best friend.

Now he was nearly a stranger.

The line shuffled forward and for a second Penny could only blink blankly at the barista, trying to remember her order, and before she could stutter the words out, Ethan leant round her, saying something her brain couldn't process to the barista. She jolted at the proximity, finding herself frozen to the spot as an arm reached out from beside her to pay for her drink before she'd even reached for her purse.

"Oh," she mumbled, looking up and up until she could see the underside of Ethan's jaw above her. "You didn't—I can pay—"

Ethan glanced down like he'd already forgotten she was there and nodded slightly. "Old habits."

The air filled with everything she wanted and feared to say, her surprise at the lack of reproachment on his face, the nostalgia of being there with him again, all while the pain of how much everything had changed between them hovered invisibly too. Then the barista handed over their drinks and the moment was gone.

His eyes flicked from hers to her mouth and she watched his throat bob, frozen in place. "Bye, Pen."

She raised her hand, but he was already gone, marching out of the coffee shop and through the painted door before she could open her mouth.

"Thank you," she whispered to the air and then cursed when she sipped her drink and burned her mouth. But before the sting, she recognized the flavor—pumpkin spice. He'd remembered.

It had rained all of Thursday morning, the grass slipperier than usual and the smell of sweet apples thick in the air, making Penny feel surprisingly thirsty every time she plucked a droplet-covered fruit from a branch. Like she was in a damn shampoo advert or something.

The trees were doing their best to cocoon her from the chill in the weather, watching over her as she plucked the ripened fruits from the boughs and sprinkling her with water as the branches bounced.

But now, the sun had finally stopped sulking and was warm on her face, so Penny decided it was time for a break to try and dry her gloves a little. Her fingers looked pale and a little pruney when she yanked the gloves off and positioned them on one of the stepping stool's stairs in direct sunlight.

She'd opted for layers again that day to keep warm. She was relieved by her choice to wear thick, dark tights and a light, long-sleeved white tee under her denim dungarees that morning, but now that the sun was out she'd had to roll her sleeves up to her elbows to try to cool off.

She'd already eaten the sandwich she'd packed for lunch as a snack at around eleven, so Penny decided to just enjoy the temporary sunshine and slipped her headphones on. She stretched out her arms and legs before peeking down the rows of trees nearest her and finding them deserted, not a single person lurking amongst the green-orange leaves.

Perfect.

Music poured through the headset and she moved in time, throwing her hands in the air and spinning, rushing from one row of trees to another and skipping with extra flourish as Natasha Bedingfield begged to be taken away to a secret place. By the time the song ended, Penny was breathing hard but she was smiling, her muscles feeling looser, her mood lifted. As she paused to gulp some water, trying to catch her breath, she glanced round the orchard, stopping mid-chug at the sight of Ethan Blake in a tank top, picking apples on a ladder much bigger than her own.

There hadn't ever been a time in her life when she'd seen a man in a tank top and thought *yes*—until now.

Who knew apple picking could be such an intense, erotic activity?

No! Not intense! Not erotic! Off-limits!

Despite her better instincts, Penny couldn't look away. Instead, she ignored the whiny voice in her head and let her eyes trace the minute movements of Ethan's biceps as he reached and pulled, water droplets landing on his skin from the branches and the strong flex of his muscles making her swallow hard as his fingers closed around the fruit and dropped it into the bag he'd slung across his chest.

His usual flannel shirt was thrown over a rung on the other side of his ladder, no doubt drying in the sun like Penny's gloves. He reached up to grab an apple a little higher than his head and she nearly whimpered when his top lifted to reveal the lower half of his taut stomach, abs bunching and rippling in a way that made her stomach swoop and bottom out somewhere around her heels. And—*God have mercy on her*—were those *tattoos* winding darkly around the bottom of his ribs?

She wasn't sure at what point she'd turned off her music to better admire Ethan, but her headphones were quiet and so she slipped them off to hang around her neck as she debated whether to run or hide before she was spotted ogling him.

"Nice moves," he called and she froze, knowing that if he'd seen her prancing around, he'd definitely also seen her staring at him for much longer than could be considered polite. "Sorry, I hope I didn't interrupt your drool-fest. Can I get you anything? A hose-down maybe?"

Taken aback by the jokey edge to Ethan's words, Penny's mind went totally blank as she struggled to think of something, *anything* to say in response. After a few moments, she somehow found her voice and managed to force out a few words. "Yeah, right," she snorted, trying to come across as nonchalant rather than flustered. "I was just watching your ... technique." *OK, good, Penny. Now walk away.*

His answering laugh was warm and she realized she'd missed the sound of it in the time they'd spent apart. In all honesty, she'd never expected to hear it again, even upon her return. And yet, Ethan had seemed indifferent to her the last two times she'd seen him. She wasn't sure if she would have preferred anger to apparent ambivalence. "Hello again, Penny. If you're not going to hide in plain sight this time, then maybe we could catch up a little?"

Her inhalation might as well have been a gasp for how taken aback she was, and then her breath caught in her throat and she began choking, coughing and spluttering like an idiot. Because of course she would.

Ethan rushed over, rubbing a soothing circle on the middle of her back and then tilted up her chin when her coughing subsided. "You OK?" he murmured and he was so close she could count the individual lashes surrounding his deep-brown eyes. How many times had he soothed her like this when they were younger? Too many to count, she was sure.

"Fine," she rasped and then stared dumbly when he smiled. "You look different."

The edges of his mouth curled, a familiar cocky look that had only grown hotter with age. "Ten years will do that to a person."

"No, sorry, I just mean that you—you look good. Nice," she corrected, flustered into adding, "healthy."

He didn't hold back his laugh as he took a step away, allowing some distance to flow between them. Not that it mattered. She could taste his sandalwood scent on her tongue and those big biceps were now close enough to touch—*No touching! Off-limits!*

"I am healthy, yes. And how are you? How long are you back for?"

She opened her mouth but again her voice seemed to have deserted her as only a squeak came out. Clearing her throat, she tried again. "I'm fine. Good. Nice weather now isn't it. Great, even. Warm. Strange after all the rain, right?" Her laugh sounded odd, a little too fast and breathless, and she was rambling. "Maybe let's just . . . put this back on," she muttered, hurrying over to his shirt and tossing it to him.

He caught it easily and slipped his arms in the sleeves and honestly? It didn't help. At all.

Penny squeezed her hands together tightly as she tried to focus on what he'd asked her. "I don't know how long I'll be back for yet, probably until Christmas at least." She found herself strangely unable to mention that she definitely wasn't staying in Magnolia Springs past the holidays, but she couldn't dwell on that right now.

Ethan smiled and brushed his hair out of his face. "I bet your parents are thrilled."

"And yours?"

"Well, I don't think they know you're back but . . ." His smile widened as he took in her blush. "They're well, thanks," he said finally.

"I saw Tasha the other day," Penny blurted and he nodded, waiting for her to continue on and blinking when he realized that she was done speaking.

"Yeah, she mentioned it to me."

"We're going out again on Friday. Tomorrow," she corrected and he nodded again, awkwardness rising up between them and she had the sudden, awful feeling that she was bugging him uninvited. "Well, I guess I should—"

"It's nice that you and Tash are hanging out," he said and her smile of agreement faltered when he hooked his thumb in his jeans' pocket and met her eyes with an intensity that made her catch her breath. "Is this special treatment reserved for Tasha? Or can I get in on it too?"

She blinked at him. "In . . . on it?" Why was he being so friendly toward her? Shouldn't he have been mad? Had she meant that little to him? Great, now *she* was the one who was mad.

The thud of his booted foot hitting the ground as he moved closer mimicked the jump in her heart. "Well, you saw Tasha and chatted, made plans . . . You saw me and tried to hide under your car."

Penny frowned. "I was *not* trying to get under my car. I was just crouched down very close to it."

His laugh sent skitters of heat across her skin as he stopped in the shadow of her body. "Just think about it, Pen."

She bit back her grimace. The problem was that she couldn't *stop* thinking about it. Him. Ethan had always known her better than she knew herself, and it seemed like that hadn't changed. Sure, history lurked between them, but more than that was *heat*. Some spark that hadn't faded away reigniting the embers at just the sound of his laugh.

"I thought you'd be mad at me," she said, and it was true.

"Why?" He seemed genuinely confused and Penny wasn't sure whether to laugh or cry. "Is this about me buying you the coffee?"

"The coffee? No. I mean, yes, I wanted to thank you for it. But I mean about the way I left things before. When I left." She tugged on her sleeve and fidgeted her boot in the grass near her foot.

"We were dumb kids," he said, dismissively, surprising her.

"How were *you* dumb?"

Ethan's smile dropped and when he leveled her with

a surprisingly serious look, Pen wasn't sure she was breathing. "Because I let you go."

The sky darkened above them, but she barely noticed as the heat of Ethan's eyes swallowed her whole. A raindrop hit the ground next to her and she jolted at the sound.

More rain hit the grass, the scent of damp earth rising up around her, and Ethan smiled as he backed away, like he hadn't just broken her heart and mended it all in one sentence.

"Have a good time with Tasha tomorrow," he said and she was fairly certain she nodded as he walked away, leaving her standing alone in the rain.

7

Before she'd left Magnolia Springs, there had only been one bar Penny had gone into—primarily because they didn't check IDs too closely for anyone under twenty-one who wanted to drink. The Old Church had been closed and reopened sometime while Penny had been gone in the city and was now called Cocktail Club.

When it came to small towns like Magnolia Springs, change was slow and not always welcomed. But the same couldn't be said for Cocktail Club, which was thriving on a Friday night. It seemed to be vaguely jungle-themed with colorful lights that changed depending on the time, neon slogans on the dark wallpapered walls, and leafy green plants in gold planters that separated the booths. Strangely, it worked and Penny felt surprisingly at ease in the space with its low-lights that made it feel like she couldn't be watched too much by the room's inhabitants.

She smoothed down her top, checking the sweetheart neckline was still in place, and brushed a piece of lint from the ruched detailing on the front. It was an outfit she'd worn many times and knew she looked good in, her black, distressed skinny jeans adding an edge to the otherwise too-sweet top with its ruffled mesh sleeves—she'd picked it out deliberately, wanting to at least feel confident in her outfit if nothing else. She'd been nervous to see Tasha again, especially now that she'd had a few run-ins with her brother, but Penny hadn't had long to dwell on her nerves because Tasha had arrived first and was waving her over to one of the tables in the center of the room.

They shared a semi-awkward hug and picked up the cocktail menu. The drinks were relatively reasonably priced, especially compared to what she was used to in the city, and the music wasn't so loud that she couldn't hear Tasha recount her day. It took a couple of minutes for the initial awkwardness to ease, but then the two of them had quickly fallen back into sync as if it had only been a matter of days, not years, since they'd last hung out. Penny realized that she'd missed having a girlfriend to gossip with while she'd been in the city. She supposed it was one of the benefits of having known someone for the majority of your life: even when time got in the way it didn't change the familiarity that every conversation held.

"So how's it been, being back on the orchard?" Tasha asked, studying Penny's face. At the mention of the orchard, Penny took a big gulp of her margarita, trying to think of anything but Ethan's toned shoulders in that tank top. "Are you hating it?" Tasha pressed, and Penny couldn't help but smile at how well her old friend still seemed to know her.

"It's been surprisingly OK," Penny replied, willing the image of Ethan's face, the way he'd looked at her as they'd stood among the trees, from her mind. "I don't remember it making my body ache so much as a teenager, though."

Tasha laughed, the sequins on her short-sleeved top catching the lights and shimmering. "Ethan said he bumped into you a couple times."

Penny was surprised by how casually Tasha mentioned this, but she nodded, trying to seem unfazed. "Yeah, I saw him."

"He said you hid from him."

"Maybe."

Tasha rolled her eyes as she sipped from her glass. "I know I told you to avoid him but I didn't mean you had to stop, drop, and roll at the sight of him."

"I didn't roll," Penny protested and cleared her throat, looking for a change in subject before the prickle of guilt in her throat made her blurt out something stupid like:

Is it possible to be in love with someone you haven't seen for ten years? Or, *Hey, Tasha, when you say to avoid your brother, does fantasizing about him count?*

"Anyway, enough about me! What are you doing now?" Penny asked, desperate to talk about something else that didn't involve Tasha's brother, especially with the warning Tash had given her not so long ago.

Tasha sipped her drink, her pink lipstick leaving a perfect imprint on the rim. "I run the library."

"Oh wow, that's perfect." Tasha had had her nose in a book almost as often as her phone when they'd been growing up. "How long have you been doing that for?"

Their comfortable chatter continued as Tasha filled Penny in on what had (or, more accurately, what *hadn't*) changed in Magnolia Springs over the last decade. Penny was surprised to find that she was actually having fun, feeling totally at ease in Tasha's company. When it hit nine and Penny began to feel like it was getting late, it occurred to her that maybe she was getting old. But, she reasoned to herself, if she wanted to be able to drive home she needed to cut herself off after this drink anyway.

Part of her wasn't ready to leave yet, though. It was easy to remember why she and Tasha had been friends, her good sense of humor and kindness shining through as Penny enjoyed their comfortable chatter.

Tasha leant in close. Her third margarita was nearing the dregs, and her rose-gold eyeliner made the intensity of her brown eyes even more apparent as she asked one of the questions Penny had been dreading all night.

"So why'd you leave San Francisco?"

"Oh, you know." Penny laughed, looking away from Tasha's eyes and instead signaling to the waitress for another drink. She'd get a cab home if she had to, but this conversation required another cocktail. Or three. "My parents needed me."

"And?"

Penny sighed, shoulders slumping as she drained the last of her drink, casting around for a way to derail Tasha's line of questioning. She began to stand, preparing to go in search of another margarita. "You know, I might go to the bar and—"

"Pen."

Penny's ass hit the stool as she sat back down abruptly, reminded of the other aspect of Tasha's friendship that had always been invaluable, if only slightly frustrating: Tasha was never afraid to call Penny on her bullshit.

"I quit my job. Spectacularly," Penny blurted. There was no point in lying to Tasha; she'd always been able to tell when Penny was talking out of her ass. "My boss was an asshole. Like, with a capital 'A'. I couldn't take it anymore." She shrugged. "I snapped, screamed at him in front of a restaurant full of people, quit mid-shift, and drove back to Magnolia Springs the next day."

Tasha's mouth hung open and she slowly shook her head. "If I didn't know you so well I would have thought you were lying."

"Yeah, not so much. Just the sad truth." Penny understood the reaction. She was generally more inclined to apologize to the waiter for them getting her order wrong than to kick up a fuss, *ever*.

"It brought you back here to us though, which I can't be too sorry about," Tasha said, a small smile curving her mouth. "You know I'm a big believer of *everything happens for a reason*."

"Things have definitely been *happening*," Penny muttered. "But yeah, I'll be helping my parents at the orchard for the foreseeable future. Until I can find a new culinary job anyway."

"Well, I'm glad you're here anyway. Just do me a favor?" She waited for Penny to nod before continuing. "Next time you leave, promise you'll say goodbye."

Penny's eyes pricked and she bit her lip as she nodded. "I promise."

"Pinky?"

She laughed but offered out her pinky finger, locking it around Tash's. "Pinky."

"Wow, looks like the band's all back together."

Penny's smile dropped as she looked up and found Shelby Patterson standing beside their table. Coda Simpley, one of the girls who'd followed Shelby around like a lost puppy at high school, was hovering behind Shelby's shoulder, looking totally uninterested in the conversation. Penny hadn't got a good look at Shelby when she had passed her in the street a few days ago, too flustered by the whole coffee-soaked-jeans situation, but now she had no choice but to take her in, from her blonde balayage to the hem of her shimmery tasseled dress.

Admittedly, Shelby looked great, but knowing she was Ethan's ex-fiancée had the observation curdling in Penny's stomach. Wasn't it a rule somewhere that the mean girls were supposed to get ugly and humbled after high school? Yet here Shelby stood, just as gorgeous as ever and, reluctantly, she could understand the appeal Ethan might have seen. *Shelby* had her life together. *Shelby* wasn't living with her parents. *Shelby* wasn't working the same job she'd had at sixteen.

Or, at least, Penny assumed that was the case.

Sure, Shelby looked good. But wasn't it all a bit too *much*? Magnolia Springs wasn't really a tasseled-mini-dress kind of place; even on a Friday night it was more of a jeans-and-a-nice-top kind of vibe. But Shelby drew the eye and, unless she'd grown a whole new personality in the ten years Penny had been gone, there was nothing Shelby liked more than attention.

"Not quite the full band," Penny replied, smile a little tight as she forced it back into place. She knew it was petty to bring Ethan into the conversation, even if she hadn't mentioned him by name, but she couldn't help herself. "So good to see you, Shelby. And you, Coda."

Coda barely reacted as Shelby sniffed, looking Penny up and down before turning her gaze on Tasha, her eyes becoming impossibly more frosty. Penny held back her scoff, feeling like she'd been transported back to high school. She'd only seen Shelby twice since getting back to town, but her mean-girl act was already wearing pretty thin.

"Natasha," Shelby said, cocking one hip forward and folding her arms across her chest.

Tash raised one eyebrow. "Shelby," she said evenly and Penny's eyes bounced back and forth between the two of them; if there was one person who could hold their own with Shelby, it was Tasha. "You have a nice night, now."

Her shoulders stiffening at the clear dismissal, Shelby tossed her long hair over one shoulder and strutted away on heels so high Penny had vertigo just looking at them, Coda rushing after her.

"What the hell was that all about?" she asked once Shelby was out of earshot. They'd not got on with her particularly well in high school, but that was forever ago and this tension seemed . . . fresh.

Tasha sighed, watching Shelby wind between tables until she settled in a pink booth in the corner. "I remind her of my brother."

Understandable, somewhat. The siblings were actually fraternal twins, and did look somewhat alike. "I heard she and Ethan were engaged."

Tasha grimaced, her empty glass hitting the tabletop with a clang that made Penny's teeth ache. "It was short-lived."

She dropped her eyes to her drink then peeked up at Tasha. "Why?"

Apparently the question had been the wrong thing to ask, because Tasha's mouth snapped shut and her nostrils flared before she said, "I don't want to talk about this with you."

Penny frowned, reaching out to touch Tasha's hand. "If Shelby's giving you a hard time, you can tell me. Ethan and I are history, Tash."

"Are you?"

"I nearly crawled under my car to hide from him," she pointed out and Tasha's lip twitched. Penny leant back and then wobbled as she remembered the bar stool's low back. "I promised you I'd avoid him, and I swear I will."

If only her thoughts were as easy to control, Penny would be able to meet Tasha's eyes with no problems at all. But surely she couldn't be held responsible for where her brain wandered or what she dreamed about without her consent? It was her history with Ethan that kept muddying the waters for her mentally, that was all. Like reaching for a cigarette even after you've given up smoking—Ethan was a habit she'd quit years ago, but now she was back, running into him left, right and center, so of course the temptation would grow stronger again.

The lighting above their table shifted to a deep purple, signaling happy hour, and Tasha shrugged. "Yeah, but I know what you two are like. Do you remember when you first started dating?" Penny hesitated and then nodded. "Well, I'd warned Ethan away from you just before that. You were my best friend and I didn't want to share. Plus, I figured it would be awkward if you guys broke up."

"But . . . we dated anyway?" Penny was a little taken

aback—this was the first she was hearing about the reservations Tasha had had when they were younger. But a lot had changed since then. Penny was an adult now, they all were, and she'd learned from her mistakes.

Tasha's chin dipped in agreement. "There never was any keeping you two apart." She hesitated, biting her lip. "I've only just got you back, Pen. I don't want you two doing something you'll regret that makes you run off again."

"Things are different now," Penny protested and then smiled and thanked the waitress for bringing over their next round of drinks. "There's a lot of history between us and seeing him after all this time . . . Well, I won't lie. It hurts, because I know I screwed up back then and I hurt you both. I don't want to do that ever again."

What Tasha had said was true: Penny knew that she and Ethan had a connection that was buried deep inside her chest, that twanged whenever she saw him, but Tasha was right to warn her away. She wasn't staying past Christmas—and Penny had already broken Ethan's heart once.

Tasha covered Penny's hand with her own and squeezed lightly. "Thank you for telling me that. I'm sorry it hurts you to see him. If it helps, I don't think he holds it against you." Tasha took a gulp of her drink and then smiled sweetly. "Neither do I. It was a long time ago."

"I just—" Penny blew out a shaky breath and tried again. "I tried to tell you guys I was leaving, so many times, but as soon as I brought the topic around to our plans after high school you guys were so firm. So clear. Neither of you understood why anyone would want to leave here, but *I* did. It was dumb, and wrong, but I was scared that if I talked to you, you'd persuade me to stay." Tears burned in Penny's eyes and she blinked quickly. "And if I'd stayed, I wouldn't have known if I could have made it, if I could have had the career I wanted." Her laugh was wet as she took a long sip of her drink. "I mean, it turns out I *didn't* make it, but hey. At least now I know." She rolled her eyes. "Sorry, I just . . . You deserved an explanation." Tasha was quiet, just listening intently, and she seemed to understand that Penny didn't want to delve any deeper right then, allowing her to change the subject. "That's enough talk about the past and me and your brother. What's new in your love life?"

Tasha squeezed her hand and then shrugged as she withdrew. "Nothing to tell really. At this rate I'll have to go into the city to meet someone." They laughed and continued chatting, and Penny was relieved to feel that the air between them was lighter. By the time they'd finished their drinks the lights in the bar had turned a sweet pink that made Tasha gasp. "Oh my gosh, we need to go. Those lights mean last call."

Penny shook her head. "No way, it's—" Her eyes

found the time on her phone and widened. "Oh shit. How is it almost midnight?"

Tasha giggled and Penny couldn't help but join in. "How are you getting home?"

"I was originally going to drive home but it looks like I'm going to have to call a cab and come back for my car tomorrow."

"No, no. That's silly, plus they'll charge you an arm and a leg to go all the way out to your parents' place. I'll call Ethan, I'm sure he won't mind dropping you off— or you can stay at my place?" Tasha already had her phone up to her ear and Penny could hear it ringing from across the table, immediately recognizing the deep tone of the familiar voice on the other end of the line.

She must have zoned out, because the next thing she knew, Tasha was hanging up and then freezing in place as she looked at Penny apologetically.

"Shit, I'm sorry. I wasn't thinking. Is this going to be OK? Him picking us up?"

No. "Yeah, of course. I'll need to head back to my parents' though if that's OK. I'm supposed to be getting up early to go to yoga with my mom."

Tasha giggled and then clamped her hand over her mouth as she looked at the collection of margarita glasses on the table between them. "Good luck with that."

The door to the bar opened not too long later and the bartender called out that they were closing to the newcomer, who raised their large hand in acknowledgement.

Ethan.

His eyes, the same shade as Tasha's, quickly found the table where Penny and Tasha were sitting, taking the two of them in, and he grinned at the collection of margarita glasses the waitress was collecting from their tabletop.

"I'd ask if you guys had a good time but I can see that you did," he teased and Penny could feel the warmth in his voice all the way down to her toes. "Ready to go?"

They stood to follow him and Penny stopped abruptly as a blur of blonde hair moved between them. "Ethan!"

He turned and smiled, a fond look crossing his face, and Penny felt her stomach sour for reasons that had nothing to do with the alcohol, and everything to do with Ethan's ex-fiancée. "Shel. You OK? Got a way home?"

Shelby nodded but her fingers curled around his arm and Penny had to look away, an unreasonable urge to pry those fingers off of Ethan rising up and fading only when she caught Tasha watching for her reaction. She smiled weakly and Tasha linked her arm through Penny's, forgiving her weakness without a word.

"Are we leaving or not?" Tasha said, interrupting whatever Shelby had been saying, and Penny coughed to hide her laugh.

Ethan rolled his eyes, the action good-natured, as he gently turned away from Shelby and ushered the two of them toward the door, calling out a goodbye as they went. As Ethan tucked Penny and Tasha under his arms and led them out to his car, Penny couldn't resist the petty urge rising in her. She turned under Ethan's arm, throwing a smug look Shelby's way as she watched them leave.

8

Yoga was tricky on a good day. Yoga with a margarita hangover? Diabolical.

"And let your body elongate, stretching into our downward dog. Breathe for ten counts, imagining every vertebrae in your spine perfectly in line as you scoop into our C-position. Good, and lift with your abdominal muscles into our tree pose—"

Penny was lost at 'elongate'.

The instructor was very soothing, with a calm and confident voice that might have been reassuring if last night's margaritas hadn't been threatening to make a reappearance on Penny's yoga mat.

At sixty-five, her mom was in better shape than Penny. She'd transitioned easily from downward dog to tree and had lowered herself to the mat preparing for a move the instructor called 'the twist'. It sounded as ominous as it looked.

It was at this point that Penny tapped out.

Luckily, there were bathrooms back by the studio's entrance foyer and she managed to make it there in time to regret indulging in happy hour's two-for-one deal.

When she was done, she decided to wait for her mom outside in the fresh air in the hopes of cooling her feverish skin.

It was surprisingly bright out, the sky clear from the previous day's heavy rain, and as she leant against the brick exterior of the studio, Penny felt herself relax in a way that the yoga teacher hadn't managed to coax out of her.

Last night had been good. More than good, even. She'd cleared the air with Tasha and it felt like she had her best friend back. She'd also woken up to find her car parked outside of her parents' place, a note left on the inside of the windshield that said nothing but '*E xx*'. The gesture warmed and confused her simultaneously. For one thing, she must have been way drunker than she'd thought, because she didn't remember giving Ethan her car keys when he'd dropped her off. But the fact he'd taken the time to drive her car back out to the cottage that morning ... It was possible Ethan hadn't meant anything by it—after all, he was a nice guy who did nice guy things—like driving drunk girls home and later delivering their cars. But the whole thing had given Penny a fuzzy feeling inside which in turn had made her feel guilty, like there was something going on between her and Ethan that she hadn't told Tasha about despite her not initiating anything.

Penny sighed, tilting her face up into the breeze and

enjoying the way it cooled her clammy skin as she tried to force all thoughts of the Blake siblings out of her head.

Magnolia Springs was almost exactly the same as it always had been. Early morning coffee groups drinking from their disposable cups as they walked through the park, the kids' soccer class finishing up on the green, the line outside of the bakery long enough that she knew the fresh bread and cakes had to be as good as she remembered them. As reluctant as she was to admit it, none of the bakeries in the city had compared to Crumbs & Co.

A row of trees lined the edge of the park behind the boutiques ahead of her, magnolias blending with oak, and she was surprised at how much the leaves had changed in the week she'd been back, shifting from green-yellow to the true orange that would eventually deepen to red.

"Wasn't that wonderful?" Angie beamed as she stepped up next to Penny, making her jump. "I grabbed your mat for you."

"Thanks, Mom."

Angie sucked in a deep breath and rolled out her shoulders, a look of bliss passing across her face that made Penny smile. "I love this time of year."

"Same." She linked her arm through her mom's and steered them in the direction of the bakery. "Only one thing could make this morning better."

Chuckling, Angie didn't fight her as Penny joined the line. "Cinnamon buns?"

"Exactly."

Twenty minutes later and with their baked goods secured, they began the walk back to the car. Angie had driven them into town and had parked in the parking lot by the grocery store, whereas Penny usually opted to park by the church where it was quieter and she didn't run the risk of bumping into a ton of people she'd rather avoid.

They were mostly quiet as they munched on their pastries, Penny practically inhaling hers.

"Did you have a good time yesterday with Tasha?"

Penny nodded, scuffing her sneakers on the ground and earning a tut from her mom. "Yeah, it was nice to catch up. We bumped into Shelby there, actually." Before Angie could say anything, Penny held up a hand. "No, I didn't get the low-down on what happened with her and Ethan."

Angie looked disappointed but brightened quickly as they approached an older woman who seemed familiar. "Oh, look!" The excitement in her mom's voice had Penny inwardly cursing. They'd been *so close* to reaching the car unscathed. "Terri! Hi, how are you? You remember my daughter, Penny?"

Terri. The nausea that had abated after she'd left the yoga studio was back in full force as Penny met the eyes of Terri Blake. Ethan and Tash's mom. Oh God, what if she had heard them gossiping about Shelby?

"Of course I do!" Terri beamed and Penny relaxed slightly. Maybe she wasn't holding a grudge for the way Penny had left things with Ethan and Tasha all those years ago. "Tasha mentioned you were visiting."

"Yeah," she said lamely and glared at her mom when she nudged her. "We went for drinks yesterday, it was nice to catch up," she added and Terri nodded.

"Well that's just lovely. It's so nice to see you girls back in touch."

Was that a dig? Penny couldn't be sure.

Mr. and Mrs. Blake had always been nice to her when she was a teen, and she'd spent a *lot* of time at their house between her visiting Tasha and Ethan. Time had been kind to Terri, further softening the lines in her white skin and lightening the blonde of her hair to a gray-white that looked sophisticated rather than aging.

"Well, if you have time before you rush off again, you should definitely come by the house for lunch with the family."

Definitely a dig. "I'd love that," Penny said, nearly stuttering. Maybe it was her overwhelming need to be liked, or that she'd thought she was getting past the tension being back in town had caused her, but Terri's wide smile put Penny on edge.

The quiet extended for a beat too long before Angie ushered Penny to her car with a hurried goodbye to Terri.

"Imagine that," Angie mused as she settled behind the wheel. "Bumping into Terri Blake."

Penny rolled her eyes and then jolted when her mom swatted at her. "Sure, you guys live in the same tiny town and go to the same stores but the chance of bumping into each other is astronomically small."

The sarcasm in her voice didn't go unnoticed.

"Well, *actually*, oh-wise-daughter-of-mine, Terri and Keith only moved back to Magnolia Springs this year."

Now that *was* surprising. "I didn't know they'd left."

Angie lifted her brows in triumph as they joined the main road and turned left toward the bridge that would take them over the river and further out of town. "Yes, well, you miss a lot when you run off for ten years without visiting your mother."

Ouch. "I'm sorry." She genuinely meant it too, and maybe Angie could tell because she softened and reached over to pat Penny's hand as the branches of the magnolia trees behind her swayed gently in the breeze beyond the window. "Why did they move back?"

A shrug. "I only know what I've heard, that Terri didn't like the new town and they couldn't settle."

"Hang on." Penny turned in her seat to eye her mom. "When you say they moved away, you mean they moved from the old town to the new town?" Penny snorted and then grabbed the oh-shit handle on the car roof when her mom took the bridge entrance at a speed that nearly had Penny flying out of her seat.

"Well the new town isn't the same," Angie defended. "It's all condos and high-rises. It's a completely different vibe."

Penny wasn't sure what was more disturbing, her

mom using the term *vibe* or the fact that she didn't seem inclined to slow down for their exit off of the bridge either. "Mom—" Her ass left the seat and her head grazed the roof. "Next time, *I'm* driving."

"Pssht," Angie said. "I've been driving these roads all my life and you know what?"

I've never crashed, Penny mouthed and nodded when her mom said exactly that.

"I've never crashed! So you just mind your manners now."

Dutifully, Penny shut her mouth and tightened her grip on the roof handle—but also silently vowed that it was the last time she'd let her mom have sugar before getting in the car and driving.

It wasn't until Sunday night that Penny considered her mom might have had a point about Penny being out of touch with the goings-on in Magnolia Springs. She'd deliberately gone out of her way to avoid learning anything about her hometown while she'd been off in the city chasing her dreams, as if the shadow of the place might be able to reach her miles away. Or maybe she was just worried that she'd get sucked back in.

Small-town life, small-town gossip . . . It was a rabbit hole and Penny was diving in head-first in the way any girl of a certain generation would: social-media stalking in bed.

There had been a shockingly cold wind that day, making the trees outside clack against her window loudly, and Penny had decided the best way to combat the chill was to stay in bed all day—barring breaks for snacks and hot chocolate. She'd also put on her thickest pair of fluffy socks and added a fuzzy blanket on top of her coverlet to ensure maximum toastiness.

Then, once cozy, she'd begun her deep dive.

In all honesty, Penny hadn't had much use for socials before. She had accounts, but they were barely used, and while she wished it was because she was too busy living her life to photograph it, the reality was that she didn't do anything noteworthy. Most of her time was spent either thinking about work, preparing for work or actually working. Maybe because if she'd stopped for two seconds, she might have lost her nerve and come running home to the cloistered safety of Magnolia Springs.

At first she'd felt silly logging on, because who would she care to stalk online? As it turned out, *everyone*.

Within an hour she knew that Coda Simpley had holidayed in Barbados last summer, that Mrs. Ashley had welcomed her first great-grandchild last fall, and that Ethan Blake looked distractingly, *unfairly*, hot with his shirt off.

She hadn't intended to fall so far down the path of stalking her ex online. In her defense, she'd initially been looking at Shelby's page filled with pouting selfies, French-tipped cocktail boomerangs, and tanned bikini pics, until she'd stumbled across a photo that had a lump rising to her throat.

The ring was sparkly, the stone large and appearing

even brighter against the light-orange tan of Shelby's hand. Ethan wasn't even in the picture, but she'd tagged him in the caption. Always a glutton for punishment, Penny had followed the tag to Ethan's page and was surprised to find quite a lot on it.

Pictures of him at a desk, head bent low and shadows falling across his face in an arty style that was clearly part of a work portfolio. Then there were photos of him with family, friends, and Shelby, baking bread with Shelby's niece, picnicking at the springs on the far side of town, at a concert for a band she didn't recognize . . .

Penny scrolled further back, unable to take her eyes away from the bright colors on the screen as Ethan's life unfolded before her: everything she'd missed. Would it all still be there if she hadn't left? For some reason the pictures made her heart speed up and tears prick at her eyes. She'd been so caught up all those years ago in what she'd be missing in San Fran if she stayed in Magnolia Springs, but she had never stopped to wonder what she might miss out on if she left. Now the proof was there, right in front of her. Would that have been her face squeezed in next to Ethan's at the top of a Ferris wheel instead of Shelby's? Her chest tightened to the point of pain before she pushed out a strong breath.

Then there were the photos she spent an embarrassing amount of time studying: beach volleyball.

Ethan had always been athletic, but this was something else.

The majority of the photos were action shots, some

in black and white like they were shooting for *GQ* and not just Instagram, but there were a couple of photos of Ethan standing still, hand raised up to shield his eyes from the sun. Sand covered his chest, clinging to the droplets of water from the ocean spray, and his smile was wide, like he'd just finished laughing.

Hindsight was a bitch, and she would just have to learn to live with her regrets.

She rolled onto her side, fluffing the pillow under her head and cursing when her phone slipped out of her hands. She jolted to catch it, fingers clasped awkwardly around the screen.

Once again comfortable, Penny returned her eyes to the screen and Ethan's abs as something caught her attention out of the corner of her eye.

A red heart.

Eyes flaring wide, Penny sat bolt upright as a cold sweat broke out across her skin. "No. No, no, no." She face-planted the pillow and rubbed her face roughly against the cotton as she shook her head.

The only thing worse than cyber-stalking your ex? Getting caught.

Her finger hesitated above the screen before she tapped, unliking the post and hoping Ethan would assume the notification was a glitch. What other reason would there be for his ex to be sniffing around at his photos from *five years ago*?

Penny thumped her head against her pillow repeatedly

with a groan, stopping abruptly when her phone buzzed. Dizzy, she fell very still before cracking open one eye and peering at the notification that had popped up on her home screen.

Ethan_Blake: Indulging in a little light stalking on this fine Sunday evening?

She shouldn't reply. That would only add fuel to the fire, right? Or maybe he would take it as an admission of guilt. Undecided, Penny was still hesitating when another direct message buzzed into her inbox.

Ethan_Blake: And yes, in case you were wondering, my abs really do look like that. Even five years later.

"Ugh," she muttered, staring at the message and clicking to open it before remembering, too late, it would show as *read*. "Crap. Stupid, stupid . . ."

FindAPenny: I have no clue what you're talking about.

Ethan_Blake: *photo attachment* Strange, that looks like your name in my notifications

FindAPenny: . . . I hate you

His response took long enough that she'd thought that was the end of the conversation, until another message popped in.

Ethan_Blake: Don't worry. If you had more than two photos on your account I'd probably be stalking them too

Heat rose in her face and she dropped her phone to the covers before sitting up to retrieve her hot chocolate and taking a long sip. This wasn't flirting, was it? This was just two friends, chatting. Her phone buzzed again and she snorted when she unlocked it, seeing his name pop up in her notifications.

Ethan_Blake liked your photo

Ethan_Blake liked your photo

FindAPenny: Now who's the stalker huh

Ethan_Blake: See you tomorrow ;)

She stared for longer than was necessary in order to read his message. Tomorrow? He was working at the orchard again? Why was he even working there in the first place? By all accounts he seemed to have a thriving business working as an architect and interior designer—or, at least, that's what his business's Instagram page had made it look like.

And how did he know that she had a shift tomorrow too?

Thoughts swirling, Penny turned her phone over so she couldn't stare at the message for any longer. If only she could quiet her brain in the same way.

9

Penny had been feeling jumpy all morning, ever since she'd arrived at the orchard. She was half expecting Ethan to appear around the corner at any moment, likely catching her in some kind of embarrassing situation as seemed to be her norm now.

But so far, she hadn't seen a trace of him.

She'd deliberately worn her coziest, scruffiest outfit to the orchard, not wanting to look like she'd dressed up for him if she wore something too nice. So she'd settled for a beat-up pair of mom jeans that had a rip in the knee and an oversize sweatshirt whose sleeves were long enough that only the cuffs were keeping them above her hands. Casual. Unaffected.

Why does it matter? Her inner voice screamed, and she tried to focus on the task at hand as she squinted against the watery sunlight. The wind had eased off that morning, but the chill in the air remained, reminding her uncannily of cold nights by the bonfire that took place on the green in the center of town to celebrate fall. Maybe she could suggest that her parents set up a stand with warm apple cider—mostly because *she* loved warm apple cider, but it would also kick-off the buzz in the run-up to Halloween Orchard Fest in late October.

Unfortunately, her thoughts hadn't settled even after clearing half the tree of its load.

Maybe he'd been joking, she reasoned. He could have been playing off of the whole 'stalker' thing, rather than literally meaning he'd see her today. She sighed, shaking her head at herself as she made her way down the steps of her ladder to deposit another load in the bigger tub.

You're here to pick apples, not pick up men.

But thinking about Ethan as only a *man* didn't feel right. There was too much between them. He'd been her best friend since they were kids, and her boyfriend since they were about fourteen. Ethan Blake wasn't just some guy, he was *the* guy. Her first love, maybe her only love really. *So far,* she reminded herself. Because Ethan wasn't her future, he was her past, regardless of the lingering connection between them.

She worked methodically, figuring the harder she focused on harvesting the less time she'd spend debating the way Ethan Blake made her feel, and pulled apples down from the large tree at a pace far quicker than usual while trying to dodge the fall leaves that sprinkled around her like confetti.

It was only rational, she supposed. Being back in this town, with these people, it was easy to fall into old patterns—and Ethan was the person she'd had the hardest time convincing herself to leave behind the first time. And she *was* leaving again, she couldn't let herself get caught up in emotions that were just a result of nostalgia and admittedly toned abs.

The sky had darkened a little, the sun having vanished behind a cloud and refusing to reappear, and Penny worked to keep one eye on the sky, not liking the way the air was feeling. The prickle of static along her skin, the slightly dew-heavy moisture surrounding her . . . If she wasn't careful, she'd be caught in a storm.

On the one hand, if it was the kind of storm that brought wind as well as rain then it was likely the winds might shake free some of the apples waiting to be harvested—but on the other hand, it might chuck them around so much that they were only good for jam or the horses in the stable next door.

She increased her pace, moving as fast as she could without putting herself in danger so that she could at least finish this tree and pack the apples safely away. The wind picked up, changing from a light breeze to a more insistent push that made her wobble.

Nearly done. Just one more section . . .

She reached up, stretching for the top branches of the tree that she'd stupidly left for last. The wind blew harder, her fingers slipped on the glossy skin of a red apple, and she shrieked when her footing slipped.

Two hands came at her with a blur of speed and scooped beneath her before she could hit the ground. Long-lashed pools of brown met her eyes as she gasped, grateful that Ethan had somehow appeared just in time for him to catch her. "Need a hand?" He placed her gently on the ground, his sturdy arms able to lower her easily.

"Sorry," she croaked and swallowed before trying again. "I lost my footing. The wind—"

Ethan nodded and she pressed a shaky hand to his cheek, assessing his pallor. He smiled but it was weak. "Glad I got to you in time. Can't believe you're still out here."

"How did you know?"

The disapproval that puckered his brow moved her fingers and she dropped her hand quickly, having forgotten it was pressed to his face. "Your car was still here."

He let go of her slowly, his body brushing against hers as his hands steadied her with a palm to her ass that he quickly removed, color staining his cheeks.

She cleared her throat, willing the heat in her own cheeks to die down—a task that was probably impossible given that her body was still fixated on the brief warmth of Ethan's hand on her butt. "I want to finish up this tree and then get out of here before that storm hits."

He nodded, face turning serious as he climbed up the other side of the ladder and began pulling apples down a little faster than she could. "I'll help you finish up. The road still floods when the weather gets bad, so we should get out of here before we get stuck."

Flash floods on old country roads had always been a pain in her childhood, and now she wasn't sure her little bug would survive a drenching.

Once she felt steadier, she helped lower the apples he collected into the tub at their feet. They worked in companionable silence for a while and in its echoes all Penny could think about was the feel of Ethan's arms around her, the way he'd clasped her to his chest like something precious, even as she tried desperately to focus only on the task at hand. It didn't help. The warmth of his fingertips pressing into her skin was as good as a brand.

The clouds rolled in, getting darker and thicker, like the evening had come around instead of the afternoon. But there hadn't been any thunder yet, so for now they still had some time left to finish up and get out of there. Her pace increased, fingers searching for purchase on the smooth surface of the apples.

"So you work here." She hadn't phrased it as a question, but he clearly heard it there anyway as she bundled a haul of apples into a cloth and walked it down the ladder to the larger tub at the base of the tree.

The wind kicked up, ruffling Ethan's hair as he nodded. "Yeah, it gives me an excuse to leave the house, get some fresh air. Meet people." He added the last with a quick grin flashed in her direction that she pretended not to see.

The ladder clanked as she climbed up the other side

to help him, reaching for the next branch and jerking back when her shoulder brushed against his.

"What about you? I thought you were a chef."

She nodded, careful to keep her distance as she twisted another apple free, its sweet scent filling the air as thunder rumbled quietly enough that she almost missed it. "Yeah, I was. I am. I'm just taking a break while I decide where to go next."

He hummed like that was a completely reasonable thing to do and she was relieved when he didn't push for more information. Their eyes caught and held and Penny jumped when the next clap of thunder seemed to be right overhead, the sound so loud she dropped the apple she was holding as the noise rippled through her.

"We should probably go."

No sooner had she said it than lightning flashed and the heavens opened, warm rain falling from the sky in a deluge so heavy that a fine mist filled the space between the trees, cloaking the orchard.

They hurried down from the ladder and grabbed a handle each of the large tub of apples, the rubber slippery in their hands as they wielded it between them. Normally they'd leave it behind when they were done, but with the weather raging around them the fruit wouldn't have lasted five seconds.

More thunder cracked and mud squelched beneath her boots, the fresh smell of rain and trees strangely soothing even as she tried to blink water out of her eyes to see where she was going. The weather had surged so quickly, so unexpectedly, they'd be lucky to make it to the small shop at the front of the orchard, let alone back home.

Ethan shielded her from the rain as they arrived at the door to the shop and Penny fumbled for the keys. The shop wasn't open every day; she'd only brought the keys with her today so that John, their afternoon harvester, could collect up the apples and leave them in the shop for sorting later.

The rain fell harder, pouring down with a renewed vigor as though it knew they were close to escaping it. Strands of her hair fell about her face in what was probably a wet mess, but all she could focus on was the cool metal in her hands and the heat of Ethan at her back.

A click sounded and the door finally swung open for them to drag the apples inside and then slam the door.

She tried the lights and was unsurprised when they didn't turn on. It was a fail-safe for storms that their generator cut power to avoid an electrical fire. It was lucky they kept battery-operated lanterns in the store for times like this. Penny was pleased that she remembered where they were, a little dusty but still functional as she flicked the switch on and a warm glow bathed the wooden walls and floor. The counter where her mom normally worked was empty and the ceiling felt lower than usual because the warm light didn't quite reach the roof.

"I don't suppose you have a heater?" Ethan said, hair dripping down his face as a shiver ran through him.

"Just blankets," she managed to get out through chattering teeth. They kept them on hand for the Halloween Orchard Fest; if it was dry, people used them as picnic blankets to sit on, but they also came in handy for drying people off after apple bobbing and keeping the chill at bay for children or the elderly if they stayed outside too long in the cool fall air. Plus, it never hurt to have a stash for situations like this.

"Right," he said, accepting the tartan one she passed him. "I suppose we should get naked, too."

Had she been struck by lightning? "What?"

"Our clothes are wet," he said, and she would have thought he was being matter of fact if not for the twitch of his lips. "If we want to conserve body warmth, we should get naked under the blankets."

"I think we'll manage with our clothes on," she choked out and he chuckled.

"Yeah, I guess." He sighed in mock disappointment and she laughed, the sound breathless. "Oh hey, there's a fireplace. Could we get a fire going to dry off?"

Penny considered the hearth, tucked away in the corner behind an armchair that was more decorative than practical, before nodding. Logs were already in the grate with matches and kindling in tidy little containers on the mantle. In all honesty, she'd forgotten the fireplace was here. She could count on one hand the number of times she'd seen a fire lit in it, but right then some warmth sounded too heavenly to refuse.

The rain continued outside, the rhythmic drumming of droplets on the roof making her eyes feel heavy as the sparks caught in the grate. They sat as close to the fire as possible, nestled comfortably in the blankets.

"OK," she said, shooting Ethan a stern look as she slipped off her shoes and socks and placed them in front of the fire atop the brick lip of the grate. "Don't read into this. I just can't deal with wet socks."

He laughed. "I remember. You walked home barefoot one summer when we swam in the springs with Tasha because your socks were wet and you refused to put them back on."

Penny shuddered, the mere thought of forcing her foot into a wet sock enough to make her cringe. "That was a good summer."

They'd been fourteen, almost fifteen, and it had been one of the hottest summers of their lives. Tasha had convinced them to go swimming with her and, while she was off chatting to some other friends, Ethan had pulled Penny into a little rocky hollow hidden from the view of their friends and kissed her for the first time. He'd tasted like sunscreen and the orange Popsicles they'd taken out of her mom's freezer. Penny found herself becoming lost in the memory, as though, in the cocooning warmth of the fire and blankets, she could almost feel the ghost of his lips, hesitant against hers.

Ethan nodded, a warmth in his eyes that had nothing

to do with the reflection of the fire, and she wondered if he was remembering their first kiss too. The lantern's glow clad him in a golden wash and his hair had started to curl around his ears where it dried; she swallowed and forced herself to look away, to not trace the shape of his shoulders beneath the damp shirt he wore, or the fullness of his parted lips as he breathed in the warmth. She didn't want to think about what she looked like right then, but at least her shivering had subsided. Thankfully, the sound of the rain covered any awkward silence that might have otherwise taken over and instead the space felt cozy, safe.

"Thanks for staying to help me," she murmured, glancing at him and then looking away from the openness on his face and instead watching the fire dance and pop in the grate.

"Of course," he said, like it was really that simple and she wondered if, for him, it was. He wasn't mad at her, he even seemed *happy* that she was home, so why did she feel like she was waiting for the other shoe to drop? "So, what's new?"

One eyebrow cocked as she considered the absurdity of the question, of catching up *now* of all times. Though, it was probably the best chance they'd get considering she couldn't run off unless she wanted to be swept away in a flash flood. "Well, I moved back to my hometown."

Ethan leant back on his hands and wriggled his toes in front of the fireplace. "Moved back? I thought you were just visiting."

"I am," she rushed to say. "I just don't have a firm exit date yet. Probably after Christmas."

"Do you miss it? The city?"

She fiddled with the sleeve of her sweatshirt and lifted one shoulder in a half-shrug. "Honestly? Not really."

He chuckled and she glanced up to find him watching her. "Is it strange being back?"

"Yes." No hesitation, no need for her to think about it. "Are you the only one allowed to ask questions here or . . .?"

He pretended to think about it before smirking at her. "I guess you can ask some too—if you even have any left after last night, stalker."

She scrambled to her feet, looking anywhere but at him as she blushed, desperate to change the subject. "You know, I think I remember my mom mentioning that they keep a stash of cider under the counter for when she and dad work late in the summer," she muttered, moving across the room and rummaging beneath the workspace until she pulled open the bottom drawer. "Jackpot. Want one?"

"Seems silly to say, what with all the water outside, but I'm actually incredibly thirsty."

She giggled and made her way back over to her spot next to him in front of the fire and pulled a can free from the box, passing it over to him. "Summer fruits OK?"

"Anything except—"

"Elderflower," she answered, nodding, and then

busied herself with pulling out her own can. "Well, cheers. To thunderstorms."

"To reunions," he murmured, and the crack of their cans opening was nearly as loud as the thunder they'd heard earlier. They sipped their drinks slowly, the cider a little warm and flat. But it was sweet and the fire made everything feel cozier, the gentle heat enough to warm the small space.

"So last night—" she began, at the same time that he spoke.

"Can I kiss you?"

Her mouth dropped open and for a second she forgot how to speak. "What? No. Of course not. Why would you—"

"Are you seeing someone?"

"Well, no, but—"

"Then you should let me kiss you. For old time's sake. For the goodbye we didn't get." He smiled and it wasn't one she'd seen him wear before. Sad but not. "Because I'm sitting here with you, the girl I loved and who broke my heart when she left, and for the life of me, I don't know why I didn't go with you. Follow you."

This was not what she'd expected at all. "Ethan—"

"Are you telling me you don't feel it too?" he challenged, leaning a little closer and smirking when she scrambled up to her feet and took three steps away. "Do you feel like the spark between us faded in the last ten years? It hasn't for me."

No. "Yes."

He raised an eyebrow as he pushed to his feet, mimicking her pose but staying where he was. "If I'm wrong, it's OK. I won't bring it up again," he said and she relaxed until he continued. "But I think you made a mistake before, when you left. You know it, I know it, hell, the whole town probably knows it because what's between us is obvious and that's just the kind of place this is."

He wasn't wrong, but this . . . she wasn't prepared for this.

"Tasha—" she tried and he silenced her with a look.

"I don't blame you for what happened. We were young, you had dreams, I had too much pride to admit that you might need more than just this town, than me or Tasha."

Penny couldn't tell if it was just her or if the room had risen in temperature by a million degrees. She was half-surprised steam wasn't rising from their clothes, even as she knew logically that nothing had changed inside the shop. It was him. Ethan. He was the one setting her ablaze with things she couldn't want, things she'd *promised* not to have.

You already broke his heart once. Tasha's disappointed eyes, the frown she'd wear, all of it ran through Penny's mind in the space of a heartbeat. And yet . . . *And yet.*

"We're not just dumb kids anymore, Pen." He took a step closer. "We're all grown up now." *Step.* "I'm not the nervous eighteen-year-old you remember." *Step.*

"If you'll let me . . ." *Step.* "I'll show you what you've been missing out on."

She couldn't speak. Couldn't *breathe*.

Ethan's hand cupped her jaw and he moved slowly, like she might spook and run at any second as he brushed his thumb over her bottom lip and looked into her eyes, waiting for her decision.

Her senses filled with him, the sandalwood scent of his skin and hair, the sweet cider on his breath and the heat in his eyes. Before she could think it all the way through, she was nodding and Ethan was closing the remnants of the distance between them.

Kissing Ethan Blake was like coming home. Easy as breathing, familiar but altogether new. His mouth teased hers with an expertise he hadn't had before, wringing gasps out of her when he tasted her mouth like he couldn't drink her in fast enough. The warmth of the fire was lost in the heat of his kiss and when he tugged her closer she didn't resist, her hands falling to his shoulders and then moving with a mind of their own until they were twined in the damp strands of his hair.

One of his hands tightened on her waist as the kiss deepened, his tongue doing its best to coax all of her secrets and desires out of her and into him. Her body was pulled flush against his and the evidence of his arousal was firm against her hip, his low moan telling her he wasn't as in control as she'd believed.

When he pulled back, she followed. Not ready for the kiss to end.

He chuckled under his breath as they panted, eyes like warm chocolate as they roved over her face. "Have dinner with me."

The heat in the room vanished, as though he'd pulled it out of the atmosphere with his words. She took a breath, held it, ready to say yes, *willing* herself to accept even as she shook her head. Disappointment made her dizzy, or maybe that was the lack of oxygen, and her breath left her raggedly as she muttered, "I can't."

Penny had made Tasha a promise and it was bad enough that she'd broken it once by letting Ethan kiss her.

He dropped his hands and retreated several steps. "I see."

"Ethan, it's not—"

"I think the rain stopped," he said, giving her a tight smile as he grabbed his shoes and strode to the door, taking her heart with him. He closed it without looking back, calling behind him, "Drive safe, Penny."

10

The art of avoidance was harder than Penny had thought. Yet for a full week she had managed just that. Sure, it had taken some creativity—Ethan somehow managed to be *everywhere* at any given moment. Still, she'd persevered.

He'd taken to arriving at the orchard at the same time as her. At first she'd thought this was a coincidence, so she'd pretended to be on a call in her car until he'd left, but after two days she'd instead opted to arrive later in the morning—only to find him on a coffee break, laughing with her mom in the shop hut where she was working the cash register. Ethan had watched her pull in and park and had wordlessly handed her a pumpkin spice latte, still hot.

She'd tried leaving late to avoid seeing him and had thought she'd been successful until she saw the note on her windshield. *Drive safe. E.* So even when he wasn't physically there, he was still finding ways to stay present in her mind and it infuriated her. Why did he have to make this so hard for her? She was *trying* to do right by him, and Tasha.

Dodging him? He was somehow one step ahead. Ignoring him? He made it impossible to do so when they were in front of her mom and he was being *charming*. At one point she'd even climbed up *into* an apple tree to avoid a passing Ethan, but it wasn't like she could stay up there forever.

. . . Could she?

Fed up, she'd even decided to forgo a shift in favor of relaxing in town, grabbing a coffee and a cake. The triumph had been sweet—and short. Because who was waiting inside Crumbs & Co? Ethan. Blake.

Penny was trying to hold on to the promise she'd made to Tasha and yet it was like the whole world was making it as difficult as possible, like some kind of face-your-ex conspiracy.

Avoiding Tasha wasn't exactly *necessary*, but it helped Penny feel a little better. How was she supposed to look her friend in the face when she'd sworn to steer clear of Ethan and had, instead, kissed him? Maybe it would have been easier if the kiss had been horrible, or even just *fine*, but it hadn't—it had been . . . *everything*. And she hadn't stopped thinking about it for the past week. She'd only just resolved the lingering tension between her and Tasha and now . . .

Ugh. Why did Ethan have to put his stupid, warm, full mouth on mine?

Maybe if Penny told Tasha, she would understand. It wasn't like Penny had orchestrated the kiss, or even gone looking for it. It had been an accident. *A really hot accident.*

Penny had just grabbed her morning pumpkin spice latte from Coffee Affair on Saturday when a flash of blonde hair made her freeze like a deer caught in headlights. Surely Ethan hadn't tracked her down on the weekend?

"Pen!" Tasha waved and relief and anxiety curdled in Penny's stomach at the prospect of facing Tasha. There was no way Penny could pretend she hadn't seen her, not when half the cafe was looking Tash's way. Did she tell her? Or did she just chalk what had happened up to the thunderstorm and the heat of the moment?

"Come and join me."

Penny's feet dragged a little as she walked over to the small wooden table Tasha had claimed and pulled out the chair opposite her. Her ass had barely hit the seat before Tasha was leaning in close and fixing Penny with a shrewd look.

"You've been avoiding me."

Penny choked on her sip of latte. "What? *No!*"

"Penny." There it was again, that no-nonsense tone that Tasha only pulled out when she knew her best friend was bullshitting.

Unable to meet her gaze, she instead looked down at her to-go cup and the pale brown label that wrapped all the way around it. "I've just been super busy."

"Too busy to answer my texts?"

She shrugged. "I lost my phone for a bit. Put it down and just couldn't find it again, you know how it is."

Tasha's face said she did not, in fact, *know how it is*. The look only darkened when a buzzing erupted from Penny's bag.

"Oh look," she said weakly, "found it."

"What's going on?" Tasha reached over and placed one hand over Penny's, stopping her nervously peeling the wrap off of her cup. "You can tell me anything."

Except, no. Penny couldn't. Tasha had asked for *one thing* and Penny had messed it up already. "It's just been a lot moving back." There, that was close enough to the truth. It *had* been a lot moving back home, especially with Ethan continuously muddying the waters between them despite Penny's best efforts to stay away.

One eyebrow rose. "You're moving back?"

"Oh. I—Well, I don't know. Maybe? I haven't exactly had restaurants beating down my door to get me to work for them."

Tasha nodded slowly before clapping her hands together. "You know who you should talk to? Ethan."

Penny's mouth went dry. "What? No. Why would I talk to Ethan?" Her laugh sounded nervous even to her own ears but Tasha didn't call her out on it.

"One of his friends from college is some hot-shot chef. Works for a restaurant in New York. I bet Ethan would introduce you."

Intrigue made her eyes widen and her heart skip a beat. She hadn't even known that Ethan had gone to college, let alone that he'd made the kind of connections there that were enviable by anyone's standards.

"That would be amazing." If only she hadn't let him kiss her, rejected him and then done everything she could to avoid speaking to him this week. Even if there was no animosity between her and Ethan, Penny didn't think he would want to help her with this. "Do you know what this guy's name is?" Maybe she could look him up, see if it was even something she'd be interested in before she embarrassed herself further by approaching Ethan. *If it's paid work and not in Magnolia Springs, then you're interested.* Although, she wouldn't be able to leave until the busy period died down at the orchard. She couldn't leave her parents high and dry like that.

Like you did before. Pushing the negative voice away, she refocused on what Tasha was saying.

"I can't remember his name off the top of my head but I've got the restaurant saved in my phone, I'll text it to you in a minute. Anyway, did I tell you about the library project I'm running with the elementary school? You know I love the kids, but my *God*—you wouldn't believe the noise, Pen!" Tasha swiftly changed topic, launching headfirst into a long list of complaints about how the schoolkids didn't respect the library *at all*.

Penny was perfectly happy to let Tasha's ranting wash over her, caught up in the prospect of reaching out to this mystery chef. It was exciting to think she might finally have a clear way out of Magnolia Springs again but she couldn't deny that she was also confused at the mix of emotions that the idea of leaving brought up in her. By the time Penny finished her coffee, she had left the cafe with a promise to get breakfast with Tasha during the week and the name of a restaurant.

She'd worry about how to get Ethan's help later.

It turned out that 'some chef in New York' had been an understatement on Tash's part. Nicolo Taften wasn't *a* chef in New York, he was *the* chef in New York. He didn't just work for a restaurant, he *owned* his restaurant—and was one of the youngest chefs to ever receive a Michelin star to boot. And, somehow, Penny's only barrier to getting an introduction? An ex she'd recently spurned. *Great*.

Though, it was for Ethan's own good even if he couldn't see it.

Warm, afternoon sunlight spilled into her parents' living room where Penny sat on her phone, learning everything she could about Nicolo. Seeing Tasha at the coffee shop had left her feeling a little hollow and it reminded Penny, uncomfortably, of how she'd felt in the days leading up to her leaving Magnolia Springs ten years ago. Back then, even her parents hadn't understood her need to leave, though they'd supported her anyway, but the weight of keeping the secret from Tasha and Ethan had been heavy. She didn't want to feel like that again, but here she was, already hiding the truth from Tasha and preparing to leave. To try to cheer herself up, she made a fancy hot chocolate from her mom's stash and put on her coziest peach-colored sweater to snuggle up in as she looked at Nicolo's menu.

The sofa dipped as her dad sat down on the other end of it, lifting her feet up and dropping them in his lap as he set his tea down on the raised table by his arm of the sofa.

"Looking at anything interesting?"

She sighed and pulled her legs under her as she sat up. "Just a restaurant in New York."

"You got an interview? Honey, that's great."

There was nothing but pride in her dad's voice, even at the prospect of her leaving again, and she smiled. "No, but it might lead that way." She hesitated and then said quietly, "Ethan knows the owner."

"Ah." Philip smiled, understanding lighting his face. "That boy would move the heavens for you."

"I'm not so sure." The words came slow, faltering, as she finally spilled her guts about what had happened with Ethan. "I promised Tasha that I would steer clear of Ethan, for all of our sakes, but he's making it so *hard* and I don't understand why."

"Do you think it was fair of Tasha to ask that of you? Especially if Ethan's none the wiser?"

Penny paused, thinking about it. She hadn't considered that before. "I mean, I understand why she said it. I made a mess when I left last time."

"But that was a long time ago," he pointed out and she nodded slowly.

"He kissed me," she confessed and the relief was instant. Keeping it inside this whole time had been a gargantuan effort. Maybe for some people it would have been weird to talk to their dad about this kind of stuff, but they'd always been close. And, more than that, her dad gave the best advice—no holds barred. "The other night, when the thunderstorm rolled into town. We got stuck at the orchard together and waited out the weather in Mom's shop."

Her dad nodded, brows furrowed as he listened to her talk. "Well, I think it's clear to me why he's making it so hard for you to avoid him, Pen."

"It is?"

He patted her on the arm. "He doesn't want to be avoided, honey. Maybe you and Tasha have this all worked out between you, but Ethan's a person with a say in all this as well. You've cast him in a role that he clearly doesn't want. Now, whether or not you feel you can be friends with him is up to you."

"But Tasha—"

"Should have nothing to do with you and Ethan," Philip said firmly.

She sighed. "I guess. I just don't want her to hate me."

"I know it feels like a bit of a pickle, but really— what kind of friend would Tasha be if she didn't let you and Ethan work this out for yourselves?" He took off his glasses and cleaned them idly with the hem of his sweater as she reached for her mug and took a drink, cradling it in her palms as the steam curled up to warm her nose. "But I still stand by what I said earlier, especially with what you've just told me. Ethan's a good man, he cares for you. I can't believe he wouldn't help you if you asked. As for the rest . . . Well, that's for the two of you to figure out."

"Maybe," she murmured, playing with a loose thread of the floral fabric arm of the sofa. She couldn't help feeling like her dad was simplifying things a little too much, mainly because she *did* care about what Tasha would think and feel. Besides, if she was being honest, she'd tried not to dwell on what Ethan had said to her. Like if she didn't think about it, she could pretend the words weren't there, spoken into reality and haunting her dreams when she let her guard down. "I don't want to make things complicated with him." Philip nodded and she continued in a smaller voice. "I don't want to hurt him again."

Her dad reached over and squeezed her hand. "Maybe that's for him to decide."

She nodded but was still unconvinced even as she felt ready to move on from the maudlin conversation. Even her hot chocolate wasn't enough to lift her mood. "Where's Mom?"

Philip waved a hand and crossed one leg over the other as he unfolded his newspaper, the smell of ink oddly comforting. "Well, normally she sees her gal-pals on a Wednesday for brunch but one of them, Karen I think, couldn't make it so they rescheduled brunch for today."

"You didn't want to join them?" she teased and laughed when he gave a mock shudder.

"I'm just fine with my crossword, thank you." He glanced up at Penny and eyed her over the top of his glasses. "But I wouldn't say no to a sandwich. If you're making one."

Laughter left her easily as she stood and made her way to the kitchen on the other side of the cottage's ground floor. "Fine, but I'm not cutting off the crusts."

"That's OK, honey. I need more curly hair on my chest anyway."

She rolled her eyes, glad her Mom wasn't there to see her do it and give her a scolding. The bread in the bread box was thick and fluffy, making her mouth water as she looked at it. She hadn't really done any cooking since she'd left her job in San Fran, not beyond pouring milk onto cereal and assembling the odd sandwich, and for the first time since she'd arrived in Magnolia Springs she realized that she missed it.

The floorboards creaked under her socked feet as she poked her head around the doorway to the lounge. "Do you think Mom would mind if I made us dinner tonight?"

Her dad's eyes lit up as he smiled. "Not at all."

She nodded, a little hesitant, and repeated the motion with more confidence. "OK, great."

What would it be like to cook without the pressure of a head chef screaming at you that the entrees were late? Or overdone when they weren't? Working under her old boss had made her good at ducking flying plates, but she couldn't say whether it had actually made her a better chef. She missed cooking for the joy of it, trying something new, experimenting with a new flavor or dish . . .

The contents of the fridge were a little uninspiring so she grabbed her keys and her dad's sandwich, handing it over to him before slipping on her shoes. If she was going to cook dinner, she was going to do it right. And that meant doing the one, dreaded thing she'd managed to avoid since she'd arrived back home: going to the grocery store.

In Magnolia Springs, there was only one general superstore to choose from, though there was also a local market just outside of town, as well as a few artisanal shops. Penny *hated* the grocery store. It was loud and busy and they moved everything around a dozen times a month, making the experience wholly frustrating.

Thankfully, she'd picked a rare quiet moment to come in and get out with the short list of groceries she needed to make chicken parm. It was one of her favorite dishes and she hadn't made it in literally years because she'd had no time to cook for herself while working at the restaurant in San Francisco. It should be a crime for a *chef* to have to live off microwaveable meals.

It was more than a little strange to be walking around the town's grocery store as an adult, though.

Everything seemed smaller than she remembered and, all told, she was actually on the verge of enjoying herself when she pushed her cart around the corner of the next aisle to grab some herbs. Instead, she immediately stopped in her tracks and backed up to remain unseen.

Running into Ethan at the grocery store wouldn't have been ideal to begin with, but to see him there with his *ex-fiancée*? Penny grimaced, hoping they hadn't seen her before she'd backed away. Enduring small talk with the two of them when everything was so confusing between her and Ethan right now might be more than Penny could handle.

So, like the scaredy cat she was, she waited in front of the aisle end where bags of chips had been stacked on the plinth and shamelessly eavesdropped.

Ethan's low chuckle made her heart beat faster even as her stomach dropped to the floor at Shelby's answering giggle. *What could be so funny?*

"We always did have a good time together," Shelby was saying, and Penny dared a glimpse around the corner. Her hands curled into fists at their proximity, the way Shelby overtly leant into Ethan and batted her eyes at him was ridiculous. The consolation Penny had was that Ethan didn't seem to be reciprocating.

"I know, Shel. I just think going for drinks would be a bad idea. I don't want to blur the lines." Ethan's voice was smooth, gentle, and Penny held her breath to listen more closely. "Besides, I thought you were dating someone now?"

Shelby scoffed. "Nothing serious. Not like us."

Us? Penny bit her lip and forced herself to remain still. It was bad enough that she was snooping on their conversation, let alone if she went charging in to—

To do what? You're just friends.

Her shoulders sagged and her cart wobbled as she leant her weight into the handles. God, what was she doing? Decision made, she'd started to leave when the sound of her own name made her pause.

"Is this because *Penny's* back in town?"

"I don't know what you—"

"I'm not stupid, Ethan. I've seen the way you look at her."

There was a tense beat of silence that had Penny's hands tightening on the handles of her cart as she waited to hear what they would say next.

"I don't think it's any of your business, Shel," Ethan said, so softly Penny almost missed the words. "I'm sorry you're hurting. But what I feel for Penny is between me and her."

What I feel for Penny—what did he feel for her? And why did the words fill her with relief? OK, now she really *did* need to leave. But she also really wanted some fresh herbs for the meal. She hovered in place, deliberating for a few moments longer, before deciding to bite the bullet and move round the corner. It had been quiet for a little while now, so with any luck Ethan and Shelby had moved on.

The wheels of her cart squeaked a little as she got

it moving again and barreled into the next aisle with the careless abandon of someone who *definitely hadn't* been eavesdropping, only to find her performance was for nothing and the aisle was empty.

She grabbed the herbs she wanted and checked her mental list, realizing she'd got everything she needed. Except . . .

"Wine," she muttered, heading back out of the aisle and turning left to grab the last-minute addition to her list. Then, as soon as possible, she was getting the hell out of here.

Grocery stores, she thought and sighed. *Trouble every time.*

Her mom was still out when Penny got home, so she unloaded the groceries from her car without any interference, swapping her boots for slippers as she came in the door. After she'd laid out everything she needed on the counter and set the oven to preheat, she tied her old apron round her waist and smiled at the small hole in the top of the pocket on the front. She'd had the thing for years and had secretly been a little bummed that she'd forgotten it when she'd moved out. Penny had assumed her mom would have thrown it out—it had certainly seen better days—but instead it had been left hanging on its usual peg on the back of the kitchen door, like it had been waiting for her all this time.

The methodical movements were like muscle memory for her, she'd made the recipe so many times, and it soothed her. Brain shut off, internal worries fading, Penny focused on slicing and flattening the chicken breasts and heating oil in a pan. It had been a long time since cooking had felt calming for her; she was too used to the extreme pressures of cooking for hundreds of people and constantly being told she was doing it wrong by her boss—despite never receiving a single complaint from the customers. *This* was what she loved, and as she placed the chicken into the hot oil to fry, she wondered why she was fighting so hard to get back to a career that had been slowly killing her.

11

If Penny hadn't cooked last night's dinner herself, she might have been worried that the flips in her stomach were from food poisoning—that, and the constant nausea. Unfortunately, the real cause stood less than three feet away with his back to her as he pulled down apples at a rate that was impressive, bordering on super-human.

"Hey."

The muscles in Ethan's back tensed and relaxed beneath his flannel shirt in the time it took her to blink. "Hey."

Silence flowed between them, heavier than usual and filled with all the things he'd said—and everything she hadn't.

"So you're done hiding from me then?" He turned and she steeled herself for the reproachment she was certain she'd find on his face, only to be shocked when she instead found only soft amusement. "I have to say, you scaled that tree pretty fast."

"I was very motivated."

He laughed and some of her tension leaked away

as the sound spread out around them, catching in the branches of the trees. "What can I do for you, Penny? Unless you've changed your mind about—"

"I haven't changed my mind," she said quickly, not wanting to hear him say the words again as she clasped her gloved hands tightly together and fidgeted with the leaves on the ground with her boots. "I . . . Well, actually I was hoping for a favor."

His brows lifted and his cocky smirk grew as he leant on the side of the ladder like he had all the time in the world. "Oh?"

"Tasha mentioned you had a friend in New York that runs a restaurant and that maybe you could put in a good word for me."

"Yeah, she might have mentioned that to me."

Her breath left her in a rush of relief. "Oh, that's great."

"What word do you want me to use?"

She stilled, unsure, and he prowled forward with purpose, stopping just a few breaths away from her. His jeans were wet around the hem from the dewy grass and the long sleeves of his blue flannel shirt and white Henley were pushed up, revealing his tanned and toned forearms, and *goddamn* she just couldn't stop her eyes from lingering on them as he looked at her.

"Infuriating?" His eyes flashed and she held her breath when he reached up to tuck a strand of loose hair behind her ear. "Beautiful?"

"Um," she said, her voice cracking and making

her wince. "I was thinking more like 'talented' or 'punctual'."

His lips twitched as he scrubbed a hand over the slight stubble on his jaw. "Are you?"

"Am I what?"

His lips twitched as he raised one eyebrow at her. "Talented and punctual."

"I—Y-yes."

"Then prove it." He backed away, smile widening as he took in her flustered state. "Have dinner with me." He lifted a hand before she could protest. "A *platonic* dinner, if it makes you feel better."

"How does that prove—"

"Well, I can't recommend just anyone to Nicky." One hand slid into the pocket of his jeans as he observed her, the wind playing in his hair. "So let's discuss this over dinner, where you can demonstrate your *talents*."

Despite the fact that she'd handed him the word, he managed to make it sound dirty, the teasing tone of his voice only adding to the innuendo.

"My place, at seven?"

"Tonight?" she squeaked and then bit her lip. "I—"

"Great. Looking forward to it."

How had this gotten so out of hand so quickly? She decided it was better to cut her losses and retreat before he managed to get her to agree to anything else.

This is not a date. She nodded to herself in the mirror, pretending like she couldn't see the spots of high color in her cheeks or the bitten-puffiness of her lips as she smoothed her hair for the umpteenth time. *It's just dinner. Platonic. It's not a date.*

And yet, she'd changed her outfit three times and got all the way to the front door before realizing she looked ridiculous in her flirty summer dress. Firstly, it was freezing outside, what with the cold snap arriving sooner than expected and sticking around, but also the frills on the long bell sleeves were bound to be a hazard in the kitchen.

This time when she approached the door, it was in her favorite pants—bootcut green corduroy—a plain, dark tee, and her comfiest boots.

. . . And her mom was waiting for her.

Angie narrowed her eyes as she took in Penny's outfit. "I thought you were going on a date?"

"No," Penny said sharply. "It's just dinner. That I'm cooking. For a friend. Kind of like an interview."

"Hm." Angie looked unconvinced. "I heard you were seeing Ethan."

What? "From who?" God, if her mom knew then that meant everyone did, or would soon enough. Tasha was going to kill her. *Play it cool, Pen.* "I mean, yes. It's dinner with Ethan, but only because it's his friend who runs the restaurant in New York and he wanted to make sure I wasn't all talk before recommending me."

"New York." Angie raised her brows, like this was news to her. "Well, good luck on your not-a-date."

Penny's phone buzzed and she cursed when she saw

the time. Great, she was already eating her words when it came to being *punctual*. "I have to go. I'll see you later."

"Make good decisions!" Angie called, the words half smothered by the closing of the door. Penny rushed to her car and pulled out of the drive so quickly she was surprised there wasn't a cloud of dust left in her wake.

She'd gone back and forth over what to make for Ethan. It needed to be something that wasn't too complicated, but was still impressive, and vegetarian because apparently Ethan didn't eat meat any more—she could thank her internet stalking for that helpful tidbit.

Her phone rang and she answered it with her car, assuming it would be Ethan wondering where she was. Instead, Tasha's voice came from the speakers.

"What are you doing right now?" There was suspicion in Tasha's voice and Penny sighed. There was no point in lying to her.

"I'm driving to Ethan's," she said and then blew out a breath. "He's making me cook him dinner before he'll recommend me to Nicky. The restaurant guy."

"Right. Nicky," Tasha replied and Penny was relieved that there didn't seem to be any anger in her voice. "But that's good; I'd heard you were on a date with my brother and I thought, *that can't be right because I specifically asked her not to mess around with him.*"

Penny's laugh sounded too high-pitched even as her

dad's words came back to haunt her. *Was* Tasha being unfair? Either way, now didn't seem like the right time to question it. "Yep. No date here. Just dinner. With a friend. Like an interview," she repeated what she'd told her mom and hoped it sounded less bogus the second time around. "Platonic," she added.

"What're you making?"

"A cauliflower and chickpea curry with rice." Tasha hummed her approval and Penny cut her off before she could say anything more. "I'm nearly at his place I think, so I've got to go."

"Good luck," Tasha said and it managed to sound like a threat as Penny hit the button on her steering wheel that would end the call.

Ethan lived fairly close to Penny's parents, at the south end of town, but still over the bridge where the river split the residential area. She pulled up to the curb and turned off her engine, sitting there for a second to just breathe and regain her composure after Tash's phone call.

The neighborhood was nice, quaint, with actual white picket fences separating immaculate lawns from the sidewalk and small houses that looked like modern cottages but went back far enough to be one-story mansions. Whatever Penny had been picturing when it came to Ethan Blake's house, this wasn't it. It was just so . . . *grown-up*.

Of course, that realization had her mind jumping back to the husky tone of Ethan's voice when he'd stepped in close and told her they weren't dumb kids any more—and he was right. So why did being around him make her feel like she was still seventeen and nervous to lose her virginity to the only boy she'd ever loved?

Before she knew it, she'd been sitting in the car for five minutes in silence while her thoughts raced, but she knew it was time to get out when the curtains in the house across the street started twitching in curiosity. The last thing she needed was to be hauled out of the neighborhood for loitering.

The slam of the car door seemed too loud in the night air, the rushing of the river in the distance the only sound beyond the faint noise of television sets in the nearby houses. This was clearly a family-centric area and it made her wonder why Ethan had bought a place here. Had Shelby lived here with him? Had this been the place he'd thought they'd raise their children? Her stomach dropped and she licked her dry lips, wishing she could forget even thinking about it.

She snagged her bag of groceries from the trunk and tried her best to push away all thoughts of Ethan and Shelby and their hypothetical children. It was none of her business who he did or didn't have kids with, *especially because this isn't a date.*

The front door opened so quickly it made her freeze in place as relief made Ethan's eyes widen and his smile grow bigger.

"Sorry I'm late," she said lamely and then held up her bag of groceries for him to inspect.

"If the food is good, then I'll leave it out of my report for Nicky," he teased, stepping back so she could pass over the threshold and into his home.

It smelled like sandalwood inside, with high ceilings and warm lighting that made the place feel cozy in spite of the large space.

"I'll show you to the kitchen."

She followed him silently, taking in this space that was all Ethan's; she was surprised to find she liked it. The finishings looked like real oak and there was just the right combination of cream walls versus pops of color in the soft furnishings—a purple throw on the sofa, a collage of photographs on the wall in the hallway. Part of her wondered if this was Shelby's doing—but it seemed too . . . sedate for any home she imagined Shelby decorating.

The kitchen was big enough to fit the entirety of her parents' first floor into, twice over, and Penny couldn't help her wide eyes as she took in the stainless-steel appliances and sleek countertops. The space was inviting and already warm despite the oven and stovetop not being on and she was grateful she'd opted for short sleeves and a dark color to avoid looking like a sweaty mess. A collection of equipment was already laid out on the counter, presumably for her to use while cooking, the curve of the colander and straight lines of the trays putting her strangely at ease. This, at least, was familiar territory.

"You approve?"

"It's gorgeous," she said honestly and Ethan smiled.

"Thanks. I designed it myself."

Her head snapped around so she could stare at him. "Tasha said you went to college." Of course, how had she forgotten that he worked as a designer? She'd assumed that meant corporate building design, but apparently it translated to homes too.

He nodded. "Yeah, just the one in the city up past the new town. Architecture and art history, minoring in culinary art." *Culinary art?* Her shock must have been written all over her face because he chuckled. "It's where I met Nicky."

"Why—"

"I wanted to understand you better," he said, the words a little quiet and she shivered despite the comfortable temperature. "This was the thing you loved enough to choose it over me and I wanted to know what you felt. To understand."

His words shook her and she bit her lip until she was sure her voice wouldn't waver. The space felt too big around them, despite being full of furniture and gently lit by the soft overhead lights. Maybe it was just that Ethan's words had left her feeling small, uncertain of her decision to leave. "That's not really what happened. I didn't leave because I loved cooking more than you, or Tasha. I just knew that you wouldn't get it and that if I wanted to give myself a real shot at the career I wanted, I needed to go."

This was not the way she'd wanted to have this conversation—though, admittedly, she hadn't particularly *wanted* to have it at all.

"I'm not trying to make you feel bad," he said softly. "Let's just . . . Start over. OK? Welcome to my home, I'm happy you're here."

The breath in her body left her in a whoosh of relief. "I'm happy to be here too."

Ethan smiled. "I have a confession to make," he said and she fell still in her path around the island, fingertips brushing the cool stone. What more could he possibly have to say? "I know you brought groceries, but I thought we could make things a little more interesting." He took a covered tray out of the fridge and set it down in front of her before removing the towel on the top.

"What's this?"

"This," he said, eyes lit up with mischief, "is your pick of ingredients for tonight."

"What?"

He grinned. "I thought it would be fun to give you a challenge. Since you were late, let's give you a time limit to prove your punctuality too. What do you think?"

What did she think? She needed a new job, and she desperately wanted the opportunity that Nicky could provide. "Sounds great." Her eyes ran over the items on the silver tray before she frowned. It didn't give her a lot to work with—six eggs, a variety of vegetables, and some veggie faux-bacon that looked *very* questionable. "What about seasonings?"

"You can use whatever you want," Ethan confirmed, leaning his hip against the island as he watched her. "But your main ingredients are here."

"Do I have to use them all?"

"Yes."

She nodded, mind whirling as she thought about the possibilities. It would be hard, but not impossible. "How long do I have?"

"Thirty minutes." He chuckled at the disbelief on her face. "Starting now."

Thirty minutes was *nothing*. She would have used the majority of that time alone just searching the cupboards for equipment if Ethan hadn't already laid out a collection for her. She washed her hands and then grabbed a tray, lining it with foil before ripping open the packet of 'Smokey Fakon' and laying out the thick strips before turning on his oven.

"What even is this stuff?" she muttered as she looked at the strips and jumped when Ethan replied.

"Quorn I think."

She rinsed her hands and looked up at him where he watched her from his place on the opposite side of the counter. Seats ran along the length of the other side breakfast-bar style and she couldn't ignore the prickle of awareness across her skin that came from knowing she was being watched. "Honey."

"Sweetie."

A startled laugh fell out of her and she rolled her eyes. "No, I need some honey. Do you have any?"

He rounded the counter and handed it to her from a cabinet up high near the stove; she could see there were other seasonings in there too beyond the basics and she couldn't help wondering whether Ethan had become a decent cook thanks to his minor in culinary art. She drizzled the not-bacon with honey and then gestured for him to pass her some salt and pepper too before sticking the tray into the warm oven as he sat back down.

Then she set to work, chopping vegetables with wild abandon and pushing them into piles for later: peppers, mushrooms, zucchini. Once she was done, she grabbed a large pan and drizzled some oil into the bottom and allowed it to heat through before throwing in the vegetables.

"Time check?"

"You have fifteen minutes left."

Crap.

Leaving the vegetables to brown, she checked on the fake-bacon and turned off the oven when she saw it was done. Then she stirred the vegetables and grabbed another bowl that she cracked all the eggs into, seasoned with salt and pepper, and set about whisking until it was ready to go in the pan with the vegetables. She lowered the heat and pushed the egg and vegetables together, leaving it to cook while she grabbed two plates and another bowl, whipping up a quick side salad of lettuce and tomatoes with sesame oil and balsamic vinegar as dressing. All the while, Ethan watched her silently. She'd never cooked for him before, nothing beyond cakes or pies when they were growing up anyway, but the feeling wasn't uncomfortable. Not many things were when it came to Ethan, Penny was realizing.

Omelet done, Penny folded it and then cut it in half, placing one piece on each plate and grabbing the warm honeyed veggie bacon to add atop the golden yellow wrap. Tongs in hand, she tossed the salad and added it to the plates before stepping back and raising her arms above her head in victory.

"Done. Time?"

"Five to spare."

She grinned and it faded only when she saw the heated look in Ethan's eyes. "Ah, good. Well, I guess I should get going."

He raised an eyebrow, half smiling as he grabbed the plates and walked toward the adjacent dining room. "You're kidding. After that performance? You have to at least eat the dinner with me. For all I know, it tastes awful. And you've already plated up for two, it would be a shame to let one go to waste."

She spluttered, about to retort when his laughter reached her. "Fine."

Not a date. This was still part of the interview. She just needed to eat a couple mouthfuls, and then get out of there. For some reason, now that the zone she got into while she cooked had passed, she was suddenly all the more aware that they were alone in Ethan's house. Just them. With, presumably, a bed somewhere in this place. Teenage Penny would have been frothing at the mouth for such an opportunity.

Platonic. Platonic. Platonic.

"Do you want a drink?"

"Soda would be good if you have it." The adrenaline was fading and the shakes would set in soon if she didn't eat or get some sugar in her. She thanked him when he returned with a can in hand and some silverware.

"I won't deduct any points for the lack of knives and forks. I imagine in a restaurant the customers already have those." His eyes twinkled as he sat down next to her instead of opposite like she'd expected. Like everything else, the table was light brown oak and the walls were painted cream, but the little nook felt warm and cozy, separated as it was from the rest of the kitchen. A tall turquoise floor lamp in the corner gave the room a warm glow and full-length matching turquoise drapes covered the large window. The table could easily seat six, but he'd chosen to sit right beside her and she had to fight the urge to shiver whenever their arms brushed.

"There's a points system now?" she said lightly, trying to keep things casual as she cracked open the can of fizz.

He shrugged. "Sure, why not. But don't think you'll

be getting any bonus points for flirting with the judge. Shall we dig in before this gets cold?"

She gaped. "I was *not* flirting. I'm just making conversation. You know, that thing polite people do?" She huffed and waited for him to take the first bite before trying her own food, wanting to see his reaction.

"Keep telling yourself that, Pen. The only thing I've seen you ogling more than me is my kitchen set-up." He chuckled at his own joke while she scowled and then placed a forkful of food in his mouth. His eyes popped wide at the first taste and he chewed quickly before looking at her in surprise. "That's really good."

"You could be a little less shocked," she grumbled and then forked in some of her own food and nodded. Other than the weird veggie bacon, it *was* pretty good. "Not bad for a half hour in an unfamiliar kitchen with a random list of ingredients."

"If you always cook like this, I might just have to keep you around." He grinned before taking another bite and she couldn't help but feel a little smug as he hummed his enjoyment while eating. "So I told you I minored in culinary art."

"Yeah." She eyed him warily, wondering where this was going.

"What I didn't tell you is that I'm an *awful* cook. Nicolo is the only reason I passed the course." He laughed at the shocked look on her face. "You want me to create a mock-up of a versatile, multi-functional space with art nouveau styling? I'm your guy. Crème brûlée? Casserole? Not so much."

Her laugh surprised her and she put her silverware down to sip her drink so she didn't choke. "You can't make casserole? It's like, the easiest dish in the world. You basically just chuck everything in one deep dish and put it in the oven."

"You make it sound so simple," he mused. "I suppose it would seem easy to you; my girl has talent by the bucketload."

My girl. He'd said it flippantly, as though it was the most natural thing in the world for him to call her that. So why did the words make her heart beat faster? Squashing the feeling down, she raised an eyebrow at his goofy behavior. "Were you sneaking wine in the kitchen when I wasn't looking?"

"No." He smiled and it faded slightly when he added, "I've just missed having you around. You being here . . . it's nice. It's more than I thought I'd ever get to have with you again." She looked away, guilt stirring, and he seemed to sense it because his hand covered hers on the table. "I wasn't trying to make you feel bad, Penny. I'm just saying . . . I'm happy you're here."

The room looked a tad blurry as she blinked. "Me too."

Their conversation continued as they ate, feeling more comfortable after Ethan's words, and Penny stretched contentedly when her plate was clear. "I hope you don't expect me to clean up. You don't need a minor in culinary arts to be good at washing up."

Ethan laughed and the sound caught her off guard, melting through any lingering defenses. It had been a long time since she'd heard him laugh like that, carefree and deep, just genuine joy. "Well, maybe you can show me how to cook like you sometime."

"Maybe," she mused, a smile tipping up her mouth. "We could start with casserole and work our way up from there. I was only kidding though. Do you want a hand washing the dishes?"

"Nah, that's what I have a dishwasher for."

She blinked. "You're not planning on putting that skillet in there are you? That needs to be hand-washed."

He waved off her concern as he stood. "It's survived in there once, it'll survive again."

She stood with him, reaching to catch his arm before he could head back to the kitchen. "No, it's OK, I'd rather just clean it for you." Her words faltered as she realized how close they were standing and she let go of him, her fingers grazing his arm.

Not a date. Not a date. Not a date.

She could smell his aftershave, count the freckles on his face, feel the rapid rise and fall of his chest against hers as the scant distance between them fell away. She wasn't sure who moved first, and in that moment she didn't care.

Their lips met, once, twice. A tingling, curling

sensation rose up from her lower belly to her chest and her doubts fell away as his tongue coaxed her mouth open. A plate fell to the floor and she barely noticed, the crash sounding like it was a million miles away. Her hands were in his hair, tugging at the soft strands, and his lifted her up with his palms under her ass as she linked her legs around his waist.

Ethan tasted sweet, like the honey from dinner, and when his tongue stroked hers she moaned breathlessly, loving the way his hands tightened on her body at the sound.

His fingertips dug into her ass, kneading and grasping frantically as his mouth devoured hers, the taste of him wrapped up in all of her senses until she couldn't tell where she ended and he began, only that she needed *more*.

As if he could read her mind, Ethan lowered her onto the table, pushing the remaining dinnerware out of the way and not even flinching when it hit the floor as his hands traced up the sides of her body. Her legs around his waist pulled him closer just as his hand found the edge of her bra beneath her shirt and bypassed it completely, squeezing over the cup until her nipples ached for his mouth.

They were pressed together, his hardness jutting into her as they tasted each other's mouths and then the seam from her pants pressed into *just* the right spot.

"Ethan," she gasped, and he moaned in return, hips rocking into her and pressing her clit against that seam again and again until she cried out, trembling, and his shout was hoarse as his own release followed, triggered by hers.

Her head was swimming and she blinked a few times to get the dizziness to abate as she tried to reclaim her breath. God, he'd made her come harder with their clothes still on than any other guy had managed with her clothes *off*.

As her heart slowed to its natural rhythm, Ethan lifted himself up and away and she caught a glimpse of the blush in his cheeks and the wet spot in his jeans where he'd come.

The room was in disarray, silverware and plates on the floor, and the remains of her soda was spreading across the table, the ends of her hair getting caught in the puddle as she sat up.

What had they just done? Dry humped like goddamn teenagers on his dining room table? But she couldn't deny that it had felt *good*.

Ethan cleared his throat, like he was just as taken aback by their display as she was. "You, uh, don't have to sleep with the boss to get the job by the way." It was a lame attempt at humor but she tried to smile anyway as she accepted his hand off of the table. Tried, and failed. Because now that her mind was thinking clearly again, she knew this had been a mistake. It was one thing for her to break her own heart when she left Magnolia Springs again in a few months' time, but to mess around with Ethan's? Unacceptable.

"Tasha's going to kill me," she muttered and Ethan's eyes narrowed in on her like he'd heard the words.

"What does my sister have to do with—"

"It's late." She cut off his words with a nod, unsure if she could trust herself to be there alone with him when all she could think about was following him back to his bedroom and finishing what they'd begun. "I should get going. I'm sure you're right, the pan will be fine."

"I—"

"See you later." She spun on her heel and this time she was the one who ran away from him. The night air hit her with a sharp chill of reproachment, like it too knew what she'd just done and was judging her for it, and she shivered as she climbed into her car and let her head drop down to rest against the wheel.

She was so screwed.

12

How many times could she screw up in just one month? Penny felt like she should have reached her limit by now, except the hits kept coming.

The drive home after leaving Ethan's hadn't been long enough to clear her head, so she parked her car in the driveway at her parents' and grabbed her coat and scarf from the backseat of the car. Wrapping them tightly around herself, Penny tried to breathe deeply, to center herself as she observed the mist her breath made and shoved her hands deep in her pockets to stay warm.

She sucked the cold air down greedily, hoping it might cool the fire Ethan had heated in her blood, or that it might sedate the part of her that was tempted to get back in her car and walk straight back into Ethan's arms. Because there was no doubt in her mind that he had a lot still to give ... and so did she. But would it end up hurting them more than if she'd just stayed away?

Leaves crunched under her boots as she followed the familiar path that curled around the side of her parents' cottage and led into the fields. The rhythmic thump of her feet on the ground kept her heart beating steady as the trail opened up to a dirt path, a sparsely held together fence on one side, bathed in moonlight.

It had been ten years since she'd last *truly* kissed Ethan Blake, and now she'd done it twice in the space of a month. Yet, despite the time that had passed, the feel of his mouth was still as deeply ingrained in her skin now as it had been when she was seventeen. Something burned between them, but she couldn't work out whether pursuing it would leave her hurt or just hot.

The sky was a clear and deep indigo that darkened the longer Penny walked, stars winking in and out in a sprawl so bright she stopped to crane her neck up and look at them. You couldn't see stars like this in the city.

When she finally looked back down, her vision swam and the stars were etched on the inside of her eyelids.

Somewhere, an owl hooted, likely searching for mice in the field, and no matter how many times Penny tried to empty her head, she kept finding herself back in that moment at Ethan's. The smashing of the plates as they'd hit the floor, the silverware bouncing like silver streamers as it hit the hardwood in a clash that should have been deafening. But the only sound she could recall was Ethan's heavy panting, the way he'd mumbled her name under his breath like a prayer.

She stopped walking once she reached the place where the fencing shifted into a more solid presence. Colton's land. His fields ran all the way from there to up and past the orchard. His stables were directly opposite, just across the way, and Penny clicked her tongue gently, hoping one of the horses might still be out.

Colton had never minded before when Penny walked on his land, especially since it bordered her parents', so she strolled down further. Heavy footsteps had her head jerking up and around and she smiled when a horse as black as the night surrounding them leant its head over the fence and sniffed at her hands eagerly.

"I'm sorry, I didn't bring any treats."

The horse didn't seem to mind, just snuffled its nose in her hands and let her stroke up to the soft center of its head for a scratch as it huffed warm air into her palms.

Maybe coming to Magnolia Springs had caused more problems than it had solved. She didn't know what to do—pretend like Ethan hadn't made her come without even removing her pants? Confess to his sister and let her mete out Penny's punishment? Run again? Not that she had anywhere to run to—and her savings would only last her so long. But, she couldn't help thinking as she stood out under the stars with the horse's mane beneath her hand, the truth was . . . she didn't *want* to run again.

She'd been desperate to leave Magnolia Springs as a teenager, but now that she was back she wasn't sure why. Had she changed? Had the town? Sure it was annoying that everyone knew everyone and all their business, but it also meant there was almost always a friendly face around to tell you *good morning* or offer a smile.

The horse, apparently grown tired of waiting for treats that didn't come, decided to walk away and Penny knew she needed to get home too. It was getting late and the cold air was biting at her skin; already her ears had begun to ache from the chill, so she pulled up the hood on her coat to warm them as she began her walk back to the cottage.

Once again, Penny had made a mess of things and now she had to decide whether to clean it up or lie in it.

She'd walked further than she thought, and by the time she reached the cottage it was nearly eleven. The tiny yard light was still on and she smiled at the familiarity of it all, the fact that her parents still left the light on when she came home after dark.

The warmth rushed over her as soon as she stepped inside and Penny shuddered, the last of the cold trying to cling to her bones as the heat dove in. She unzipped her coat and hung it on the hook, poking her head into the kitchen and instead heading the other way, to the living room when she found the light off. Murmured voices from the TV pulled her in and Penny strode past the hot log burner before dropping into the gray armchair opposite her parents on the sofa.

"How did it go?"

Terrible. Wonderful. "It was OK."

Angie nodded in response and Penny was grateful that her mom was too engrossed in the film they had on to notice Penny's disheveled state. There was still soda in her hair where it had spilled on Ethan's table while they were—

"So what are we watching?"

"Oh, it's nearly over now, honey. It was your father's pick this week."

Penny nodded. It was probably either an action flick or had something to do with space, the army, or was based on a true story. Her dad was nothing if not predictable.

Still, she sat there quietly in the warmth and let her eyes get heavy to the sound of the TV and her parents' chatter.

Penny still hadn't made up her mind. The whole short drive to the orchard the next day she went back and forth with herself. She could only hope Ethan wouldn't be there today, otherwise they were about to leave 'kinda awkward' in the dust in favor of 'excruciatingly uncomfortable'.

She'd have to face him eventually, she knew that. But doing so now, when she wasn't sure what her own thoughts about all this were, only meant she'd make more of a mess of things. Plus, when it came to him, she knew she couldn't keep up her resolve. When it came to Ethan, she was weak. There was no denying it anymore, not after the events of the previous night.

There was no sign of his truck outside the shop and she breathed a sigh of relief as she stepped out of her car and grabbed her equipment for the day. It was cold again but in a way she found refreshing rather than dreaded being out in. Dew coated the grass and dotted the open gates to the orchard like little gems, glinting in the morning light, and Penny regretted wearing her sneakers, knowing they'd soak up the moisture and leave her toes cold.

Good progress was happening in the orchard with nearly half the trees harvested and still a few weeks leeway before the weather turned too much for the fruit to survive. The annual bonfire in mid-October was fast approaching, which meant the heat was on to harvest as much as possible before the Halloween Orchard Fest happening two weeks after that. Penny couldn't believe so much time had passed since she'd been back in town. It had nearly been a month but it had flown, while at the same time making her feel like she'd never left at all.

Penny pulled on her gloves and analyzed the tree in front of her, deciding where to start first. Today's only aim was distraction—she planned to work so hard that Ethan wouldn't have the chance to invade her thoughts at any point during the day, or, if she exhausted herself enough, her dreams later on.

The apples were still firm and droplets of water flicked up at Penny as she pulled the fruit free and dropped it into the bucket.

By the time midday came around, she was overheating in her sweater and was more than ready for a break. Though, admittedly, she was still no closer to a decision when it came to her next steps with Ethan or whether to tell Tasha what had happened. On the one hand, she was dying to discuss it with someone, but on the other . . . Well, there was a very real possibility that Tasha might murder her.

Penny grabbed her coat from atop the bucket but didn't put it on, still sweating from the physical exertion of the morning. She turned around to grab her car keys, debating what she wanted for lunch when the skin at the back of her neck prickled.

She knew who it would be before she even turned around—which is why she didn't.

"Hi," she said, still looking at the tree.

"Hey. Saw you working and wondered if you wanted to grab some lunch together?"

Lunch. Like she'd fall for that again. Dinner was supposed to be just that, and yet somehow it had ended with a swift, and somewhat embarrassing, orgasm. "I don't think that's a good idea, Ethan."

Don't look at him. She knew that if she looked at him, she'd give in to whatever he wanted. *Do. Not. Look.*

If Penny ever had to face Medusa, she'd be screwed.

"Fine," he said and she turned in time to see him shrug. "Coffee, then." A dimple appeared in his chin when he grinned and she melted.

"One coffee," she warned. "And no funny business."

He raised his hands in mock surrender. "I'm pretty

sure you were the one who couldn't keep their hands to themselves, Pen."

Her mouth dropped open as he folded his arms and raised a brow in challenge. "I did *not*—"

"My car or yours?" he called over his shoulder as he walked away, flashing another grin at her obvious outrage.

"Mine," she grumbled, following him at last. "I'd need a ladder to climb into yours." *Overcompensate, much?*

Except, he wasn't overcompensating. At all.

"I think we've established that I can easily lift you up, Penny." His voice was rough and she bit her lip, not meeting his eyes as she unlocked her car. It flashed its lights cheerily as she rounded the driver's side.

Exactly, she thought but didn't say. *He* had been the one lifting her up into his arms and sweeping the dinnerware off the table—of course he'd been the instigator.

. . . Hadn't he?

They climbed inside and she turned on the engine while he buckled his seat belt. Déjà vu hit her out of nowhere, her body flashing hot and then cold as she remembered how dangerous it could be to have Ethan Blake in the car with her looking like *that*. A lot of time had been spent in cars together when they'd been teens, making out near the springs or behind the church because the lights in their parking lot had been broken.

His fingers were long and nimble, artist's hands,

sliding up the black belt to remove the kink at the top, the muscles in his forearms cording. Blond hair fell into his face when he looked down to clip in the buckle and she nearly reached to push it back.

Old habits were hard to break, but she'd really thought she'd managed to kick the addiction that was Ethan Blake in the ten years she'd been gone. She realized now that it had been easy enough to think that when she didn't have to see him all the time. Clearly her resolve was much weaker than she'd thought.

"Are we going? Or did you lure me into your car under false pretenses?" There was that cocky smirk again and damn if it didn't look good on him. He'd always been sure of himself as a teen, but this was somehow *more*. It was the kind of confidence that said, *yeah, I know you want me, even if you don't want to admit it.*

She blinked and threw the car into reverse, spinning around with ease as she pulled out of the orchard and headed in the direction of the bridge that would take them into town. "Sorry."

It wasn't her preference, but she didn't want to risk stirring up any further memories by parking in her usual, quieter, spot behind the church, so instead she snagged a spot near the grocery store and decided they could walk from there to the long line of boutiques and mini eateries where the coffee shop could be found.

Surprisingly, the rain had held off and the sun shone brightly, if a little watery, down on them, filtering through the last remaining leaves on the magnolia trees that lined the sidewalk. Penny avoided looking in the direction of the library, as if that could shield her from Tasha's wrath if she saw Penny out for coffee with Ethan after Penny had sworn their dinner the night before was purely platonic.

The gushing of the fountain was superseded by the chime of the church bells, signaling the new hour, and Penny focused on putting one foot in front of the other. Thankfully, Ethan seemed content to enjoy the short walk in silence, not saying a word until she thanked him for holding open the door to Coffee Affair.

"What do you want?" he asked once they reached the counter and she pulled her eyes away from the cake display and shook her head.

"Oh, that's OK. I can get it."

He rolled his eyes and leant down to say quietly, "It's a coffee. Not a marriage proposal." When she just blinked at him he sighed, turning to the barista. "I'll take a medium cappuccino with cinnamon please and she'll have a medium pumpkin spice latte."

The words reminded her of the last time they'd been here and how he hadn't even hesitated, remembering her order like no time had passed at all. She reached out and stopped him from handing over his cash, instead handing her own money to the barista. "My treat."

He must have caught the look on her face because he softened. "You know, just because you left, doesn't mean I forgot you."

There was no judgment in the words, but she flinched

anyway. Mostly because she'd done everything she could to try to forget about him, and Tasha, and Magnolia Springs in general. Not that it had worked very well, and now here she stood, right back where she'd started.

The barista handed over their coffees and Ethan tipped her while Penny tried to find them a seat. Luckily, it was a weekday so most people were at school or work. Come the holidays, this place would be packed.

"Do they still do the Christmas market?" she wondered aloud and Ethan nodded as he sat down opposite her at the corner table that ran along the back wall. She'd gravitated there on instinct and her fingertip traced the initials carved into the wood—E.B, P.L. What would her younger self think if she could see her now? Where they'd ended up? After everything that had happened, they were still back at the table they'd carved their initials into at sixteen.

"Every year," he confirmed and she couldn't help the small tingle of excitement that swept through her at the thought. She'd always loved the market growing up. The town cordoned off Main Street for a whole month and built temporary wooden huts that townsfolk and out-of-towners alike could rent to sell their wares or serve hot drinks and food. They even had a band and a dress-up Santa for the kids.

She pulled her thoughts away from the cinnamon holiday buns one store in particular had used to make every year—they were her favorite—and instead concentrated on her coffee as she avoided Ethan's stare. "Did you talk to Nicky?"

He nodded, a smirk tugging at his mouth when he said, "I left him a message yesterday afternoon."

Yesterday aftern—"But I didn't make you dinner until the evening."

"I know." He shrugged and she stared. If he had already talked to Nicky, then why had he made her come over to cook for him? Ethan's eyes dropped to where her fingers still traced their names on the tabletop. "Amazing that they haven't re-decorated after all this time, huh?"

It was, but Magnolia Springs was slow to change and this cafe had probably been here since her parents were teens. She ignored his observation and took a too-hot gulp of her latte. "Why did you make me cook for you if you'd already spoken to your friend?"

Ethan set his coffee cup down softly and when he looked back up at her, eyes soft and gleaming, she couldn't look away. "C'mon Pen, you're a smart woman. Why do you think I invited you?"

Penny bit her lip and then shook her head. "I don't—"

"Well, this is cozy."

The slightly nasal voice made Penny's nose wrinkle as she pulled away from Ethan, not having realized that she'd leant closer.

Ethan looked up and smiled, polite if a little wary. "Shelby, hey. You remember Penny?"

"Vividly," she said and sniffed. "Nice to see you." The words were curt but she was all sugar when she turned back to Ethan, a smile on her glossy lips. "I just wondered if you were around this weekend, E? Maybe we could get dinner?"

E? Gag.

His brows furrowed, a gentle look she hadn't seen on him before taking over his face. "We've talked about this, Shel. It's not a good idea. I don't want to get back together."

Shelby stiffened, eyes blazing as she looked between Penny and Ethan. "Oh yeah? So she's finally decided to take you back?" Shelby snorted and threw Penny a withering look that made her stiffen. "Well, when she runs off and leaves you in the dust again, you know where I'll be."

She strode away, the sweet jingle of the bell by the door at complete odds with Shelby's stormy exit. Clearly things in the grocery store hadn't been as resolved as Penny had hoped.

Penny's mouth fell open as she watched the exit. "I can't believe you were engaged to her," Penny said without thinking and then grimaced. "Sorry. It's not my place to judge."

Ethan shrugged. "It could be. If you wanted."

She opted to ignore his offer. "I was surprised when I heard that you two had . . . Well, been a *you two*."

He shrugged. "I didn't pursue her, it just kind of happened. We were working together on a project—one of her friends had bought a store in the city and wanted help with the interiors. Shelby knew I'd started my business recently and was trying to get my name out there, so she put us in touch." He sipped his coffee, watching Penny closely as if decoding every expression or minute movement she made. "She's not as bad as she pretends to be, you know. The project got us talking more and I realized pretty quickly that the mean girl act is mostly just a front she puts up. And then, I don't know, it just seemed . . . easy. After you left, Pen, I'd thought that was me done with dating, but Shelby and I kind of just fell into the relationship." Penny tried not to flinch at the hint of pain that underscored his words as Ethan went on. "Before we knew it, a year had passed and there was a lot of talk from her family about next steps . . . I proposed because it was what everyone wanted and expected us to do." His eyes looked far away, as if he could see it all playing out in his mind's eye.

Part of her was relieved that there wasn't some big, epic romance lurking in the shadows between Ethan and Shelby, but the rest of her just felt sad that he'd been with her just because it seemed like what everyone wanted. "What happened?"

"It wasn't right," he said, voice quiet and eyes burning as he looked up at her. "There was no real spark, no heat. Things were . . . fine. I think even Shelby was more interested in being able to say she was engaged rather than who she was engaged to."

"She seems plenty devoted now," Penny said dryly and Ethan smirked.

"Jealous?"

She snorted. "Of course not." She was sure she wasn't really jealous of Shelby, of the claim she still seemed to think she had to Ethan, but there was a feeling coiled deep in her stomach that seemed to disagree. Penny sipped her coffee and peered at Ethan over the top of the cup, dismissing the thought. "So then what happened?"

He shrugged. "Nothing, really. Things were fine. But I wanted more than *fine*. I wanted to miss her when she was gone and think about her day and night, I wanted someone who could bring me to my knees with a look and could wreck me with one kiss. I didn't have that with Shelby. We both deserved better than each other."

The words took her aback, even as they made her mouth run dry. She hadn't expected that level of passion and intensity from the relatively simple question, but maybe she should have known better. Ethan had never been scared to say what he wanted. She had half a mind to ask what Shelby had meant by Penny 'finally' taking him back, but was scared of the answer he might give. Instead, she sipped her coffee and let the quiet fall over them while she gathered her thoughts.

His empty cup hit the table with a *thunk* that made Penny jolt. "Actually, no. I don't know why I'm bothering to hide this from you. The real reason Shelby and I didn't work out was you."

"So everything you just said—"

"Was true," he allowed. "But everything I described? Everything I want to feel in a relationship? That's how I felt—still feel—with you, Pen. How could I have had that and *not* compare Shelby to you?"

Her heart quickened and she gulped. "But I only just got back into town."

"When you know, you know. And I knew it wasn't Shelby," he murmured and her heart thudded faster, all of her attention boiling down to focus on his soft confession. "I couldn't marry Shelby. Because for me it's always been you, Pen."

She swallowed once and then again when the lump in her throat didn't clear. "You blew up your relationship... for me?"

For a moment his confidence wavered and he ran a hand through his hair as he let out a long breath. "I broke things off with Shelby because we both deserved better than to settle."

Their eyes caught and held and she was the first to blink. "I don't know what to do with that information. By the end of the year, I'll be leaving again and—"

"And you don't think I'd come with you?"

She bit her lip, admittedly not expecting that response.

"Look, you need time. I get that. I'm just saying... Give me a chance. Hell, give me till Christmas and if you're not in love with me at the end of it I'll pack your bags myself and pay for your gas."

"That's a little overdramatic," she said, rolling her eyes, but his face was entirely serious. That was one thing she'd forgotten about Ethan in their time apart, how intense he could be once he set his mind to something. He didn't give up until he had what he wanted.

And what he wanted now was her—she couldn't say she minded the feeling, being someone's sole focus and only desire.

"What do you have to lose? Christmas is just about three months away. If it's so ridiculous, then what do you have to worry about? I'll even set up a meeting for you with Nicky, regardless."

She hesitated, more than a little tempted even as her common sense told her this was a messy, stupid idea. "I need to talk to Tasha."

He rolled his eyes. "By all means, summon a committee," he said casually and she nearly choked on the last of her coffee when he smirked. "I've already waited ten years. I can wait a little longer."

13

"Did you think I wouldn't find out?" There was a coldness in Tasha's voice that was evident even over the phone and Penny grimaced. "First dinner, now coffee? In what world does that add up to you staying away from my brother?"

"Tasha—"

"Oh, I've got to hear this," she snapped. "What, it wasn't really coffee? He was just helping you brush up on your interview techniques for Nicky?"

"Tash—"

"You always do this! Ten years and nothing has changed, you still pick him over me. I wanted to be friends again but how can I do that when you lie to me?"

"Tasha!" Penny put her car in park and took her phone off speaker, lifting it to her ear. "Open your door. Please." Her voice wobbled and Tasha must have heard it because she went silent as Penny stepped out of her car and waited for a door to open.

The only direction she'd gotten from Ethan was that Tasha lived on this street, she hadn't known the door number. Movement caught her eye and Penny walked in the direction of the moving red smudge, unable to see if it was Tasha standing by the door through the haze of tears in her eyes that she couldn't hold at bay any longer.

"Fuck," Tasha whispered, her face falling and anger dissipating as she took in the blotchy redness of Penny's face and the dampness of her eyelashes. Her voice echoed through the phone Penny still had clasped to her face until Tasha took it and gently lowered it. "I'm still mad at you," she warned and Penny nodded, crying harder, and then she was being wrapped in a firm embrace. "Come on then, let's get inside."

Penny sniffed, relaxing as the familiar bergamot smell of Tasha's perfume washed over her, though her tears kept falling as they made their way through the entrance and into the small, brightly colored kitchen. Everything was decorated in shades of orange and white, the bright, happy colors matching Tasha's personality perfectly. The kitchen counter was a little cluttered—a half-drunk mug of tea and an open package of cookies lying discarded, no doubt when Tasha had gone to open the door.

Penny steeled herself, remembering the words she'd rehearsed in her head as she'd driven over. "I'm sorry, Tasha. Really. I never meant to put Ethan first, ever. I've just never thought about it as an either-or situation. You're my best friend, he was my boyfriend. But

I totally get how it might have seemed that way, especially when we were kids. I really am sorry."

"*Was* your boyfriend?" Tasha raised her brows and Penny nodded and shrugged simultaneously as she sat at the small round table next to the big modern window.

"I'm not—We're not—" She blew out a breath and accepted the hot mug of tea that Tasha pushed her way. "He said things to me that I don't know what to do with, Tash. We saw Shelby at the coffee shop and she was obviously upset and it just opened a whole can of worms. He said he'd felt like he was settling with her because he couldn't help comparing what they'd had to what we'd had." Penny slumped forward, despair making her fold herself down until her head hit the table softly. "What am I supposed to do? I've tried staying away from him, I've tried pushing him away—nothing seems to stick." A tear leaked from her eye and ran down her face. "Just tell me what you want me to do, because I don't know any more. All I do know is that I don't want to hurt him—or you."

"Do you love him?"

The blunt question took Penny off guard and her head snapped up, fingers clenching around the hot mug of tea. "I—That's ridiculous. It's been ten years."

Tasha's eyes scrutinized Penny's face and then she sighed. "So you do."

"That's not what I—"

"It's OK. At least this way I know you're serious, not just chasing some high-school high." Tasha watched her steadily before pulling the package of cookies further open and offering them to Penny. "I'd rather have you as a sister-in-law than Shelby any day."

"Did you know? About why they broke up?"

Tasha shrugged. "He said it just wasn't right between them."

A lump rose in Penny's throat and she swallowed hard. "He told me he waited for me. All that time. Whereas I was off trying to do everything I could not to think about him, or you, or everything I left behind when I ran to the city." She bit into a cookie and chewed in silence as Tasha watched her swallow. "I don't know if I deserve that kind of devotion."

"Maybe that's not for you to decide," Tasha said and Penny was surprised at how well her friend was taking all of this—especially given Penny now knew that she'd essentially screwed things up for Ethan after she'd left, despite her not knowing about it back then. Which, really, made her feel worse. The idea that while she was alone and miserable in the city, fighting for a job she thought was her dream, Ethan would have been falling in love with and kissing and *marrying* someone else with her none the wiser. If she had come home and he'd still been with Shelby . . .

"We kissed," Penny confessed, pushing the hypothetical thoughts away as her stomach dropped at the memory of the kiss. She forced herself to make eye contact with Tasha. "The other night at dinner. I never meant for it to happen, and I left straight away but . . ."

"The damage was done," Tasha said, a small smile on her face. She sighed. "It wasn't fair of me to try to keep you guys apart, especially with your history. You two are like magnets, and I can't fault you for loving him. Just, please, if you're going to pursue this, don't hurt him. Are you still planning on leaving?"

"Yes," Penny said without thinking, before her confidence faltered. "I mean, I think so. Working with Nicky would be an amazing opportunity. Ethan said . . ." She cleared her throat and continued, "He said he'd come with me."

Tasha didn't seem surprised. "That tracks. He said some things over the years that made me think he'd regretted not going with you the first time you left. You have time to figure out what you want this time, though. But maybe don't discount anything too fast? Ten years might not have changed much between you and my brother, but Magnolia Springs is different now and so are you." Tasha shrugged. "Maybe it'll grow on you."

"Like a fungus," Penny muttered, making Tasha snort, even as she thought back to the calm she'd found under the stars last night.

"Plus, it'd be nice to have you around more . . ."

Penny bit into a chocolate chip cookie and hummed happily around the bite. "We'll see."

"So tell me more about this kiss—but bear in mind this is my brother we're talking about."

When Penny returned to her parents' cottage, she knew there was an inquisition coming. She noted the tell-tale long looks, the particularly generous measure of wine in her glass, and, to top it all off, her mom had made meat loaf. So when Angie Larkin leant forward, hands steepled beneath her chin as Penny put the first bite in her mouth, she wasn't surprised.

"So, what's new with you, honey?"

The meat loaf was a tad dry while somehow being soggy, a confounding experience for the senses, meant to throw the recipient off balance so her mom could better extract whatever information she wanted to know. The CIA had nothing on Angie Larkin.

"Not much," Penny said, taking a gulp of her white wine to dislodge the meat loaf clogged in her throat—another deliberate choice, alcohol loosening the lips. "Things are going well at the orchard."

"Great, great . . ."

They resumed eating, the quiet prickling along Penny's skin as she shared an amused glance with her dad who was used to his wife's antics.

"Well, I had a great day." Angie placed her silverware delicately on the edge of her plate as she dabbed a napkin at her mouth with enough demureness that you would have thought they were in a five-star restaurant and not having family dinner in the cottage. "I heard something very interesting today, actually. You remember Coffee Affair in town, don't you darling?"

Philip nodded. "Of course, dear."

"Well, apparently our daughter was in there with a boy yesterday."

Penny bit her lip to bury her smirk, suddenly remembering all too well how it had felt to be fourteen with her first proper crush. "Yes, I had coffee with Ethan."

"Well, why didn't you say so when I asked?"

A shrug in response made her mom's frown deepen. "It was just coffee."

"And dinner," her dad added and she shook her head at him.

"Whose side are you on here, Dad?" Penny turned to him, shocked at the betrayal.

"What? I want the details too," he said, mouth twitching.

"Fine, yes, and dinner."

"So?"

Penny pushed the meat loaf around with her fork, glancing up to find her parents watching her intently. "What?"

"What does this mean? Are you together? Dating?" Angie fired the questions one after the other and Penny took a long sip of her wine before she replied.

"I don't know yet."

Angie threw her hands up, napkin fluttering in the

air as she pushed back from the table. "Talk to her, Philip. I'm not getting any younger here, Penny, and I want grandchildren."

Her mom huffed and left the room, and Penny met her dad's eyes across the table, finding a warm amusement in his as they set their silverware down at the same time, meat loaf largely untouched.

"Shall we order pizza?" he asked and she laughed.

"Only if we can get cheesy garlic bread too."

"Done." He hesitated as he stood up to clear their plates. "Did you think about what I said?"

She nodded. "Tasha and I talked. It's all good. I just don't know where I'm at with Ethan. He's so . . ." She sighed, searching for the words. "He knows what he wants, has done for a long time apparently, and his life is so together and I—Well, I just got back in town after screwing things up in San Francisco. I don't know how long I'm staying here or where I'm going next."

"Does he need you to know those things?" Philip scraped the last of the meat loaf into the garbage with a satisfied look on his face before rinsing the plates and placing them in the sink.

"Well, no."

Her dad shrugged. "Then maybe you just cross that bridge when you come to it."

Was it really that simple?

"I guess," she muttered, pulling up the website for the local pizza place in town to scroll through their deals.

"Besides," Philip added, a twinkle of mischief in his eyes that made Penny sit up and pay attention, "maybe Magnolia Springs will surprise you if you give it another chance. Maybe you'll want to stay after all."

The chances of that happening still seemed slim, but she could also admit that it hadn't been absolutely terrible being back here for the last month or so. In fact, compared to being in the city where everything was constantly changing, it had been a nice change to stay somewhere that was so familiar.

She sighed, deciding to take her dad's advice and think about it later. "OK. Hit me with your toppings, Pops."

14

It had been all hands on deck at the orchard lately to try to clear as much of the remaining harvest before the Halloween Orchard Fest. The annual bonfire was next week, and the festival would be upon them soon after. Penny couldn't deny how excited she was for her first Orchard Fest in ten years. It was the perfect mix between cozy and spooky fun, with apple bobbing, an apple pie bake-off, apple carving, and so much more.

Ethan still hadn't heard back from Nicky, and while there was a small part of Penny that had been holding out hope that he might be able to offer her an escape from Magnolia Springs, she found that she actually didn't mind as much as she'd expected to. Working with Ethan had been a lot more enjoyable since things between them had started feeling more comfortable, especially now that she knew Tasha wasn't going to murder her for hanging out with her brother. She liked the easy routine she'd settled into with Ethan on the days that they shared shifts. He brought her a pumpkin spice latte in the morning and usually worked a couple rows away from her (at her request, because otherwise she'd found she had a tendency to get distracted by the sight of him between the trees). Then, they'd take a short lunch break in town before getting back to the orchard to finish their shifts.

One Tuesday morning, they were lucky enough to have some sunshine and when Ethan wandered over to check on Penny from his section across the way, she was surprised to find a basket and blanket in his arms.

"What's all this?"

He smiled and it was nearly as bright as the sunlight that arched overhead and filtered down through the leaves, making her squint. "Lunch."

"O-kay," she mused, accepting the hand he offered to help her down from the top of her stepladder. His palm was warm in hers and the green of his open shirt brought out the flecks of gold in his eyes. She was so entranced, she nearly misstepped and fell. She would have done, anyway, if Ethan's body hadn't moved closer to her in that moment, pressing her back against the ladder in mid-descent. Her arms automatically came around him, his head coming up just shy of her chest, and for a moment the orchard disappeared, the birdsong falling away, until there was only Ethan, his eyes on hers, his mouth tantalizingly close.

He smiled and she couldn't have stopped her lips from responding even if she'd wanted to. "This is so soft," he murmured, tugging gently at the hem of her chenille navy sweater. "Not so sure that this is practical though," he added, running that same hand lower, over her short black skirt and down over the thick black tights she had on underneath. She could feel the heat of his hand on her thigh even through the material.

"Oh?"

"Someone might walk past you on this ladder and get an eyeful," he said, smirking, and she snorted, gently pushing him away to continue down the ladder and onto the grass.

"Ethan Blake, are you telling me you looked up my skirt?"

"Maybe," he teased and then shook his head. "Neon green underwear is certainly a choice, Pen."

She rolled her eyes, knowing full well that her panties were black and that Ethan was far too chivalrous to do anything as crude as peeking up her skirt. Not that she was sure she'd mind.

Her stomach chose that moment to growl and Ethan chuckled. "Let's get you fed."

He laid out the red checkered blanket a few paces away, underneath the shade of two apple trees that had already been cleared of fruit, and patted the space next to him as he sat down. "OK—bear in mind that you never did follow up on showing me how to cook, so this is all very rudimentary. It's hard to screw up sandwiches, but who knows. We can't all be Penny Larkin in the kitchen."

She giggled but accepted the sandwich bag he passed her. "What's in it?"

"What do you think?"

PB&J. It had to be. She unwrapped it and took a bite, smiling at the taste that reminded her of childhood summer days at the springs and school field trips on the bus, sharing lunches. Despite his lack of culinary skills, Ethan had been something of a mother hen, always the one to pack sandwiches and snacks for her and Tasha. PB&J was his signature.

"It's good," she mumbled around the bread and Ethan grinned, reaching over and brushing his thumb over her bottom lip, wiping away the raspberry jam, and then sucking the digit into his mouth.

"Delicious," he said, smirking at the blush that heated her cheeks. "Apple slice?" He held out a small tub and she took a couple pieces, crunching through the sweetness happily as the wind rustled the leaves above their heads.

"Thank you for this," she said when her mouth was free of food. "We should do this again in the summer, I'll even bring orange Popsicles." They were a staple of their childhood too, and Ethan grinned.

"Oh? You're planning to stick around till next summer, huh?"

She blushed again and stuttered as she tried to correct the slip. "Well, I—"

He laughed. "It's OK, Penny. We can have orange Popsicles wherever we end up next summer, even if it's not here."

She reached for his hand and squeezed gently. "OK."

"Now, can I interest you in a slice of pie?"

Her eyes widened and made grabby hands at him. "I could kiss you right now."

"I'd let you."

She laughed and tried to look anywhere but at Ethan's mouth. "I was talking to the pie."

"Ouch." He grinned at her as he passed over a paper plate and fork and she couldn't be sure that she wasn't drooling. The first bite made her eyes widen and Ethan nodded, looking smug. "Angie's finest." Her mom had made pie for Ethan? Life was so unfair. Though, at least he was sweet enough to share it. "And don't give me that look. She only gave me the pie because I mentioned taking you on a picnic."

That made her feel a little bit better. The breeze flipped up the corner of the blanket and Ethan moved closer, his thigh pressing against hers as she offered him a forkful of pie, feeding it directly into his mouth while she giggled. She wasn't sure she'd ever had a more perfect afternoon.

After one particularly long and grueling shift at the orchard a week later, Penny wanted nothing more than to have a long soak in the bath and then to sleep for a million years. So when her phone rang with an unfamiliar number as she was about to exit her car back at her parents', she nearly didn't answer.

"Hello?"

"Hey."

She sucked in a sharp breath of surprise. "Ethan. Hey."

"Are you busy right now?"

Bath and relaxing evening long forgotten, she shook her head. "No. Why?"

"Want to catch a movie?"

That was the last thing she'd been expecting him to say. "A movie?"

"Yeah, they're like photographs but they move and tell a story." There was a smile in his voice when she snorted. "Meet me in town?"

"Sure. Oh, and Ethan?"

"Yes?"

"Where did you get my number?"

"Tasha."

Penny's eyes pricked and she smiled. "OK. See you in a few."

The only movie theater in town also doubled up as a bowling alley on its far side, with three screens for movies and a large confectionery counter dedicated to popcorn, candy, and slushies on the back wall as you walked in. She wasn't sure she could remember the last time she'd been in there, but the smell of popcorn took her back to being sixteen and coming to watch the latest *Pirates of the Caribbean* movie with Tasha and Ethan—though Tasha had moved seats half-way through because Penny and Ethan had spent most of their time occupied by their mouths rather than watching the screen.

She was the first to arrive and, after pacing anxiously by the popcorn counter, she decided to distract herself by scanning the posters in the lobby in the hopes of finding something good to watch. Their options were the new Reese Witherspoon movie—an all-women ensemble heist—a cheesy-looking horror flick about puppets, or a re-screening of *The Notebook* as part of a promotion they were running called "Old but Gold".

Ethan wasn't one for horror, and she couldn't take crying in public to *The Notebook*. But she'd wait for Ethan to arrive before grabbing tickets, in case he'd suddenly become a horror-buff in the time they'd been apart. Instead, she headed to the popcorn counter and ordered two large buckets with extra butter and two mixed-flavor slushies and then waited for the order while internally spiraling. After ten years, she was on a date with Ethan. That, in and of itself, was nerve-wracking enough. But now she was worrying that maybe he didn't like popcorn and mixed slushies any more. Maybe he was a nachos or corn-dog guy. She had to admit to herself, she didn't know much about Ethan *the man*—after all, it had been ten years! Maybe this was a poor choice for their first actual date. It wasn't like they could chat during the movie so she could get to re-know him. Or worse, what if he didn't think this *was* a date? Maybe they were just two friends who kind of liked each other and had a lot of history, watching a movie. But movies were a common date, weren't they? It had been so long since she'd been on one that Penny wasn't sure if she was overthinking, underthinking, or, hell, even thinking at all. Her nose wrinkled and she was thrown out of her panic spiral by the food and drinks being placed on the counter.

"I grabbed us some tickets for the heist chick flick. Hope that's OK?"

She jumped and glanced over her shoulder to find Ethan waiting. "Hey. Yeah, that's great."

"Figured you wouldn't want anyone to see you ugly cry to *The Notebook* in public," he teased and she rolled her eyes, even though he was right. She blinked away the annoying prick of tears in her eyes as she realized that he really did remember the little things after all this time.

Rather than respond to his jibing, she presented his popcorn and slushie. "Here."

He chuckled. "Didn't feel like sharing like old times?"

Actually, she'd worried herself by how much she'd wanted to share with him like they'd used to do as kids. So she'd deliberately got them separate snacks, that way she could avoid the warm brush of his fingers against hers in the popcorn bucket and placing her mouth in the place his had been on the straw. There was only so much temptation any one person could take.

"Sorry if you're not into popcorn any more. I can get you nachos instead, if you like? Or a corn dog?"

He gave her a sideways look as he led them away from the counter. "I like my popcorn and slushies the way I always have, sweetheart. You feeling OK?"

She nodded vigorously and this seemed to make things worse, his frown deepening. But he didn't pry, letting her keep her anxieties to herself.

They wandered over to the roped-off entrance to the screens and Ethan presented their tickets to the attendant before ushering her ahead of him with a hot hand at the small of her back.

"Predictions?" she asked once they were seated, relieved when they settled near the back but not in the very back row that teens congregated in to make out. She would know. They'd once been those teens in the back row.

"Hmm, I think Reese Witherspoon is secretly the bad guy."

Penny rolled her eyes. "Are you just trying to let me win?"

His laugh warmed his eyes and she had to look away before she drowned in their depths. "Go on then, show me how it's done."

She bit her lip. "I think one of them is going to seduce a guard of some kind to pull off the heist."

"A classic trope," he said, nodding.

They'd been playing the predictions game for a long time and falling back into the pattern was easy thanks to its familiarity. It felt comfortable playing it again with Ethan, even as her heart raced at his proximity and the brush of his arm on the rest between them. Typically whoever picked a prediction that came true in the movie got to pick the next one. Sometimes there were no winners, but it didn't stop them coming up with all kinds of nonsense guesses.

"I'm glad you agreed to meet me," Ethan murmured, his low voice raising the hair on her arms and sending a tingle across her chest. "I take it your talk with Tasha went well?"

She nodded. "It was dicey at first, to be honest. I know she's just trying to look out for both of us but it took a little while to convince her that our friendship isn't at risk if anything happens between me and you. And then many cookies were eaten, and things got a little easier from there. I do get where she's coming from though, especially after how everything went down last time." Ethan didn't say anything, allowing Penny to finish her thought as he simply nodded in understanding. Before she could lose her nerve, Penny blew out a breath. "Ethan? Is this a date?"

His eyes flicked over her face, assessing her. "Do you want this to be a date?" She hesitated, biting her lip before nodding. "Then it's a date." He smiled when she relaxed and leant in to kiss her on the cheek as they settled back in their seats.

The previews came to an end, the screen briefly going completely black as the movie prepared to play. The theater was relatively empty and the darkness felt cozy until the brightening of the screen threw their surroundings into sharp relief.

Ethan's face looked pale in the bright light and when he turned to find her watching him, she jerked her gaze away quickly. She'd been up front with Ethan about her feelings, and her concern over her eventually leaving Magnolia Springs behind, so why did she feel guilty? Like a nerve was twanging under her skin, Penny couldn't stop fidgeting, unable to focus on the movie, or anything besides Ethan's warmth beside her. She didn't need to fight this feeling anymore, but she also felt like she couldn't give in to it either. Had it been so long since she'd last been happy that the sensation now felt completely foreign?

A hand covered hers, squeezing gently, and her eyes darted down to find Ethan's hand intertwined with her own atop the shared armrest between them. Maybe it was the darkness of the room that had her burning, the freedom of being unobserved, but her body felt like a live wire as Ethan touched her.

When her fidgeting started up again ten minutes later, Ethan leant in with worry furrowing his brow. "If you want to leave we can," he said, as Reese Witherspoon pouted adorably on-screen.

"No, it's fine," Penny murmured, wriggling in her seat to get comfortable. "Just can't relax and get my brain to switch off."

"Oh." A small smile pulled at Ethan's lower lip as he settled back in his chair. "I see."

They didn't say anything else and Penny tried to focus on the screen and the inevitable heist build-up. But then Ethan let go of her hand and surprise, maybe a little hurt too, made her fingers clench.

Except, his hand didn't stop moving and instead dropped, reaching over the armrest and landing on her knee. She started, popcorn spilling from her bucket, and when he squeezed her knee her breath caught.

"What are you doing?"

He smiled. "Relaxing you."

His hand on her leg was the *opposite* of relaxing, and then he started to move. His fingers trailed over her knee and carefully stroked upwards in a line of fire so delicate she thought she might lose her mind.

"Ethan—"

"Shhh. I've got you. You can be quiet for me, can't you?"

His hand reached the waist of her jeans and he looked up at her for approval before flicking open the button and smoothly lowering her zipper.

Her gasp was lost in the loud music that flooded the room, but Ethan knew, had seen her chin tilt and mouth part and rewarded her by slipping his hand under her jeans and cupping her over her underwear.

Penny glanced to her right and was relieved that the rest of their row was empty, as was the row behind them. Nobody could see him torturing her, but even if they could, she wasn't sure she'd care right then. Not when she could feel her own wetness mounting against the friction of his large hand.

She wasn't the only one affected, though. Ethan's eyes were closed, his bottom lip sucked into his mouth as he rocked his hand against her heat. Her hips canted forward and his finger slid under the boundary of her underwear, making them both jolt.

There was a brief moment then, as if they both realized that there would be no going back from this, then the bubble of time popped and his hand pressed against her clit.

He stroked into her arousal, the curl of his fingers proprietary as he teased her entrance and found her soaked. Ethan muttered something under his breath that she couldn't hear over the music playing, she stared at the screen without really seeing it as the tip of his finger pressed into her and she gripped the armrests, trying for some semblance of control.

"Is this OK?" The words were husky and uttered straight into her ear, making her shudder as his finger pressed into her more fully, curling and rubbing in a way he definitely hadn't known how to do when they were in high school.

"Yes," she panted and his smirk was there and gone in a flash of light from the screen.

"Good. I think you can take more, baby. Don't you?" His palm pressed flat against her and the added pressure to her clit made her legs strain open wider. "I think you *need* more, but you have to be quiet for me, Penny."

She nodded, the movement frantic and eager, and was rewarded with the press of a second finger at her entrance, stretching her out as the pressure inside her built. Her eyes fluttered close and Ethan tutted.

"Eyes on me, baby," he growled and then chuckled low and dark when he felt the rush of moisture his words generated. Their eyes locked and he bit his lip on a groan as the filthy sound of what he was doing to her was lost in the soundtrack of the movie.

"How's that, Penny? Are you feeling calmer now?" The speed of his slow thrusts increased and her hips rolled against his hand as small whimpers were wrung from her lips. The motion of his hand froze. "Shhh, only quiet girls get to finish."

Her mouth snapped shut and she begged Ethan with her eyes, relieved when he resumed fucking her with his fingers. Each drag of the digits against her inner walls had her muscles coiling, the pressure mounting higher until she ground desperately against his hand.

"God, I've fucking dreamed about this," Ethan groaned in her ear. "I can feel how close you are, Penny. Fluttering around my fingers. You want to come?"

She nodded, her pussy clenching around his fingers.

"Then come," he said, voice hoarse, as he curled his fingers inside her, pressing against a spot that made her gasp just as his mouth came down on hers to capture the sound. He stroked her through the orgasm, murmuring praise in her ear as she soaked his hand, and her muscles slowly relaxed.

Her heart was beating so fast she had to take several calming breaths as Ethan withdrew his hand and rebuttoned and zipped her jeans before raising his fingers to his mouth and curling his tongue around them like he was sampling the nectar of the gods themselves.

Then he grinned like that wasn't the hottest thing she'd ever seen and said, "Shall we finish the movie?"

He held her hand throughout the rest of the film and Penny felt drunk with the way her muscles tingled, the release he'd given her making her sleepy and warm. She hadn't meant to fall asleep, but when Ethan nudged her awake, the credits were rolling and his smile was soft.

"Hey, sleepyhead. Want to get a late dinner?" The yawn that left her was so big her eyes watered, interrupting her response and making Ethan grin. "Or we could make that a rain check?"

"Can we rain check? Do you mind?"

He pressed a kiss to her cheek and helped her stand from her seat. "Not at all. I already filled up on popcorn anyway."

She glanced down and narrowed her eyes at the two empty buckets. "You always were a snack thief."

"I make up for it with my dazzling wit and good looks."

Penny was still laughing when they walked out of the movie theater and into the cool night air, shivering lightly at the shift in temperature. Ethan draped his jacket over her shoulders and she smiled, breathing in the sandalwood scent that lingered on his clothes.

"Do you mind if we just sit for a minute? I need to wake up a little before I drive home."

Ethan chuckled. "Sure. Come on." The town square

was fairly quiet, as most of the shops shut by seven, with only a few passers-by walking to and from eateries, the odd car driving past making the only sound aside from their footsteps. She smiled when she realized where he was leading them.

The water had slowed to a trickle and the stone rim of the fountain was mostly dry as they took a seat on the edge. Once it hit a certain time in the morning the fountain would turn back on in full force, ready for the new day, but in the evenings it was turned off to conserve power.

"I used to come here all the time, do you remember?"

He nodded, looking out at the hub of their small town with a soft look on his face. "Yeah. After you left it kind of became *my* spot, though."

"Oh?"

He nodded. "It's a good place to think. And . . ."

"And?" she prompted when he fell silent.

"And it made me feel close to you," he murmured, his eyes avoiding hers. His confession was so quiet she had to hold her breath to hear the words. "Not even necessarily in a romantic way—you were my friend before we were ever more, and I missed that. *You*."

Well, she was certainly feeling more awake now. "When I moved, I tried my best to not miss you, or anyone here really. I worked double shifts until I was so exhausted all I could do was go home and sleep, but you and Tasha and this stupid place snuck into my dreams sometimes anyway."

He turned to her and the streetlights in the distance reflected in his dark irises as he watched her intently. "Why didn't you want to miss us?"

She shrugged. "A hundred reasons. It hurt, it made me want to run straight back home, but I knew I'd screwed everything up when I left and thinking about that, about how I must have hurt you and Tasha and my parents, was too much."

His hand found hers, their fingers intertwining easily as Ethan lifted their joined hands to his mouth and pressed a kiss to the back of hers. "I'm sorry you went through that alone."

There was a lump in her throat that made it hard to swallow. "It was my choice, I guess. I always thought, at least you and Tasha still had each other after I left."

"Eh," he said, wrinkling his nose. "We were both busy doing other things at first. I went to college, Tasha started her internship at the library in the new town. Maybe if you'd stayed, it might have been different."

"Maybe," she whispered and he squeezed her hand.

"But right now, I think it all turned out OK in the end. Don't you?"

15

October had hit fast and hard, the remaining leaves on the trees turning red overnight and blanketing every sidewalk and open space in town until it seemed like something out of a fall Pinterest board, especially now they had built the annual bonfire on the green by the stores.

Penny had agreed to meet Ethan and Tasha by the church at seven and, as she wrapped on her scarf and slipped temporary heating pads into her boots to keep her toes warm, she couldn't help feeling just as nervous as she was excited. This was her first outing with all three of them since she and Ethan had begun seeing each other again. At least, that's what Penny thought they were doing. They hadn't really had the *define the relationship* talk yet, especially because it had been a hectic few weeks getting the orchard as ready as possible before they started setting up for the Halloween Orchard Fest. They'd both been too exhausted to do much more than hang out at his house, watching the occasional movie or just talking. It had been nice to spend more time around each other without feeling the need to rush into things. He brought her coffee in the morning while they worked at the orchard and she cooked them dinner at least once a week, but it hadn't progressed beyond that. She'd always left before it got too late, and he'd been a perfect gentleman which had been nice . . . and a little annoying.

She got the sense that he was holding back because he thought it was what she wanted. And to begin with, it had been. But now . . . It had been almost two weeks since their movie date and she was getting antsy to take things further. Maybe it was this thought that had made her pick out her tightest black jeans, the ones that made her ass look phenomenal, and the scoop-neck red sweater that made her eyes look extra bright and her hair intensely dark. Then, to top the outfit off, she'd grabbed a matching red beanie with a pom-pom on its top, remembering Ethan's fondness for her in hats. And anyway, it was bitterly cold outside and she wanted to be both toasty *and* cute.

"I'm off to the bonfire!" she called out to her parents as she left the cottage. They were upstairs, still getting ready, but would be joining the rest of the town for the festivities. Her car was cold when she climbed inside and she blasted the heat as she turned on the wipers, brushing off the brown leaves that covered her windshield. She pulled out of the drive smoothly and turned the car toward the road that would take her into town. If her parents had been ready on time they could have carpooled, but she hadn't wanted to interrupt them based on all the giggling coming from their bedroom.

There *was* one other thing she was starting to feel nervous about, besides hanging out with Ethan and Tasha together for the first time in years.

Ethan's deadline.

He hadn't mentioned it again since they'd had coffee a few weeks ago, so she couldn't be sure how serious he'd been. But whether it was his imaginary Christmas deadline or her own self-imposed departure date, it felt like time was becoming scarce and she was no clearer on where she was going next or whether she and Ethan were in this for the long haul. She'd like to think so, but it was still so new. Equally though, everything felt so familiar, so natural between them, like they knew each other so well already, not least because, once upon a time, they had. But she wanted to get to know the person he was now, even if their connection felt as strong as ever. She kept turning the conflicting thoughts over in her mind as she drove into town, no closer to figuring out her answer by the time she parked her car behind the church and stepped out. She could already smell the sweet smoke from the bonfire in the air and felt her nerves ease at the familiar scent as she walked past the fountain and toward the green, looking for Ethan and Tasha.

Ever since she was a kid, Penny had loved the annual bonfire. There were stalls dotted all around selling warm cider and hot chocolate, cakes, and fries, but the main draw for Penny was, of course, the bonfire itself. She'd mentioned to her mom about having a stand for the orchard there, offering to help with running everything so it wouldn't be too much work for her parents, but the applications had already closed for vendors by the time she'd mentioned it. Still, there was always next year. *If she decided to stay, that was.*

She spotted Tasha and Ethan pretty quickly once she'd made it through the small crowd of people standing by the entrance. Seeing them together almost threw her off. She hadn't noticed the night they'd gone for drinks but now they were older the resemblance between them was uncanny—they'd always looked alike, given that they were twins, but it seemed more obvious now than when they were growing up.

Penny lifted her hand and waved, relieved when Ethan's face lit up and Tasha beckoned her over. "Hey," she called and then hugged them both once she came to a stop in front of them. "Hope you weren't waiting long, my parents were running late so I had to leave without them in the end."

"We would never expect you to be on time," Tasha said, grinning widely as she smacked a kiss onto Penny's cheek.

"Hell might freeze over," Ethan added and Penny shot him a mock glare.

"You guys are *so* funny. Truly. I can barely breathe for laughing," she said in a monotone and then couldn't help laughing when they did. "What are we in the mood for? Cider? Hot chocolate?" Penny linked one arm with Tasha's and held out her other hand to hold Ethan's as she led them toward the large park where the bright flames could already be seen.

Tasha's stomach growled. "I guess food first?"

Most of the food trucks that were typically dotted all around town had congregated around the town square for the night. They found a cart selling veggie corn dogs, hot dogs, and beef dogs that smelled surprisingly good and got one of each to share at a picnic table nearby, alongside hot wine for Tasha, cider for Penny, and hot chocolate for Ethan.

Penny wrinkled her nose at the idea of hot wine—she couldn't imagine anything quite as gross—but Tasha seemed to be enjoying it well enough.

Once the hunger in their stomachs had been sated, they stood up and moved closer to the fire. A small barrier had been erected the whole way around, presumably to prevent any accidents, but otherwise everything was just as Penny remembered it. The sky held fragrant smoke, the stars just peeking through, and the wood crackled and popped like it was its own song. They sat on the grass a few feet back from the flames, enough to feel the heat but not close enough to sweat. Penny was grateful it hadn't rained the night before otherwise the wet mud would have been a pain to navigate.

They chatted between themselves for a little while, reminiscing about bonfires from their childhoods and how so little had changed in the intervening years. Tasha perked up as she looked out over the flames, clearly having spotted someone she was interested in talking to, and she stood up with her wine in hand to cross to the other side of the bonfire. "I'll see you guys later, I want to say hi to Tayla from work."

Ethan wrapped his hand around Penny's waist and they sat quietly, sipping their drinks. It was one of the things she'd loved most about dating Ethan all those years ago—they'd never felt the need for mindless chatter. They had plenty to talk about, but sometimes just enjoying the silence was perfect.

Her head lowered onto his shoulder and his hand tightened on her hip, like he wanted to bring her as close as possible, and she understood the feeling.

His corduroy jacket was soft under her cheek and his hands were warm on her body despite the lack of gloves, but then Ethan had always done well in the cold. Penny, not so much.

"Do you want to move closer to the fire?" he said, as if he'd had the same exact thought, and she smiled.

"Sure, my nose is getting a little cold."

He laughed, tapping the tip with his finger and then following it with a kiss before he stood and offered her a hand. "Come on then, let's—"

Something warm splashed onto Penny, trickling down her cheek as sticky sweet wine collected in the strands of her scarf and the ridges of her puffer jacket.

"Oh my gosh! I'm *so* sorry, Penny. I tripped over my own feet. I'm just super clumsy, right, Ethan?"

Penny's hands curled into fists as she pushed to standing and Shelby's eyes widened, like she hadn't realized they were the same height. Her face was carefully blank, her manicured nails lightly holding a now-empty paper cup as she tried to mask her sneer.

"It's fine," Penny said, biting back her frustration, not wanting to cause a scene in front of the whole town. Ethan opened his mouth, as if to argue, when Penny shook her head. "I hated this scarf anyway."

Shelby nodded sympathetically, pushing her bottom lip out in a small pout that probably helped her get her own way more often than not. "Why don't you go home and change? I'll look after Ethan while you're gone."

If Penny had been a cat, her hair would have stood on end as she eyed Shelby. She'd tried to have a little empathy for Shelby after Ethan explained what had happened between them. It couldn't have been easy loving someone who wished you were someone else and for the last few weeks she'd even felt bad for Shelby after learning how her relationship with Ethan had ended. But Shelby had taken it too far now; pulling a stunt like this was beyond desperate. Penny steeled herself to say something, but before she could get a word out, Ethan stepped in.

"Seriously? This crap is beneath you, Shel. We've

been broken up for over a year now, at some point you need to move on. I have." Ethan sighed and Penny wished she could have felt happier that he was defending her, but the wrecked look on Shelby's face made it hard to feel triumphant at that moment. "My place is closer, Pen. Come on, let's get you cleaned up." He turned his back on his ex-fiancée without another look at her and tugged Penny away gently by the hand. "I came with Tasha, so are you OK to walk to my place? Or we can take your car but I figured you wouldn't want to get the seats all sticky." For some reason, tears swam in her eyes and he pulled them to an abrupt stop when he noticed, cupping her face between his palms as he looked down at her. "What's wrong? Did I say the wrong thing?"

She shook her head quickly, blinking away the tears. "No, no. I'm fine. I'm sorry. It just bugs me that you have history with her and God knows how many other people in this damn town. It's stupid, really."

He smiled, the look gentle and a little amused as he wiped his now-sticky hand on his jeans. "I have more history with you than everyone else in this town combined."

She sighed, slipping her palm into his and angling them in the direction of the footpath that led to the residential corner of town where Ethan lived. It was less than a twenty-minute walk that would have been OK on a regular day, but tonight she could feel whatever Shelby had spilled on her solidifying in her hair.

"Sometimes I just really don't miss small-town life, you know? Everyone knows everyone and everything, and there's always someone who wants to make small talk or that remembers you when you were a kid . . ."

Ethan chuckled. "I promise to never subject you to small talk." She couldn't help her giggle and he softened at the sound. "But really, Magnolia Springs isn't all that bad, Penny. It's where you met me, after all."

Put like that, she couldn't deny that maybe Magnolia Springs did have a few things to offer.

They walked in silence, the comfortable kind, the smell of the bonfire and sickly sweet alcohol hanging around them in an invisible haze, but they were far enough now from the fire to be able to see the sprawl of stars above them.

"Thank you for stepping in with Shelby. That couldn't have been easy."

He shook his head. "It was long overdue. I can handle her saying stupid crap to me, but that . . . It was too far."

She squeezed his hand and he smiled, lifting it to his mouth to press a warm kiss to her knuckles that made her stomach swoop in response. The grassy path soon morphed into sidewalks and they crossed the road as they headed into Ethan's neighborhood and, before long, approached his door. She was familiar enough with the front of his house at this point. They'd cooked together in the kitchen a couple times, eaten food at the dining table together, and made out on his sofa until she decided it was time for her to go. But until now, she hadn't been further back into his house than the living room.

Her boots unzipped easily and she handed her ruined scarf to Ethan who walked away to presumably throw it in the trash. Thankfully it had caught most of the drink, so her coat was only a little sticky and easily cleaned up with a wet wipe. The ends of her hair, on the other hand, were another matter. She would need to shower to get the sticky mess out of her hair.

"Pen?"

"Yeah?" she called back and slowly wandered toward the voice when Ethan didn't respond. It felt silly to be nervous to approach. She'd been in his house so many times, so why did this feel different?

Ethan's head popped out from behind a doorway down the hall and he arched a questioning brow at her when he found her standing still, hovering between the boundary line of the hall and living room. "You coming?"

"Um. OK."

Her steps were short and hurried and she was a little breathless a few seconds later when she stood in front of him. A slow smile was taking over his face and she got the impression he thought she was funny for some reason.

His bedroom was plush, with more of the same cream walls he had in the rest of the house and one feature wall in a light greige that was echoed in the throw on the end of the bed and the dark carpet. He'd turned on both of the bedside lamps and their muted light put her at ease as anticipation thrummed through her veins.

"What now?" she whispered and that smile widened into a full-blown grin.

"Well, I'd assumed you'd want to shower, but we can clean you up another way if you prefer."

She gulped. "Oh?"

His hands fell to either side of her waist as he leant in close and she got a glimpse of the bedroom behind him. "Both options require you to wear a lot less clothes."

Now *that* she could get behind.

Like he'd seen the answer in her eyes, his laugh was low and made heat curl in her lower belly. His hands were gentle as he pulled her body against his and touched his mouth to hers, teasing her until she relaxed and sighed into the kiss.

He walked backwards, bringing her with him, and she was helpless to resist when his hands slid up to cup her jaw, tilting her head to the side so he could kiss her throat. Small nips and quick licks made her whimper and she felt him smile against her skin.

"Can I take this off?"

She nodded and he lifted her sweater deftly, slipping it up and over her shoulders, and then lifting the tank top she wore beneath up and over her head until she was left in her bra.

His eyes darkened and his hands twitched, like he was holding himself back from reaching for her. "I like this." He ran one fingertip over the lace that covered the plain black bra and she raised an eyebrow.

"It's nothing fancy." And it wasn't, just one of her everyday bras, but he was looking at her like he would devour her if she asked, so she unhooked it and let it fall to the floor.

Ethan knelt on the carpet, his soft blond hair tickling her stomach as he undid her pants and eased the fabric down her cold legs, warming the skin with his palms, until she was left in her plain black cotton panties.

His breathing was ragged when he leant back to take her in, the heat in his eyes unmistakable as he licked his lips and reached for her only to pause when she took a step back.

"I think you're a little overdressed."

Ethan didn't hesitate, reaching over his head to grasp the neck of his Henley and lifting it over his head in one smooth motion that made her weak at the knees. He had to work out beyond working on the orchard, because he was hiding a decidedly muscular body beneath the shirt.

Then he reached for his jeans.

Her mouth went dry as the denim brushed over toned thighs and crumpled at his ankles before he kicked the fabric away, leaving him in only a pair of tight gray boxers that showed off the dimples in his lower back when he bent down to kneel at her feet once more.

"Better?" he rasped and she nodded.

"Much."

His mouth lifted on one side in a crooked half-smile that faded into hunger when he leant in close, digging his nose into her underwear as he mouthed at the material, making her arch into his touch. "This," he groaned, voice rough with lust as he looked up at her from his place on the floor. "This is what I think about constantly, ever since I had my hands on you at the movies."

Her eyes widened. She'd had a couple of boyfriends in the past who'd gone down on her, but it had never been anything to write home about. But the way Ethan was looking up at her, like she was a goddess and he wanted to worship at her feet, had her tingling already and he hadn't really even touched her yet.

"Can I?" His mouth was red where he'd been biting his lip and there was a naked desire in his voice that stole her ability to talk, so she nodded.

Two fingers hooked into either side of her underwear, pulling them away and baring her to the cool air and Ethan licked his lips, nodding slightly like he was hypnotized before he brought his face closer and licked a long line over her slit. He tongued her lips, pushing them apart slightly with his mouth as he dipped inside, tracing the contours of her folds and brushing her clit lightly.

He repeated the motion and she could feel herself throbbing, desperate for his touch as Ethan continued his gentle ministrations. Teasing her, she realized.

"Ethan," she whined and his laugh was full of heat, but she didn't care because he obeyed and finally pressed his mouth firmly to the apex of her.

His tongue worked, massaging her bud and coaxing moans from her throat that she might have been embarrassed about if she could think beyond the pleasure his mouth wrought. She swayed and his hands slid up her calves to clasp her to his face more firmly, nudging her thighs apart with his shoulders as he pressed nibbling kisses to her clit, making his way down until his tongue could spear her opening.

At some point her hands had found his hair, holding him exactly where she wanted as her hips rocked over his face and ground down as she hovered at the edge of her climax.

A warm hand slid from her ass to her front and pressed down on her clit at exactly the right moment and she cried out, body trembling as she came with Ethan's name on her lips.

He caught her when she sagged and carried her over to the bed, laying her down gently and letting her catch her breath as he kissed her hands, her chest, cherishing her more in this way than words could have expressed.

"Maybe we owe Shelby our thanks," she said when she could finally breathe again and Ethan laughed.

"I wouldn't go that far."

"The night is young," she replied, glancing up at him before lowering her eyes to take in his mostly-naked body next to her and snagging on the hardness tenting his boxers. "That looks painful."

He shrugged. "It'll go down."

She frowned. "And if I don't want it to go down?"

He looked up in surprise, smiling sheepishly. "Oh."

Penny lifted herself into a sitting position with a little difficulty, given that she felt completely boneless. "May I?" She reached for his boxers and held her breath until he nodded, excitement humming through her.

"I just didn't want you to think you had to—" Ethan's words stuttered and fell away as she closed her hand around his cock. "It's not quid pro quo, is all," he managed.

"I know." In truth, this was partly selfishly motivated. She wanted to see Ethan come undone, and from what she remembered he'd always been very responsive to head, which made sucking him off a lot of fun.

She pumped him in her hand and his eyes slid closed, a gasp making his hips lift when she straddled his legs and lowered her mouth to lick him as she stroked. He bobbed against her lips and his garbled apology made her snicker as she parted her lips and took him into her mouth. The salty taste of him sat on her tongue as she widened her jaw to take more of him in, swallowing him down and backing off just as suddenly, loving the way he whined for her.

"Penny, you need to stop or I'm—I'm not going to last—"

She smiled around him, looking up at him as he fisted his hand in her hair and cursed, hips jumping despite his words, and she took everything he gave her.

Humming happily, knowing the vibration of her throat would drive him wild, she spread her legs a little wider so she could rub herself against his thigh as her hands worked Ethan's base.

"Fuck, Penny. You're so wet. You love this, don't you? Torturing me?" He moaned and she rocked her own hips in time with his thrusting into her mouth. "Oh God, yes, ride me, Penny. Penny, I'm close. Penny. *Penny.*" Ethan's voice turned hoarse as he called for her as he came, making her grind against him faster as she swallowed.

Her mouth lifted away and she smiled at him, pleased with herself even as she rocked against his leg, and the look on her face made him flush.

"I need to be inside you. Now."

She nodded and he reached clumsily for the oak nightstand next to the bed, throwing the drawer open so haphazardly he nearly pulled the whole thing out as he found a condom.

His hands came up behind her, squeezing her ass as he lifted her from his leg and positioned her instead over his cock. Brown eyes caught on the wetness she left behind on his thigh and he swallowed hard. "Get over here now, Penny. Otherwise I might combust."

She laughed and lowered herself, balancing with her hands on his corded shoulders as she sank down onto him, making them both groan. There would be time to go slow later, right now she just needed him, to feel him inside her.

Ethan clearly agreed, wasting no time in thrusting all the way, the sounds of their bodies meeting filling the room as she moaned his name and rode him harder than she had his thigh.

She was lost in him, in the depths he somehow reached as he held her to him like she was something precious. Her arms wrapped around his neck, twining in his hair as he drove deeper into her, his hands pressing her to his chest.

They moved as one, her body pressed flat against his as his mouth claimed her, taking her moans for his own as they moved faster, harder, the walls shaking with their pleasure as they tumbled off the edge clutching each other close.

Finally sated, she laid against Ethan's chest and let herself catch her breath. It was like ten years of hunger she hadn't known was there had suddenly been satisfied and now she was at peace. Maybe she could have fooled herself before, but she wasn't sure she could say the same now—regardless of anything else, she couldn't let Ethan go again.

"So," she said a few minutes later as he lazily stroked up and down her spine. "How about that shower?"

"I can't believe you've been hogging this gloriousness to yourself this whole time," Penny complained as she stepped out of Ethan's en-suite with a towel wrapped around her body and another in her hair.

His shower, a walk-in, with a rainfall head and water pressure that somehow worked all of the knots from her muscles after just five minutes, was beyond luxurious.

Ethan was lounging on the bed, scrolling on his phone with the sheets draped lazily over his waist and she paused for a moment to savor the image.

"Penny, you've got a bit of—" Ethan tapped his chin and she snapped her mouth closed and narrowed her eyes as he laughed. "No, no. By all means, get a good look."

"I think I will," she retorted, marching over and whipping off the sheets so his entire body was revealed. "I played myself," she said hoarsely, running her eyes over him at a leisurely pace while he smirked. She brushed a hand over his torso, tracing the lines of the tattoo that wound around his side in a complicated knot. "Does it mean something?"

"Nah." He took hold of her hand and pressed a kiss to each of her fingers before he sat up and crossed the room to rummage in the drawers that sat against the wall opposite the bed. "I just thought it looked cool. Here." He held out a bundle of clothes and she couldn't resist raising them to her face and inhaling, the smell of him invading her senses until she felt almost drunk.

"Thank you."

"You're supposed to wear them, not sniff them," he said, laughter in his voice. "Or you can go naked, I'm fine with that option too."

She pulled off the towel on her head and threw it at Ethan while she slipped on his t-shirt. She'd borrowed some of the roll-on deodorant he'd had in the bathroom and kept getting wafts of the masculine smell every time she moved her arms, though the fabric of the shirt helped somewhat.

Not bothering with the pajama bottoms he'd offered her, she ran her fingers through her hair and winced at the knots.

"Here." Ethan sat on the bed behind her and gently pulled her down in front of him. She heard his bedside drawer open and close and then a gentle tugging sensation started as he worked a comb over her hair, untangling the knots with care.

"Thank you," she murmured, voice a little thick with emotion in the face of his tenderness. "I'm sorry we had to leave early."

"I'm not," he said and she laughed breathlessly. "I want to ask you something." He chuckled, feeling the way she tensed beneath his hands. "It's nothing bad or scary. I think."

"OK . . ."

"Tonight has been incredible. But I need to tell you, I don't do casual sex."

"All right."

One hand on her shoulder encouraged her to turn

and face him and there was a vulnerability to his expression that made her breathing speed up.

"I don't want anyone else," he continued and she reached for his hand, squeezing it. "I just want you."

"I don't want anyone else either," she whispered and the smile tugging at his mouth made her want to kiss him, so she did. "Are you asking to be exclusive?"

"I—I think I am, yeah. Is that OK?"

Relief swamped her and she laughed lightly. "More than OK."

"Good," he said, voice breathless.

"Good," she repeated and when he leant in to kiss her, she smiled.

16

Angie Larkin was a hard ass.

Penny had suspected as much for a long time, but seeing her mom in action really drove it home. With the annual bonfire done, the next big event for Magnolia Springs was the Halloween Orchard Fest, and if Penny didn't already know that her mom thrived on a deadline, then she might have been concerned they were taking too much on. The Orchard Fest had grown bigger every year until it had become a Magnolia Springs staple and Penny couldn't deny that she was excited to attend for the first time in forever.

"What do you think?" Angie asked vaguely and Penny nodded her head, knowing full well her mom didn't actually want any opinions or feedback. Penny had stopped offering them after the third time she'd been shot down that afternoon.

Most of the trees were now bare of apples, barring a few in the far corner, and her mom surveyed the land with her hands on her hips and a keen look in her eyes that Penny had seen far too many times growing up.

Usually when she had tried to get out of doing her homework to hang out with Tasha.

"Ethan!" Angie called and Penny jolted, looking over her shoulder to find her . . . *boyfriend*. The word itself nearly made her smile, like an absolute goofball. Ethan approached, looking far too edible to be seen in public, and smiled at her mom. "Now, what do you think of this . . ." Angie launched into her whole spiel again, explaining where she wanted to set up the various stations while Ethan nodded and rumbled his praises in that deep voice of his that drove Penny wild.

Until she realized what he was saying.

She tuned back in to hear him confirming their dinner plans and her head jerked up, bouncing between Ethan's smug face and her mom's delighted one.

"Wait, what?"

Ethan dimpled at her from above her mom's head and Penny narrowed her eyes. "I was just inviting your parents to the dinner party we're hosting."

"Right," she said slowly and his smile widened. "When is that again?"

"Friday."

"And who else is going to be there?"

Angie frowned at Penny as Philip walked over to join them. "Honestly, Penny. Goodness knows where you got your organizational skills from because it certainly wasn't me."

"What?"

"Well, it's almost as if you know nothing about your own dinner party, honey."

Penny glared at Ethan. "Almost as if."

Why was he springing this on her now? By way of her parents? The question must have been written all over her face because as soon as her parents moved deeper into the trees, Ethan slung an arm over her shoulder and murmured, "Figured this way you couldn't run off or hide me from your parents."

"Some warning would have been nice," she muttered and he snorted.

"The lack of warning was deliberate." His eyes sparkled as he tugged on the ends of her new scarf, a fluffy purple number she'd bought that weekend. "But what do you say? Will you host a dinner party with me?"

"Maybe," she conceded. "If you make it worth my while."

"That can be arranged," he whispered, kissing her cheek. "I thought it would be a good way to let everyone know about us, all in one go."

She hummed and slid her body around so she could look up at him. "I like the sound of that. *Us.* It does mean you're my boyfriend, right? Because in my head that's what I've been calling you since the night of the bonfire."

"Penny, are you asking me to go steady?"

She snorted. "I think we're past that point."

His eyes darkened and he leant in to press a lingering kiss to her lips. "I thought I made what I wanted from you pretty clear the night of the bonfire, but by all means, I'd be happy to give you a repeat." The words were low and hot and made her toes curl when they were coupled with the smirk on his face. "You can call me whatever you want. Honey, boyfriend, partner . . . I mean, I'd personally go with *forever*, but if you just want me as your boy toy or your boyfriend, then I guess I can live with that," he teased.

Forever. "Maybe we should start with boyfriend and see how you do." She tried to hide her smile and failed. "But I guess you're right, a dinner party really *is* in order."

A gentle breeze rustled the leaves at their feet as Ethan cupped Penny's cheek. "I'm so completely yours, you know. Will you be mine?"

He'd asked her the same thing in a dozen different ways over the past few days; she couldn't tell if it was romantic or a request for reassurance. Either way, she didn't mind. The tenderness with which he said the words made a lump rise in her throat and she nodded. "Yes."

"Good, because I really didn't want to have to uninvite everyone to our soft-launch dinner."

Dinner. Right. Her mind was already whirling, producing and discarding possible recipes to try. "Who else did you invite?"

"Tasha, your parents, and mine."

Despite the fact that she'd already bumped into Ethan's mom a few times since being back, nervousness made her palms tingle at the prospect of seeing her again in a more formal setting. Would his parents approve of them dating again? Did they hold her mistakes against her?

Pushing down her panic, she tried for a smile that felt wobbly. "Can't wait."

She met Tasha later that afternoon, having left Ethan in the capable hands of her parents to help with the festival-planning. Penny was facing an altogether bigger task: finding the perfect outfit for this dinner party.

It needed to be something mature and pretty, but also easy to move in when she was cooking. Cool enough that she wouldn't sweat through it standing over the stove, but not so skimpy that it would look odd given the colder weather.

She was probably overthinking it a little.

"Try *a lot*," Tasha griped and then smiled to show she didn't really mind Penny's whining. "This feels so weird, shopping with you on a Tuesday afternoon like school just got out and we need to spend the allowance burning a hole in our pocket."

Penny laughed and then took a long drag of her iced coffee. It was cold out, but she'd been in an anxious sweat ever since Ethan had dropped the meet-the-parents . . . *again* bomb on her. "Is it still just the same places that have good stuff?"

Tasha peered in the window of the library as they walked past and waved at the brunette woman inside.

"Pretty much. Though, a couple stores changed hands. Do you remember Candace?" Penny nodded, they'd gone to school with the bubbly blonde girl. "She runs Threads now and, to be honest, the stuff in there is super cute."

Penny wasn't sure she was ready to see more people she went to high school with, but needs must, and she followed Tasha into the store in question with only a small amount of reluctance.

The vibe inside was very boho-chic and Penny had no doubt that in the summer this store would contain a *lot* of sequins. They didn't recognize the girl behind the counter and Penny breathed a sigh of relief that she could focus on finding an outfit and not on small talk.

Racks of colorful clothing seemed to be organized by occasion rather than any other order she could make sense of, with matching shoes stacked atop the clothes on a small podium. They browsed idly and Tasha held up a couple tops for Penny to inspect and disregard due to the itchy-looking lace on the straps and front.

"I meant for me," Tasha said, rolling her eyes.

"Oh. In that case, it's cute."

"Do you guys need any help?" The girl from the counter called and Penny shook her head at the same time that Tasha nodded.

"That would be great. We're looking for a parental-approved outfit, but it needs to be cooking-safe."

The girl nodded like that wasn't a strange request in the least and tucked a strand of pink hair behind her ear. "I think a dress is probably your best bet, something with short sleeves so they don't get in the way?"

Penny headed to the carousel the girl indicated, flipping through the rack before pausing on one dress in particular that had a lovely silky texture and was a burnt orange perfect for the season. "What do you think of this?"

Tasha *ooh*ed. "I love. Do you want to try it on?"

Penny hesitated, holding the dress up against her and looking in the floor-length mirror to her left. It *was* nice. The dress complemented her hair, making the brown look richer, and her green eyes popped against the red-orange of the dress. "Should I really buy the first thing in the first place I look?"

Tasha laughed. "Well, this is Magnolia Springs, not the city, so it's not like there's a whole ton of choice around here anyway."

She had a point. "OK. OK, I'll take it." The dress rippled in the air as Penny walked it over to the counter to pay and the girl smiled as she grabbed a bag.

"So, you're a chef? Are you the new owner of the lot next door?"

Penny blinked. "No, I work in the city." *Worked*, she mentally corrected and the girl made a noise of understanding.

"Ah, I just wondered. It's been vacant for a couple months now, it used to be a Thai place."

At the mention of Thai food, Penny's stomach growled and she glanced at Tasha with warm cheeks. "Lunch?"

"Thought you'd never ask." Tasha bought the two tops she'd been eyeing and then they thanked the clerk on their way out.

A wind had kicked up, whipping their hair around them with enough ferocity that Penny knew her hair would be knotted by the time they got inside. The vacant storefront the girl had mentioned was indeed right next door; a wide window with a faded white frame offered a glimpse inside to reveal a fairly large floor space.

Penny looked away, letting Tasha lead her away in search of food, even as Penny wondered what kind of restaurant might move in there and how they might decorate. New eateries were never a bad thing, especially in Magnolia Springs where cafes and food trucks were more prevalent—though there was a semifancy restaurant in the new town, last time Penny had checked anyway.

"Hello? Earth to Penny?"

She shook her head and focused on Tasha. "Sorry, what?"

"I asked if cake was an acceptable lunch."

She snorted. "Are you looking for permission or a partner-in-lunch-crime?"

Tasha grinned and held open the door to the bakery for Penny to enter first. "Both."

17

In hindsight, Penny might have gone a little overboard with her dinner plans. But, in her defense, she was really, really, nervous.

Ethan had reassured her a dozen times that his parents weren't going to give her a hard time over mistakes that were ten years old, but Penny couldn't help feeling like the other shoe was about to drop—on her head, no doubt.

She tugged at the hem of her rust-colored dress and then at the crossover neckline, regretting her outfit choice more with every passing second. Was it too dressy? Too short? Had she sweated through the silky material?

The soup she'd made the night before was ready to go at a moment's notice, a fall blend of butternut squash with zucchini and peppers that only needed to be heated up. She'd picked up some crusty bread topped with pumpkin seeds that morning from the bakery that should accompany it nicely.

She'd stayed at Ethan's last night so she could prep as much of the food in advance as possible, but despite the warm comfort of his bed and arms she couldn't say she'd slept that well at all.

A knock at the door had her heart leaping into her throat and she stood frozen in the doorway of the kitchen, watching as Ethan walked to the door with a confidence she envied. He knew her parents loved him, so what did he have to worry about?

The door swung open and Tasha smiled, holding up a bottle of wine as she stepped over the threshold. Penny's breath of relief caught and choked in her throat when Ethan's parents and her own filed in after Tasha.

"You look like you could use this," Tasha murmured, pressing the wine into Penny's chest and snickering.

"And you could take a little less pleasure from all this," Penny hissed and then pasted a smile on her face as she accepted a hug and kiss on the cheek from Terri and Keith. "So glad you could all make it."

Bowing out of the huddle of people with the excuse of checking on the food, Penny took the chance to claim a steadying breath as she opened the oven to check the chicken. She'd opted for two different mains, one a classic roast chicken with lemon and herbs, and the other a veggie option of hollowed and roasted peppers filled with couscous, tofu, and lentils. The chicken would be ready in a half hour, which meant it was time for the peppers to go in the oven.

"Do you need any help?"

The sudden voice made Penny jump, one of the

peppers nearly falling off the tray as she turned to see Terri standing in the doorway.

"Oh, no. I'm fine, but thank you." She smiled and then hesitated. "Actually, could you get everyone around the dining table? The appetizers will be ready in a minute."

"Of course."

Penny turned back to the stove, stirring the soup in the pan before grabbing a clean spoon to dip in and taste. She nearly burned her tongue, which was good because it meant the soup was ready but annoying in the sense that it hurt like a bitch.

Turning off the heat, she lined up the bowls and grabbed a ladle to spoon a healthy portion into each dish before calling out to Ethan to help her carry them into the other room. The bread was already sliced and ready to go on a large serving platter that she brought in as Ethan set down the bowls.

"This smells wonderful, Penny. Ethan tells me you're a chef?"

Penny smiled, nodding at Ethan's dad. "Yeah, I am. I'm just home helping out Mom and Dad with the orchard for now, but I'll be back to cooking as soon as I can."

Keith nodded in approval. "Which culinary school did you attend?"

It felt like the whole room froze in time for a few seconds before Penny answered, voice tight. "I, uh, I didn't. I chose to learn on the job instead."

Her parents sent her twin looks of pride and she relaxed a miniscule amount.

"Ah. Yes. Well, how . . . practical."

Penny was sure her answering smile must have looked more like a grimace and silence descended. The clink of spoons and the crunch of the bread took over the room as they dug in and Penny discreetly checked the timer set on her phone when she was done. The chicken and peppers had about twenty minutes left.

Clearly trying to make up for the tension her husband had created, Terri sipped her wine delicately and asked, "How did you get into the restaurant world, Penny?"

She blew out a breath, relieved that this question was a little easier to answer. "I got a job straight out of high school—"

"Yes, we remember you rushing out of town," Keith muttered and Ethan's silverware clanged as he dropped it, eyes wide.

"Dad," Tasha protested and Penny shook her head.

"It's OK. Yes, I left abruptly. I'd been applying for internships and junior roles, and after a few interviews I had a conditional offer from one restaurant in San Francisco to work under their head chef twice a week and as a pot-wash the other five days. It was an amazing opportunity for someone with my level of experience." She looked directly at Keith and didn't flinch from the suspicion in his gaze. "I knew what I wanted, and I went after it. So I won't apologize for that—*but* I could have handled things better when I left. I've already apologized to Tasha and Ethan for that, but if you feel like you need an apology too—"

"That's not necessary—" Terri said kindly at the same moment that her husband spoke up.

"I'd say so. You were gone, we were the ones who had to listen to Coldplay on repeat blasting from Ethan's bedroom."

"*Dad*," Ethan growled, pink spots high on his cheeks, and Keith had the grace to look chagrined.

"That does sound like an ordeal," Penny said, lips twitching, and was relieved when chuckles rang out, dissipating a large part of the tension in the room. "It's understandable that you'd have reservations about me, but I'm not here to repeat my mistakes."

"I'll believe it when I see it," Keith said gruffly and Penny took a large gulp of wine in response.

"Let's not pretend you didn't make your fair share of mistakes when you were wooing Terri, Keith," Angie said sharply and Penny glanced over to find her dad placing a soothing hand on her mom's back. Penny's gratitude toward her mom in that moment was balanced only by her curiosity about what 'mistakes' she was referring to, and even though she was dying to ask for more details, she decided that now wasn't the time.

Keith flushed red but raised his glass in acknowledgement.

Maybe this evening would be salvageable after all.

Of course, that was when the power went out.

Plunged into darkness, Penny swore colorfully and Tasha giggled in the ensuing silence. "The chicken still has ten more minutes," she groaned and Ethan squeezed her hand from his place beside her as he turned on his phone flashlight.

"I think I've got some candles in here somewhere," Ethan muttered as he stood and began rummaging through the sideboard by the light of his phone. "Aha," he said triumphantly a few moments later, pulling three white candles in holders and a box of matches from a drawer. Quickly placing them along the middle of the table, he lit the candles so the room was bathed in a warm orange glow. In different circumstances, Penny thought, it might almost be quite romantic.

"I'll go and check the breaker, in the meantime you guys can enjoy some wine and ambience," he added, heading toward the door. His smile had returned, relaxed and easy. Penny hated him just a little in that moment for being so unflappable when she couldn't have been further from *calm* if she'd tried.

She gulped down the remaining wine in her glass and raised a brow at her mom when she frowned disapprovingly.

"OK," Ethan said, walking back into the room a few minutes later with his flashlight still lit. "The bad news is that the power is out for the whole block."

"And the good news?" Tasha asked, glancing over at Penny like she thought this might be the final blow to her sanity.

"I had a quick look and I think the chicken might be just about done."

Penny stood and blew out a breath before straightening her spine and nodding sharply. "I'll take a look. Hopefully it's ready."

Ethan followed her into the kitchen, a warm hand at her back rubbing between her shoulder blades soothingly. He kept the flashlight on and held aloft so she could see into the oven as she prodded the chicken with her meat thermometer. The juices ran clear and relief made her sag when the thermometer beeped to confirm the chicken was hot all the way through.

"Thank fuck."

Ethan chuckled and she pulled the bird and peppers out of the oven and set about carving and plating up. Thankfully, she'd kept the rest of the dish relatively simple with pre-done new potatoes and flavored rice accompanying the mains.

Back at the table in the flickering candlelight, Terri hesitantly lifted her fork to her mouth. "You're sure it's cooked?"

"Positive," Penny said, smiling as she popped a piece of chicken into her mouth reassuringly. The skin on the chicken could have been crispier if the power hadn't turned off the oven, but the meat itself was tender and juicy, so she was counting it as a win in general.

They were half-way through the main course when Keith spoke up again. "So, exactly how serious is all this then?" He gestured between Penny and Ethan with his fork as everyone in the room tensed up, waiting to hear what more he would say. "Do you have a plan?

"A plan?" Ethan had both brows raised and a warning look on his face that made Penny feel light with relief. He was on her side; it would all be OK.

"Yes, you know how women sometimes have them." He waved a hand airily as he speared a piece of chicken, oblivious to the glares he was receiving from all the *women* in the room. "Married in a year, kids in two, that sort of thing. Do you plan to marry?"

Penny inhaled so violently she choked and Tasha thumped her on the back from her left.

Ethan rolled his eyes. "Are you trying to scare her off?"

"Scares easy, does she?" Keith laughed but nobody else joined in and he glanced around, finally sensing the displeasure coming at him from all sides. "I just think it's wise to think about these things, is all. Obviously it will be difficult for you to pursue a career while you're raising the children, Penny, but then again you'll have us nearby to help with that sort of thing."

Penny didn't know what to say. "Children?" she rasped and her dad set his silverware down delicately before pinning Ethan's dad with a fierce look Penny wouldn't want to be on the receiving end of.

"Keith, this isn't the fifties. My daughter's career is just as important as your son's."

Penny started to smile, grateful that he was standing up for her, but then her mom chipped in.

"Besides, you think we're not going to be involved with our own grandchildren? As if we'd let you take the lead in teaching them that kind of misogynist nonsense."

Penny looked at Tasha with wide eyes, begging her to stop this and do something.

"Well, all right, I think that's enough wine for everyone—"

Ethan's dad puffed up, glaring at Philip even as his wife patted his hand in a way that was both warning and conciliatory. "I am certainly *not* a misogynist. My own wife is a woman."

Unsure whether to laugh or scream at what Keith was saying, Penny stood abruptly and gathered the mostly empty plates. "Well, I'll just go and grab the dessert," she muttered, avoiding eye contact with anyone around the table. And then she fled to the kitchen.

Ethan followed, looking a little unsettled as they stared into the fridge together at the mini mousses she'd prepared the day before. "I'm not sure what just happened."

"Me either."

A beat of silence passed and then, before she could stop it, a bubble of laughter worked its way out of her. Before she knew it, they were laughing, clutching at each other as the flashlights shook in time with their bodies. All of a sudden, the lights came back on, jolting Penny so hard she nearly fell, Ethan's form behind her the only thing that kept her upright. She took a few steadying breaths, her smile still spread across her face.

"I'll turn off the oven," Ethan said, breathless from laughter as Penny wiped moisture from her eyes.

"I'll get the mousse."

All in all, the dinner party was turning out to be just as bad as she'd expected, and in some ways delightfully worse, but she wouldn't have changed anything for the world. Not when she had Ethan working alongside her and a warmth running in her veins that only appeared when he was around.

"Shall we?" he murmured, gesturing ahead of him and she grinned when he swatted her playfully on the ass as they left the kitchen.

18

The weekend after the fateful dinner party was full of Halloween Orchard Fest prep. Penny sat at the kitchen table with her dad, her legs up and crossed in the chair and her sweatshirt's hood up over her head to shield her eyes from the sunlight spilling into the room. It was possible she'd overindulged on wine on Friday after everyone had left and it was just her and Ethan.

Thankfully, the ache in her eyes seemed to be the worst of the side effects and she worked slowly and methodically, looping colorful paper strips together to make the garlands they would be hanging in the trees for the festival. Her dad was moving a little quicker but had the added task of making patterns on the paper with felt-tip pens and glitter. She didn't envy him. The glitter got *everywhere*.

Her stomach grumbled and she sighed, looking up hopefully to where her mom was puttering about in the kitchen. Three pies sat on the cooling racks, the fragrant steam filling the room with the scent of apples, cinnamon, and honey. There had been one year that her mom hadn't won the apple pie competition they hosted during Orchard Fest, but she'd never let it go. Each year, she recreated her signature winning pie, and experimented with at least two other flavors. The upside? There would be a constant supply of pies in the house in the run up to the festival as her mom tried to perfect her recipes. The downside? There was no choice whether or not to partake in pie-tasting, though generally Penny didn't mind too much. Because, *pie*.

"Is it cool yet?" she whined and Angie chuckled.

"Fine, fine. Heathen." She cut a slice of each pie and placed them on one plate each before setting them down between Penny and her dad. "Wait! You need a fork, and I need to add the cinnamon sugar sprinkle on top."

Penny restrained herself just barely, eyes fixed on the golden deliciousness in front of her. "Love you," she muttered and Angie snorted.

"I don't know if you're talking to me or the pie."

"Hm?" Penny pulled her gaze away and licked her lips. "Oh. Um, both."

Philip chuckled but pushed his paper chains to one side in favor of focusing on the pies.

"OK." Angie clapped her hands together. "This one first." She pushed one plate forward ahead of the rest and pulled out her own fork. Philip went first, spearing the tip of the slice, Penny went next, choosing a piece with optimal crust to filling ratio, and Angie popped her forkful into her mouth without too much preamble. It felt nice, a little nostalgic, to be doing this with her parents. She'd taste-tested recipes before with her colleagues at the restaurant in the city, helping them with notes of flavor and texture. At least, she had done in the early days. In the past year or so, there hadn't been much time at all for experimenting with flavors and improving their craft.

Penny's mouth filled with saliva. The pie was still warm, the apple was tart but pleasantly off-set by the cinnamon sugar crust. "So good," she mumbled and Angie glared.

"Don't talk with your mouth full, Penny."

She stuck her tongue out to show she'd swallowed before repeating her analysis. "So good, Mom. Do we have any ice cream?" She loved the combination of hot and cold and how the ice cream would melt into the pie's filling.

"Yes, I think so. Try the other two first and then we can talk about ice cream."

Dutifully, they moved to the second plate and Penny nodded as the flavors hit her tongue. This pie was much more nutty, the filling more smooth and solid compared to the apple chunks of the first pie. "What is that, apple and pecan?"

Angie smiled, pleased. "Right in one. What do you think?"

"That's my favorite so far," Philip mumbled, sneaking a second forkful under Angie's disapproving eye. "What? It's tasty."

"Third pie," Angie demanded and handed them each

a glass of water to cleanse their palates first. "What do you think?"

Penny chewed consideringly. The texture was really good, less solid than the pecan and more sticky, the cinnamon sugar crust carried through reminding Penny of a pumpkin spice latte. She frowned. *What was in this pie?* She couldn't pin it down. "It's really good, what is it?"

"Guess," Mom said with a smirk.

Penny hummed. "Well, I can definitely taste the apple and cinnamon, and I want to say pumpkin?" Angie nodded in confirmation and Penny took another, smaller taste of the pie. "There's something else in there but I can't pin it down."

Philip swallowed and raised his hand like they were in class and Angie looked amused as she nodded at him. "Honey."

Penny groaned. Honey, of course. "Clever." She glanced at her dad and found a smug look on his face. "How did you know?"

"I saw her put it in the mix."

She snickered. "I think that's cheating."

Philip shook his head. "No, no. I'm just using all my resources."

Angie giggled. "I'll allow it. So, which is your favorite?"

"The first one," they answered in unison and Angie frowned, because that was her original signature recipe.

"Pie three is a close second for me though," Penny tried, and her mom sighed.

"I need new taste testers," Angie muttered. "Get Ethan and Tasha to stop in this week for pie, OK? I need impartial judges."

"OK," she agreed. "But I'll warn you that Ethan might not be unbiased. He wants you to like him, so he's likely to kiss your ass."

Philip guffawed, his heavy breath blowing glitter everywhere and earning him a glare from his wife. "He knows we love him."

"Unless he hates my pie," Angie said, winking as she pushed away from the table to grab a brush for the glitter. "Then I'm afraid he'll be banned from the house."

"Understandable," Penny said and smiled, reaching over to take one of their hands into hers and squeezing gently. "Thank you for yesterday. Having you there with me helped."

"Of course, pumpkin," her dad said gently as her mom pressed a kiss to the top of Penny's head. "Keith was being an ass."

"Philip," Angie said, swatting at his arm before she sighed. "But your father is right. I'm not sure what got into Keith. He's normally not so . . ."

"Dickish?" Penny supplied and her mom frowned but nodded. "I can't blame him for being hesitant after the way I left things before."

"Well, you just let us know if he gives you any more trouble," Philip said, the stern look on his face melting away as he peered behind Angie to try to glimpse the rest of the pies. "Now, what does a fellow have to do to get some more pie around here?"

One thing Penny hadn't missed about being in a new relationship was the early-days anxiety.

She'd seen Ethan sparingly over the past week, what with him being busy working for a client and Penny in the throes of setting up the Halloween Orchard Fest. If you'd told her a few weeks ago that she'd miss seeing Ethan around the orchard, she would have laughed and resumed climbing the closest tree to hide. But now he wasn't there and the harvest was largely complete, she missed seeing him between the rows of trees.

But it had been almost two weeks since the night of the bonfire. Two weeks since she'd done anything more than kiss Ethan in the stolen moments they'd found after work or as they crossed paths around the orchard. And while she knew that sex wasn't everything, it bothered her regardless. It made her wonder whether their second first-time hadn't lived up to what Ethan had imagined, or if it had been much better for her than him.

It was a good thing she hadn't harbored any hopes of 'getting it out of their system' by sleeping together. Now that she'd tasted Ethan again, she wanted more. Shelby was kind of a dick, but Penny had to admit that she understood why Shelby couldn't just let Ethan go, even if it was annoying as all hell.

But at least their temporary separation would be

over in a matter of moments. Ethan's client work had finished yesterday and the Halloween Orchard Fest was ready and waiting for the town to enjoy that day. Ethan had agreed to meet her there and Tasha was coming too.

Angie was buzzing around with directions and finishing touches for the decorations that had been set out. Fairy lights and paper chains had been strung in the trees, illuminating the way through the orchard to the different stations like a maze, and several tables had been set up running along the side of the shop for the apple pie competitors to leave their pastries. The scene was everything she remembered it being and more.

She shivered lightly under her sweater and decided a warm drink was needed. She hadn't wanted to ruin her outfit with a bulky coat; she'd opted for a short black skirt and thick black tights with hearts on them in pink print and a matching deep-pink oversized sweater. Her only concessions to the cold were her purple fluffy scarf, matching gloves and temporary heating pads in her boots.

She headed along the tree-path to the east until she found the table with warm apple wine and took a tentative sip, surprised to find it was actually good. The sign declared that the drinks had been made with apples from this very orchard, likely part of last year's harvest so that the wine had time to mature.

It was still early, with mostly just parents and their young kids visiting the orchard for the time being, but more people would be arriving soon. The later it got the more magical the fairy lights looked in the trees and the deeper the glow of the pumpkins set along the main path through the orchard, until the ground looked golden.

Competitive apple bobbing had been set up at the front of the orchard, with scores being kept for how many apples were retrieved in thirty seconds. The winner would get to take home the winning apple pie from the competition—though Angie had won it enough times in a row now that people had complained it was rigged. Penny couldn't say for sure one way or another, though she did have her suspicions.

A voice called her name and Penny spotted Tasha by the store in a denim jumpsuit that made her look like she'd stepped out of a cowboy lookbook, the style heightened by the barrel curls in her blonde hair. She waved and took another sip of her apple wine as she joined Tasha.

"Hey, you look cute."

"Thanks! You do too. Ethan's just inside talking to your dad about something." Tasha smirked at the instant concern that filled Penny's face. "Orchard-related, I think."

Penny nodded, like this wasn't worrying in the least. There wasn't some trend she didn't know about that involved getting a girl's father to bless a break-up was there? Like the opposite of giving permission to marry? Had Ethan's dad got to him more than she'd thought at the dinner party? *No, surely Ethan would have said something if that were the case.*

Before Penny's thoughts could spiral too far out of control, Ethan appeared sans Philip and she smiled, letting him fold her into a hug that did more to warm her than the apple wine. She buried her face in the crook of his neck, enjoying the warmth of his skin on her cold face and the softness of the faux-fur collar of his corduroy jacket.

"Hey, you."

"Hi," she breathed. "I missed you." Tasha made a fake gagging sound that had Penny rolling her eyes. "OK, come on. Let's get Tasha a candy apple before she combusts."

Tasha's face did brighten at the mention of the sweet treat and Ethan chuckled as Penny led them through the trees toward the dipping station. It was a delicacy Penny had loved as a kid but that was liable to give her a sugar crash just from smelling the caramel now that she was an adult.

Under the cover of the trees, Ethan slipped his hand into Penny's and leant in close to murmur in her ear, "I missed you too." The husky softness of his voice made heat curl in her core as butterflies took flight in her stomach.

Several kids with harried-looking parents walked past, sticky apples in hand and Tasha sped up a little until the station came into view.

"More power to you," Penny said as Tasha picked

out her apple and placed it firmly on a white stick, ready for submerging. "I think they have a cinnamon-toffee flavor this year," she offered and Tasha practically salivated as she handed the stall vendor some cash and hurried over to the vats for dipping. "I wonder if that's an apple I picked," she mused and Ethan chuckled.

"It's a wonder you got anything done, what with all the climbing of trees and frolicking that went on."

She narrowed her eyes and he laughed, the sound warming the night air as he kissed her frown away.

"I can't believe you outgrew this stuff," Tasha groaned, oblivious, as she licked the excess off her fingers while twirling the apple expertly to prevent any drips as the sugary mixture cooled and hardened. "Do you remember that year your mom asked us to run the stand and you dared me to get inside one of the vats at the end of the festival?"

She laughed at the memory, remembering how long it had taken Tasha to get the toffee out of her hair and eyelashes. "And you did it, too."

They'd been twelve at the time and Ethan had been going through his moody phase where he'd thought it was uncool to hang around with his sister. He'd missed toffee-gate in favor of playing basketball with his guy friends, and had regretted it as soon as they'd told him what he'd missed. Ethan used to have a sweet tooth almost as big as Tasha's.

It was the perfect night for the Orchard Fest: the sky was clear and the ground was mostly dry, it was cool but not freezing, and tucked into Ethan's side Penny wasn't sure when she'd last been this happy. Strange that it had taken coming back to Magnolia Springs to feel like this. She wasn't sure it was just being close to her parents, or even rekindling her romance with Ethan and friendship with Tasha, but sometimes she thought she liked the town itself. The thought was ridiculous.

For the longest time, she couldn't have imagined anything worse than being stuck in Magnolia Springs and becoming a lifer in the little town. But now that she was here ... Well, maybe Ethan had been right. Magnolia Springs wasn't so bad—and not just because it was the place where she'd first met him, but because it was her first home. Maybe her only home, considering how disastrously things had gone in the city; she couldn't say she felt much of a connection to the place. For her, it had been more about what San Fran and being a chef in the city could offer her. Now, as she watched Ethan and Tasha under the light of the twinkling trees, she wasn't sure the city would have ever been enough.

Tasha spotted several friends a little over the way, standing in line for apple wine, and took off to greet them, leaving Penny and Ethan alone. She slid her arms up and linked them behind his head, gazing up at him intently.

A half-smile pulled at his mouth. "What?"

"I'm just glad you gave me a second chance."

He softened. "I've been in love with you for half my

life, Penny Larkin. You did what you thought was right back then and, yeah, it sucked, but you're here now. Things happen for a reason. Who knows where we'd be right now if you hadn't ever left and grown into the person you are now?"

"You sound like your sister," she teased and then she kissed him, tasting his smile, and then leant back to smirk at him. "How much wine have you had?"

"Stone cold sober, baby," he drawled and her laughter made her shoulders shake.

"Are you worried this is moving too fast?" she murmured once her giggles had subsided, a melancholy filling her as they swayed under the stars without any music.

"You mean other than my dad's interrogation about our non-existent children?" His eyes sparkled but he shrugged. "Not really, but we can take this at whatever pace you're happy with. Like I said before, I may not have known it at the time but I've waited ten years to be with you, Penny. So, no, to me this feels long overdue," he whispered, kissing her fiercely. Their mouths collided, a tide of feelings rising up and swallowing them whole as Ethan tugged on her bottom lip and taunted her tongue with his. "I couldn't stop thinking about you this week."

"Oh yeah?" She leant up to kiss him again, slipping her hands beneath his open flannel shirt and tugging him closer. "Do you want to get out of here?" she asked breathlessly as they broke apart.

She had been looking forward to the Orchard Fest for weeks and there was no way she was leaving this early and missing all the fun. But she couldn't deny that right now, with Ethan's hands on her and the warmth of his body under her fingertips, she wished there was somewhere they could slip away to, just for as long as it would take to relieve the desire that was building in her.

Ethan licked his lips, his grin made of pure, smug, male dominance. "That desperate for me, Penny?" His hand slipped from her waist to curve over her ass and she nearly growled.

"Yes."

"Good."

She debated where best to go, her body burning hot with need. They couldn't stay in the orchard, not with impressionable young kids running about liable to get an eyeful. Her parents' place was closest, but it would look a little too obvious what they were sneaking off to do if she took her car.

"How do you feel about horses?"

Ethan's eyes widened but he didn't argue as she took him by the hand and led them out of the trees. The town seemed to be out in full force, standing in line to carve apples or eat pie and vote for their favorite. They slipped through the crowd unnoticed and her heart raced as they crossed the dirt road to the much quieter fields on the other side.

Her hand was clasped tightly in Ethan's as they

moved over the scraggly grass and toward the large brown barn. Colton had stopped using this space years ago when one of his horses had escaped too close to the road, the near-miss frightening everyone half to death. Luckily for Penny and Ethan, it meant one thing: privacy.

It was almost pitch-black inside and Penny left the door slightly ajar to let the bright moonlight illuminate the inside of the barn. Hay was strewn about the floor, an old tack set hung on one wall, and some graffiti had been sprayed onto one of the others. Penny wondered vaguely if this was a new make-out spot in town or if it was too out of the way for the high-school kids.

"Are you sure this—"

Penny halted his question with her mouth, the heat of his lips making her shiver as he walked them back until they leant against a wooden post. Ethan lifted her up so that her legs could wrap around his waist. "Did I mention I missed you?" she mumbled between kisses, gasping when he trailed his mouth down her neck to suck at the pulse point in her throat. "I was worried you'd changed your mind about me."

He pulled back, the moonlight bathing his face and making him glow. "Never." His kiss was tender, his hands gentle as they cupped her cheeks, and she whimpered, wanting more.

"Then why did we wait so long to do this again?"

His laugh rumbled through her as his hands slid into her hair, tilting her head back so he could kiss her deeper. "I was trying to give you space. I didn't want you to feel rushed or that this, *us*, was only about sex."

Her answering laugh was breathless. "If I need space, I'll tell you."

"Do you need space?" The question was a taunt and she answered by tightening her legs around him and grinding against the hardness she could feel through his jeans.

"What I need is for you to put your mouth to good use," she said, crying out when he nipped at her lip, the bite of pain making her breaths come hard. "What I *need* is for you to fuck me, Ethan."

The words were his undoing.

She was glad she'd opted to wear a skirt that day, and Ethan made short work of her tights, ripping through the material with his bare hands and groaning her name when he found her bare underneath.

One finger slicked through her wetness, dipping inside of her briefly before pulling back to stroke her clit. "Have you been this wet for me all night, baby?"

She nodded, barely coherent as his fingers worked her, curling against that spot inside her that made her see stars. A slice of his face was visible in the moonlight, his pupils blown wide with desire as he bit his lip, head tilting back as he swallowed hard.

"You feel so good, Pen."

She reached down to find his belt buckle, tugging at it desperately while he laughed, a dark sound that made her pulse race.

"You want me, do you, baby?" He freed himself and supported her weight with the post behind her. "You want me to fuck you right here where anyone could find us?"

"Yes," she moaned. "*Yes*."

His head notched at her entrance and she could feel the heat of his skin, the way he twitched against her sensitive flesh. He sank in one inch at a time, lifting her chin so she'd meet his eyes. "Look at me, Penny. You're going to take all of me, aren't you?" He glanced down to where they were joined and shuddered. "Fuck. That's hot."

She looked down too and couldn't help the way she clenched around him as she watched her pussy swallow him with ease. When she wriggled, needing more, needing friction, he finally stopped teasing her and began to move.

The post behind them creaked ominously but didn't give as Ethan fucked her against it, her desperate whines muffled in the collar of his shirt.

"Penny," he moaned and she wasn't sure there was any sweeter sound in the world.

She rocked against him, feeling more than a little wild with the cool air sending goosebumps over her skin and the wood of the post behind her hard at her back. His hand dropped between them, stroking her clit in the way that made her desperate for more and Ethan groaned when she tightened around him.

"Again, sweetheart. Eyes on me," he growled, the

words short as he fought for self-control and she lifted her eyes to his, still hazy from her first orgasm as he kissed her breathless. "You can take it, baby. Can't you?"

She nodded, gasping when his pace quickened and the sound of their bodies filled the barn. Moonlight sliced across them and she glanced down to watch as he bottomed out into her over and over again.

He pressed closer, the angle shifting as he supported more of her weight on his hips, and she moaned at the new depth as his hand moved between them once more.

"Now, sweetheart. Come for me, Penny."

She came, gripping him tightly as her muscles clamped down, causing him to teeter over the edge with her, chanting her name, and she couldn't describe how good it felt to be with Ethan Blake.

19

They returned to the orchard to find things still in full swing, and if anyone had noticed their brief absence or Penny's now-bare legs, they didn't say anything.

Tasha waved them over to her spot by the table laden with pies, where small pieces had been stuck onto cocktail sticks for sampling and voting. Penny hurried over, not wanting to miss out. The selection was decent, with ten pies to choose from.

"Do you have a favorite?" Penny mumbled around her fifth skewer.

"I—"

"Of course she does," Penny's mom said before Tasha could answer. "It's number seven, right?"

Tasha glanced at Penny and then at Angie. "I haven't tasted that one yet. They've all been great so far though."

Penny had to admit that it was a good answer. Knowing her mom, she might have just been testing Tasha. The pies were all anonymous, to help make things fair, but Penny was pretty sure she hadn't tasted her mom's pie yet, so when she got to number seven she braced herself before nodding. Angie hadn't been double-bluffing Tasha after all.

Angie watched them eagerly until Penny's dad came over and gently steered her away, murmuring about intimidating the voters.

Small pieces of paper were left next to a large box with a slit cut in the top for the votes to enter and Penny scrawled the number seven on it before dropping it inside. She wasn't even voting for her mom just because she was her mom, though. Penny genuinely thought Angie's pie was the best there. The crust had been flaky and crisp and the filling tasted like fall, if it were a pie filling.

"Earth to Penny," Tasha teased and Penny blinked, a little disconcerted at the sight of the twins peering at her with identical looks of amusement on their faces. "She was totally thinking about pie."

"Yep, that's definitely her pie face," Ethan said, nodding.

Penny rolled her eyes. "Ha. Ha. I do not have a pie face." A familiar figure in the crowd of passersby caught her eye and she decided to change the subject before they could argue with her. "Is that your mom?"

Ethan turned and waved. "Yep. Hey," he said a moment later, kissing his mom on the cheek after she hugged Tasha and, to Penny's surprise, hugged her as well. "Where's Dad?"

Terri glanced at Penny and away. "Oh, he, um, didn't feel like it tonight."

"That's a shame," Penny said, and she meant it. Surely Keith wasn't avoiding her? She didn't want to be the source of any tension in Ethan's family, but if Keith needed some time before he could accept that she and Ethan were a package deal then that was OK. At least, she hoped it would be.

Ethan frowned, having caught on to what his mom wasn't saying, and Penny took his hand in hers, squeezing slightly to show that it was OK. Ethan muttered something she didn't hear and Penny smiled at Terri.

"Have you had any of the apple cider yet? Come on, I'll show you to the stall."

Penny led the way through the grove of trees and only screamed once when a kid jumped out at her from behind a tree dressed up as a zombie. Of course, Ethan and Tasha had thought it was hilarious but Terri had been genuinely sympathetic as she patted Penny on the shoulder.

They grabbed some ciders and wandered through the trees, stopping at a row of stalls that some local vendors had set-up to sell jewelry, cakes, and, strangely, cheese. Tasha had seemed inclined to try her luck for another candy apple. Penny personally thought the threat of a sugar crash was a little too high, and was about to warn her friend, but before she could, Terri had leveled a disapproving stare at her daughter. Unsurprisingly, Tasha had quickly left the idea of another sugary treat in the dust.

By the time they'd finished a full circuit, a voice over a megaphone called that voting for the pie competition would be closing in five minutes.

"OK," Penny said, glancing between the Blakes, "if you haven't voted yet then you probably should. Or my mom might have a meltdown." They shared a look but nodded. "Then, while they're tallying . . ." Her lips curled into a mischievous grin as she wiggled her brows at Tasha and Ethan. "Care to try and beat my record?"

Tasha groaned. "Really? I don't want to get my hair wet."

"A likely story." Penny grinned. "Ethan?"

"You're on."

Her laugh sounded appropriately witchy as she clapped her hands together. "Excellent."

The line for apple bobbing wasn't too long and was mostly kids, seeing as most of the teen girls didn't want to ruin their hair or make-up in the water and the guys were more interested in the girls than apple bobbing. Then there was Penny and Ethan.

They stepped up and Penny smiled at Colton, who had agreed to come and help out. He placed a fresh bucket each in front of her and Ethan and then filled it with floating apples as they lowered themselves to the ground, the grass cold against her knees. Colton got a good deal out of it, as her parents let him take the used apples back to the stables for the horses.

"Are you ready?" he asked, the deep wrinkles in his face thrown into relief by the twinkly lights. "On your marks . . . Get set . . . Go!"

Penny didn't hesitate, just got right in there and immediately closed her mouth around one apple, spitting it out and over the side into the container before diving back in for another and another. It was a shame this wasn't a skill she could actually do anything with, but Penny had always been absurdly good at apple bobbing.

"And, time!"

Penny and Ethan both surfaced, gasping and soaking wet. Ethan's hair was sticking up in odd tufts but his smile was big and bright as he flicked water at her, making her squeal.

Colton looked into each of the containers and grinned when he saw Penny's. "Winner! Congrats, Penny. Here's your prize." He handed her a piece of paper and she pumped the air with her fist as she read it.

"Free pie!" she told Ethan triumphantly. "Oh, and how many apples, Colton?"

"Not quite your record, you're getting slow, girl. But fifteen isn't half bad."

"And Ethan?"

Colton's lips twitched as he looked between them. "Six."

"Well, that's a new record for you," she said, grinning at Ethan and darting away when he shook his wet hair at her like a dog. "Come on, let's go claim my pie and find Tasha and your mom."

To nobody's surprise, Angie's pie had been voted the winner and Penny was particularly delighted because, as the high scorer for apple bobbing, that meant she got to eat it.

"Maybe I'll share it with you," she said coyly to Ethan as she waved her prize pie under his nose. "If you're nice, that is," she added with a wink.

Ethan smiled indulgently down at her, leaning in as he murmured "I can be *very* nice, Penny Larkin. *Especially* for pie," loud enough so that only Penny could hear.

"A man after my own heart, Ethan Blake," she responded jokingly, trying to stop her body from betraying the bolt of heat that his words had sent running through her.

After sharing some funnel cake with Tasha and Ethan and a few more warm ciders with their parents, Penny felt she was more than ready to get warm, and dry, and maybe eat her pie in bed. They congratulated Angie one last time and said goodbye to the others before making their way to the car.

Penny drove them both to Ethan's, since he'd apparently come with Tasha, and was feeling more relaxed than she had in days—and she knew it was only partially due to the relief that the festival was over for now. It was good fun, but exhausting.

The rest was definitely a result of their activity in Colton's barn.

It wasn't a long drive, and the silence was comfortable until Ethan suddenly fell still and looked at her with wide eyes. "Um, Penny?"

"Yeah?"

"We might need to make a stop."

She glanced over at him, surprised. "OK. Where?"

"The drugstore. We didn't use a condom."

She relaxed, re-focusing on the road as she took the turn that led away from the town and toward Ethan's place. "I have an IUD, we should be fine." His breath of relief made her laugh. "Sorry, I should have told you before."

"No, no, it's OK. I'm more relieved for you than anything else, I've heard Plan B can be unpleasant."

She didn't know herself, but she appreciated his concern nonetheless.

They pulled up outside of his house and Ethan jogged around to the driver's side to open her door before she could step out. "What a gentleman," she said, smiling.

"Just wait," he said, voice full of promise that made her body perk up. He noticed and laughed. "You're insatiable."

"Don't leave me to fend for myself for too long next time," she groused and his eyes darkened.

"Noted." Then he reached down and swung her up into his arms, bridal style as he opened the front door with one hand and for some reason it was the hottest thing she'd ever experienced. "How does a bath sound?"

"Like heaven."

The water was hot enough that steam rolled off her skin as she relaxed back against Ethan's soapy chest. It turned out that his bath was big enough for two, a fact she planned to capitalize on frequently.

"I'm worried," she said softly, hating to ruin the moment but needing him to soothe the edges in her mind. "You told me I had till Christmas—"

"Penny," his murmur was exasperated and she looked up at him with her head on his shoulder. "I was exaggerating. You haven't actually been counting the days have you?"

"Well, I thought I had to make a decision before—"

"Are you happy?" His tone was calm and the gentle stroking of his hand against her stomach didn't falter when she nodded. "Do you want to be with me?"

She swallowed but nodded again. "Yes," she said hoarsely and his lips curved up.

"Then that's all I need to know. Whether we stay here or we go elsewhere, we can work that out later. As long as we're together."

"But you have your life here, your family. Your work."

He shrugged. "I'll visit, and I can work from anywhere really." The water sloshed gently as she shifted in his lap and he stilled her with a hand to her hip. "If you're not careful you're going to—" He sighed and looked down and she smothered a laugh when she felt him, hard against her ass. "Never mind."

Her smile faded slowly as the real worry she'd been battling rose up. Unable to push it back down, she voiced it. "If I did want to stay here, in Magnolia Springs, does that make me a failure?"

"Baby." Ethan rubbed her shoulder soothingly. "Not at all. You can only make the best decisions you can with the information you have. Yes, you left before but you achieved what you set out to do. Maybe it wasn't what you hoped it would be, and that's OK."

She nodded, aware that she'd never told him what had happened to bring her back here. "My boss was an ass," she said, and began to explain the toxic work environment, the long hours and how it had left her no time to have any sort of social life. "But really, the tipping point came a few months ago. My boss was being featured in some article and he was being interviewed in the restaurant so we could all hear the conversation as we were doing food prep in the back. Well, the journalist asked about this one dish, a salmon en croute with a beetroot jus, and as soon as I heard her ask about it I couldn't help but listen in. That was *my* dish. I'd worked for months to perfect it and couldn't believe that she was going to specifically mention it in the article. I thought it might finally be the break I'd been waiting for, my chance to actually get some real recognition for my work."

"Oh wow, that would have been amazing, Pen," Ethan's voice was low, but there was definitely a note of pride behind his words.

"Well, yeah, it *would* have been. But my asshole of a boss just flat-out lied. He claimed that it was his dish, that *he'd* worked for months perfecting it, not crediting me at all. When I heard . . . I just lost it."

"Understandable."

"I love to cook. Being here and cooking for myself again has reminded me why I love it so much. But working in that restaurant . . . I don't know. It's not the same." Her breath shuddered out of her as her secret hovered in the air between them. "I just don't want to let anyone down," she whispered and he turned her around so he could kiss her, his mouth a little wet from the water and steam and the smell of lavender bubble bath rising up in the air around them.

"That's not possible," he said, the confidence in his voice bolstering her. "I think you are brilliant. Talented and punctual," he teased, "kind, and a little kooky. But nothing you could choose would let me, or anyone else, down."

Relief flooded her at his words and she knew, instinctively, that he was telling the truth. Penny found herself swept up in a wave of emotion and, before she could stop herself, she rushed on, "You know, ever since I got home, I haven't actually told anyone exactly what happened back in the city. I've been so worried that people would judge me for it, would view me as a failure for quitting, so I've been skirting around the details whenever anyone asked." She paused, gulping down air to stem the tears that were threatening to spill over, before she went on. "But with you it feels different, Ethan. It always has, and I hadn't realized how much I was missing it until you came back into my life. You'll listen to me in a way no one else does, and I just *know* you'll understand. I feel . . . I feel safe with you."

"That's all I want, Pen. *You're* all I want." He spoke softly, his words tender as he brushed a hand down her cheek. Her heart swelled with emotion as she held his gaze, knowing with a surprising certainty that this was something she couldn't let go. *He* was something she couldn't let go.

"Now we just have to convince your dad I'm worth your time," she mused, breaking the tension that had hung between them, and Ethan chuckled.

"I'm a grown man, I don't need my parents' approval."

"But it would be nice to have it," she pointed out and he smiled.

"True. We'll get there. He just wants us to be careful is all."

"Well, my parents love you. Though, if you voted against my mom's pie tonight, she might never forgive you."

They laughed and she kissed him, putting all of the emotion she couldn't quite voice into it. He kissed her back just as firmly, and it quickly became molten, his hands exploring her body in the way he hadn't been able to in the barn, her mouth tasting his skin in nips and licks and kisses before she pulled away, breathless.

"Help me dry off?"

"Absolutely," he said, grinning as he stood up and offered her a hand as they stepped out of the bath together and let the water drain away.

"Ethan?" The words were soft as he wrapped her in a large towel and scrubbed his hands over the fabric to dry her off, making her feel small, precious.

"Yeah?"

"I love you."

His grin was instant and blinding. "I love you too."

He took his time drying her after wrapping another towel around his waist. The soft towel brushed over her skin, chasing stray droplets of water, and he gestured for her to tip her hair over so he could wrap it up in a smaller towel.

When she was upright once more, he took the towel from her and opened a drawer under the sink and pulled out a tub of body butter.

"Can I?"

She nodded, a flush working its way across her skin as he dipped his fingers into the tub and scooped out some cream that smelled faintly like chocolate. It was cool against her skin as he rubbed it into her chest, lifting her breasts to stroke their undersides, and raising each of her arms to massage the cream into her pale skin.

Those long, warm fingers worked their way down her stomach, curving around her hips and over her ass as they moved up her back to work her shoulders. She relaxed into his hands and leant her head back as he stroked her muscles into mush.

His towel dipped as he lowered to the floor and she watched with intrigue, only a little disappointed when it remained in place. More cream slid up across her calves, across the backs of her knees and rounding the inside of her thighs. His gaze was intent, completely focused on the task of taking care of her, and when he'd finished with the cream he stood up and reached back inside the drawer for the deodorant and brush she'd taken to leaving at his place, along with a few other essentials.

She reached for them and hesitated when he drew back and gestured for her to lift her arms, rolling the cool liquid onto her feverish skin and dotting her face with the moisturizer she liked to use, smoothing it on. It was like nothing she'd ever experienced.

When he was done, he took her hand and led her out of the bathroom. The towel around his waist fell to the floor and she bit her lip, admiring the taut muscles of his body and the dimples by his spine as he rummaged in his drawers inside the bedroom for some low-slung pajama bottoms.

That sight alone would be enough to tempt a nun. She followed him over and wrapped her arms around his waist from behind. "Do you really need to get dressed so soon?" she murmured, voice husky, and was pleased when he halted his movements. "I want to make you feel good."

His legs smoothly moved apart until his thighs were spread wide and her nipples hardened against his back when he groaned at the first touch of her hand. The familiar, warm taste of his skin was intoxicating as she pressed kisses to his neck while stroking his cock.

When she stopped, he mumbled a protest until she gently encouraged him to turn around, sank to her knees and looked up at him, following the path of her hand with her eyes as it stroked up toward his abs. His throat worked hard as he swallowed, the strong column begging for her mouth again, but she wanted to take him like this, to feel him let go under her tongue.

The veins in his arms stood out as he battled for control, leaning against the dresser and clasping the wooden top with white knuckles.

"Ethan." Her voice was silky, but he responded instantly, eyes flashing open from where they'd fluttered closed. "Can I taste you?"

His nostrils flared and his jaw worked, like it was an effort not to come from her request alone. "Yes." The words were a guttural growl and she remained where she was, stroking her hands up his damp calves, over his thighs, until her hand reached his dick again. "*Yes*," he repeated when she tightened her grip and lifted up so she could brush her mouth along his head.

"Beautiful," he rasped, unraveling the towel on her head and gathering her wet hair up in his hands, and groaning when her mouth closed around him. "You are"—he gasped—"more than anything I ever could have dreamed up. Better than any fantasy. *Penny.*"

He was close, she knew. His hips moved of their own accord and his eyes had slid nearly closed, watching her through thin slits until she pulled back and pumped him in her hand.

"Tell me what you want, baby," she rasped and his eyes burned when they locked onto hers. "Do you want to come?"

He nodded and then hesitated before shaking his head. "Not yet."

She tasted him one more time, letting her tongue swirl around his head and humming with pleasure when he gasped. "Then what do you want, Ethan?"

"You. Always, you."

The words made her breathing quicken and when he reached down to pull her up from the ground, she moaned into his kiss.

"Come on," he said quietly, leading her over to the bed and gesturing for her to sit. The sheets were cool underneath her as Ethan vanished briefly to hang up the discarded towels in the ensuite before he returned with her brush in hand. "Turn." She obeyed and felt her muscles turn to jelly when the comb touched her head and lightly began working through the tangles.

Once he was satisfied, the brush hit the bedside table with a soft thump and then his mouth was on her, peppering kisses over her shoulders and throat, trailing up to the hollow beneath her jaw until her nipples tightened and she was throbbing with need.

"These have been passed over far too many times," he rasped, brushing one hand over her breast and thumbing the nipple with ease. Her head dropped back to rest on his shoulder and he took the opportunity to squeeze her other breast firmly. He turned her gently, pressing a searing kiss to her lips before trailing more kisses down and over her chest, reaching out to encircle one nipple and sucking it into his mouth when she arched her back. "Let's rectify that."

His head bent over her, one hand cupping her breast and tweaking the nipple while his mouth lavished the other with kisses and bites that had her writhing for him. She'd always been sensitive there, but she didn't think she could come from this alone—

Her eyes widened as Ethan swapped sides, blowing gently on her wet nipple before taking the other in his mouth and when she looked down she could see the evidence of how much she affected him. He leaked at the tip, his own hand moving slowly up and down his shaft and she watched, hypnotized, until with one more flick of his tongue she cried out.

He pulled back to look at her, surprise and heat on his face. "Did you just—"

"I, um. Yep." She was as surprised as him, but what did he expect? It felt good and he looked hotter than anything she'd ever seen before, leaning over her with his muscles flexing and those gorgeous tattoos that trailed up and down his sides. "Can I—" She reached for him, wanting to make sure he felt good too, but he shook his head.

"Not yet. Lay back for me, Pen."

She obeyed, shuffling further onto the bed and letting herself sink into the mattress.

"I love you," he murmured as he lowered himself, his eyes burning into hers as he kissed her knees and spread apart her legs to kiss up her inner thighs. "All of you." He tortured her with light kisses, never applying the pressure she needed or climbing up high enough to the place she desperately wanted him, until she was a whimpering mess.

"I love you," she rasped and he smiled, his mouth tantalizingly close to her mound. "Ethan, touch me?"

"Anything you want, baby." His mouth covered her, like he'd just been waiting for her to ask, the warmth of his tongue making her jolt as he stroked up and flicked at her clit in a tease that made her gasp. "How's that, sweetheart?"

"Good, so good," she mumbled, already lost in sensation as one of his fingers pressed into her gently before withdrawing to instead tease her clit. "More."

He chuckled but did as she said, returning his mouth to her pussy and sucking until her hips lifted from the bed even as her hands wound into his hair, keeping him exactly where he was. The strands were cool against her fingers, the only source of cold as the rest of her burned.

When his fingers curled inside her she groaned, long and loud, and he repeated the motion over and over before swapping his fingers out for his tongue, tasting every inch of her until she was so close to the edge that she could cry.

The flat of his tongue smoothed over her clit and then delved back inside her as one of his hands slid up the bed to cup her breast, the twist of her nipple perfectly timed with the thrust of his tongue until she was coming harder than she ever had before.

"*Ethan!*"

His rumble of pleasure was lost in her pussy and as the aftershocks ran through her, he lined himself up with her entrance. "I just need one more, sweetheart. Can you give me one more?"

She nodded even as she moaned, reaching for him and groaning in satisfaction when he pushed into her with ease.

"Fuck, you're soaked, baby." She clenched at the words and he gasped, sinking in deeper as he pressed her legs back further. "You take me so well, Penny, like you were made for me."

Her hips lifted and the new angle made them both falter and then grasp frantically at the other as Ethan lost control completely, driving into her with an intensity that had her keening and begging for more.

"Penny—"

"Yes. *Yes*."

Ethan cried out and she echoed him as her muscles tightened once more and he throbbed inside of her, slowing as they came. Her body relaxed and her limbs fell to the bed, spent and like jelly, and he laughed shakily, the breathless sound making her smile.

"I love you," she said, equally breathless, and when he crawled up the bed to hover over her she tasted herself on his lips. They lay there like that, entwined, while they caught their breath for a few minutes before he pecked her once more and stood to retrieve a small wash cloth to clean her up. When she could move again, she nipped to the bathroom to pee, and when she emerged he was waiting next to the dresser.

"T-shirt?"

"Please."

He selected one and brought it over to her, slipping it over her head and kissing her when her head popped through the hole in the top and making her giggle.

They made their way out of the bedroom and Penny settled onto the deep sofa in the lounge while Ethan gathered snacks from the kitchen.

"Hey, did you ever hear back from Nicky?" she called and Ethan reappeared with bags of chips and cans of soda.

Ethan shook his head. "I got his assistant, apparently he's been in Japan for the last month to study the food scene there. He's back next week though, so

I'm going to try calling again—if that's still what you want?"

She hesitated. "Can I think about it?"

Warm lips touched her cheek as he settled next to her and then hit a button on a remote to turn on the electric fireplace. "Whatever you want, sweetheart."

You, she thought and when he opened her bag of chips for her before passing it over, she smiled.

20

The clean-up from the Orchard Fest hadn't been the quick job that Penny had been hoping for. Somehow, the entire process felt like it had taken longer than when they'd put it all together. They'd been out for almost two days taking down the lights and decorations, but Penny had managed to sneak a few slices of leftover pie that made the effort worth her while.

Overall, the Halloween Orchard Fest had been a huge success and Angie had been glowing with pride for the past week and a half. Apparently, some people were even calling it the event of the year, though where she'd heard that her mom wouldn't say. Probably from Penny's dad.

The harvest was, thankfully, finished now—Penny wasn't sure her muscles could've taken any more strenuous days picking now it was getting properly cold. But even after they'd finished tidying up the orchard, Penny was still keeping busy by helping her parents. She'd done multiple trips across the way to drop apples off to Colton at the stables, although this wasn't really much of a hardship when he let her pet the horses. There was also a ton of inventory that needed to be inspected, so she'd been helping her dad with that for most of the week.

It had felt like a treat to book into the yoga class that Saturday after running all over the orchard trying to help her parents, dragging Tasha along with her and her mom. It was funny how much more enjoyable yoga was when she wasn't hungover. This time, she made it through the whole class without even coming close to puking, making it a firm success as far as she was concerned. Although, it did help that she'd been too busy that week to have indulged in any margaritas.

"This was actually really fun," Tasha said, inhaling a deep breath as they stepped out into the fresh air and the wind cooled their sweaty faces.

"They do the class every week," Penny offered and Tasha grimaced.

"I'll think about it."

Penny laughed and linked her arms through her mom's and Tasha's. "This is the best part of yoga in my opinion."

"Going to the bakery when you're done?" her mom mused and Penny nodded.

"Exactly."

"Oh, hey. I need to nip into Threads real quick, is that OK?"

Penny shrugged and Tasha led them in the direction of the store they'd been in a few weeks before to pick out an outfit for the dinner party.

Opting to steer clear of the temptation of new clothes that she couldn't really afford, Penny stayed outside the store while her mom went in with Tasha. Her eyes slid to the side and landed on the empty restaurant space that was still vacant next door. It was a shame nobody had claimed it yet. The space looked like it could be really lovely, though it could use a lick of paint on the outside. She wandered over, peering through the window at the interior. Were those hardwood floors? It was hard to tell, but they were in good condition if they were authentic.

Maybe it was just that she'd been talking to Ethan more and more lately about what they might do next, or where they'd go, but it felt like Penny was seeing opportunities everywhere she went. The grocery store had a sign in the window that they were looking for full-time help, and the bakery was looking for someone to man their cash register ... There were more possibilities in Magnolia Springs than she'd let herself consider before. She just couldn't decide what she wanted—beyond Ethan, that was. The idea of working her way up again in another restaurant or starting from the bottom at the bakery didn't appeal, but she wasn't ready to give up on working with food just yet.

But a restaurant like this, in the heart of the town, would be different to what she'd had in San Fran. There, you had to fight for everything you had. You wanted to help develop a new recipe for the menu? Be prepared to put in hours of work that may lead to nothing. And there was always a part of the restaurant scene in the city that felt cold. The place she'd worked at wasn't the kind of place that had regulars, there was never any sense of community or family. No warmth. But if she had her own place . . . Well, it could be whatever she wanted it to be. She knew she had the skill in the kitchen, at least, and it would give her something beyond Ethan and her family to stay in Magnolia Springs for.

Thoughts swirling, lost in imaginary floor plans and menu concepts, she didn't hear her mom and Tasha exit the store.

"Penny?"

Startled, she looked over her shoulder and found her mom and Tasha waiting.

"You ready?" Angie asked and Penny nodded. Tasha was looking at her with a strange twinkle in her eye, but Penny opted to ignore it for now.

"Cake time!" Penny announced brightly. She was always ready for cake.

When she got home later that day, she found her dad at the kitchen table, newspaper in hand. The sight was so familiar that she chuckled.

"Hi, pumpkin," he said without glancing up. "How are you? I feel like I haven't seen you much these days."

It was true, she'd been spending a lot of time at Ethan's or at the orchard, helping with odd jobs like mowing the grass and cataloging the harvest.

"Anyone might think you missed me," she teased and he eyed her over the top of his newspaper.

"Whatever helps you sleep better, kiddo."

She snorted and set about making tea, filling their kettle and placing it on the stovetop to heat the water through. "I'm making tea, do you want one?"

"Earl Grey, please."

"Way to push the boat out."

"Oh, it's going to be wild later. This is, as the youth say, going to be a 'turnt' Saturday night." He did air quotes around the word 'turnt' and Penny couldn't stifle her groan quick enough.

"I'm begging you to never say that again."

"Deal."

The kettle whistled and Penny poured the steaming water into two mugs, steeping the leaves for a minute or two before adding a spoonful of honey to her chamomile tea and some milk to her dad's.

"Here you go."

She sat down opposite him and, after a moment, he put the paper down and looked at her. "Come on then, out with it."

"What?"

He smiled, making his eyes crinkle at the corners. "You think your old man doesn't know when his baby girl needs advice?"

She sagged in her seat, the frown she'd been holding back forming on her face. "It's stupid."

"Try me."

She fiddled with the handle on her mug, glancing up at her dad and then away again before sighing. "I'm thinking about staying."

"Here?"

"Yes. Well, here as in Magnolia Springs. Not necessarily here as in your house."

"Well," he said, reaching for his tea, "I'm relieved to hear that."

"I know, you guys need your space."

"No, no—Well, yes. But I meant that you're thinking of moving back to town. You just seem a lot more . . ."

"What?"

"Alive," he finished, like he'd been looking for the right word. "I don't know if it was the city or that job, but you always seemed drained when we visited. But here . . . You have light in your eyes again, pumpkin."

"So you don't think I'd be a failure for moving away only to come back again?"

"Absolutely not. You did what you thought was best for you at the time, and you have to do that again now."

She nodded, blowing on her hot drink. "That's what Ethan said too."

"I knew I liked him," Philip said gruffly and she laughed. "What do you want to do here in town though? I don't want you to give up on your dreams. If being a chef is important to you—"

"It is," she rushed to say and then cleared her throat,

tentatively giving voice to the thought that had been tugging at her all day. "I was actually thinking about opening something."

"Like a restaurant?"

"Yeah. Is that too ridiculous? I know I don't have a ton of experience running one but—"

"If it's what you're passionate about, then you can learn, honey. Didn't you say Ethan had a friend who was a chef? Maybe they could give you some pointers."

Penny sipped her tea, thinking over his words. "That," she said slowly, "might be a brilliant idea, Dad. Thank you." Ethan *had* said Nicky would be back from his travels this week.

He lifted an imaginary hat as he gulped his tea. "Just doing my duty, little lady."

They drank their tea in companionable silence as Penny thought about that empty storefront, excitement buzzing inside her to the point that she thought she might start vibrating.

"I think there's something I need to do."

Philip raised his hand, attention already back on his paper. "Bye, pumpkin."

She kissed him on the cheek and grabbed her keys and cell phone, shutting the front door behind her as she dialed. "Tash? Hey, I was wondering if you might help me with something."

By the time Penny parked up in town and walked over to Main Street, Tasha was already waiting outside of the empty store with an unexpected yet familiar figure next to her.

"Uh, hi, Mr. Blake," she said, confused, as she raised a brow at Tasha. She hadn't seen Keith since the dinner party a few weeks ago and as far as she knew, his opinion of her—something close to being a vapid heartbreaker who might ruin his son's life at any moment—hadn't changed.

"He's the realtor for the space," Tasha explained, clearly sensing Penny's hesitation. "And as you're practically family, I'm sure he can get you a good deal."

Penny flushed, worry rising inside her as she expected Keith to refute Tasha's words. She waited, expecting him to make fun of her for thinking this was an option for her, or maybe to tactfully try to persuade her that this wasn't the right course of action. To her surprise, though, he stayed silent as he turned and unlocked the store, beckoning them inside. As he looked at Penny again, she thought he saw something soften in his face, but couldn't be sure.

"Let's let her see the space first, Tash," he said. For once, Penny could see the resemblance between Keith Blake and his son, the approval in his warm eyes at once familiar and not. "It has a fully functional kitchen in the back, the flooring is real hardwood—with a polish, and some fresh paint on the walls, this place could look great."

Penny walked around the space while Tasha and her dad spoke softly. The ceilings were low enough that the space could feel cozy, but the windows were big enough that she could have a fresh ambience if she chose. She followed the line of the back wall and pushed through the swinging double doors into the industrial-looking kitchen. All the surfaces looked like stainless steel, a sea of shiny metal reflecting her warped reflection. It all looked relatively new, aside from a large burn mark on the tiled floor near the six-ring stove. There was a walk-in freezer and another room off to the left that looked like a staff break-room.

It was perfect.

But there was still a voice of doubt in the back of Penny's mind. Was she good enough to do the space justice? She really needed to talk to someone with experience.

"What do you think?" Tasha and her dad were still standing in the same place Penny had left them as she came back through the double doors.

"It's incredible," she admitted. "Better than I ever could have imagined, to be honest."

"Oh, Pen, this is so exciting! Do you think you're going to go for it?"

Penny wanted to say yes, willed herself to, but the doubt in her mind held her back. "I don't know, Tasha. I mean, I've never done this before. Am I stupid for thinking I can do this?"

Penny jolted when Keith's hand dropped down onto her shoulder. She'd been speaking quietly to Tasha and hadn't realized he'd been listening too.

"Can you imagine if nobody ever did anything

unless they'd done it before? Nobody would get anywhere. Imagine if we could have put man on the moon and instead decided, *Nah, we haven't done that before; better not.* You won't know whether you can do it unless you try, Penny."

Tasha blinked at her dad, apparently lost for words until she shook her head and looked Penny in the eyes. "As strange as this sounds, I think he has a point. When you left town all those years ago, it was new and scary but you also knew it was exactly what you wanted to do, and you did. So this is another big step for you, and of course you don't have all the answers right now, but that's what learning and research is for. If you think this is what you want, then I say go for it."

"Yeah?" Penny's voice was small but she was bolstered by the confident nods the Blakes offered. "OK. OK, let's do this." Tasha whooped and Keith grinned, the emotion transforming his face so that Penny once again saw a glimpse of his kids in him. "Wait, wait. Budget-withstanding, then we'll do this," she amended and Tasha snorted.

"This is Magnolia Springs, I can't imagine the real estate is that pricey."

Mr. Blake nodded. "You're making a good decision, Penny. Why don't you come back to my office and we can discuss it properly?"

She swallowed hard at the unexpected praise and flicked her eyes to Tasha who gave her a tiny nod before Penny agreed. "Sounds good."

They shuffled out of the door and Penny glanced back several times, already missing the space. Maybe Tasha and Ethan were right—maybe everything did happen for a reason.

Penny couldn't wait to tell Ethan about what she'd been planning, but had decided to keep it under wraps until the restaurant was ready to show him. She wanted the news that she was staying to be a complete surprise. She'd gone back to Mr. Blake's office to discuss the details of the lease and the price was almost *exactly* what she had remaining in her savings. She'd taken the plunge and, subject to credit checks and other legal stuff she was letting Mr. Blake handle, she would hopefully pick up the keys later that week.

It felt like it was meant to be.

But she hadn't forgotten about her talk with her dad, and his suggestion to talk to Nicky had been a great idea. Hopefully Nicky wouldn't think she was an idiot for opening up her own place without really knowing what she was doing, or even what kind of food or mood she wanted for the space.

She and Ethan had just finished dinner at Carter & Sons and were in the middle of looking at desserts when she remembered to ask him for Nicky's number.

The menu crumpled, denting under Ethan's grip as he jolted, looking up at Penny suddenly, and a plate slipped from the table to shatter on the floor. Ethan blinked at it for a second before holding up a hand so she didn't move. "Sorry, I just hadn't thought . . . You just surprised me, that's all." The waiter arrived with a broom and Ethan apologized again.

She bit her lip. "Did I say something wrong?" They were supposed to be there celebrating their one-month anniversary, it was the only semi-fancy restaurant in Magnolia Springs, located in the new town. She'd made the effort to do her make-up and had put on a wine-red sweater dress with a cowl neck that clung to her curves. Ethan looked delectable in his gray-wash jeans and navy pullover on top of a gray shirt.

"No," he said slowly. "I just wasn't expecting you to want his number any more. And I kind of thought we'd talk it over before you try out for a job in another state." Against the deep burgundy of the paneled walls behind him, he looked paler than usual, the greenery in the planter atop their booth's walls the only relief against the moody color scheme.

"Of course we would," she said, brows drawing together as she tried to decipher his tone. "I need to talk to him, that's all." She wanted the restaurant space to be a surprise, but maybe that was a mistake.

He looked up at her, eyes shadowed as he lowered the menu onto the table to look into her face more fully. "Are you being honest right now?"

She recoiled. "Why would I lie?"

"I don't know. Why would you run away without saying goodbye the first time? We've been talking about building a future together, Penny. Maybe even here, in Magnolia Springs, and now you want Nicky's number? Maybe my dad was right." There was no escape from the hurt in his eyes or the pain barely held back as he looked at her. His shoulders slumped at her shocked silence and the pain on his face stabbed her like a physical wound. "I'm sorry. I just don't want to lose you again."

"You won't." The words were soft and she reached for his hand slowly, like a spooked animal. "*I'm* sorry, Ethan. The way I left everything back then was wrong and I understand why you're worried now. But I'm not going anywhere, I promise. I just need to talk to Nicky, for advice."

"I want to believe you, Pen, I just don't know if I can trust what you're saying." His face shuttered, jaw tensing so hard she worried for his teeth. "You've made promises before, Penny."

"I know but—Ethan, *please* believe me, I'm not—"

"Oh, hi, guys!" The cheery chirp couldn't have come at a worse moment. Penny gritted her teeth and forced a smile on her face as she looked up at Shelby and her date, knowing Shelby was analyzing the tension at Penny's table.

"Hi, Shel." Ethan's voice was flat and Penny didn't miss the look of triumph in Shelby's eyes. "This isn't a great time."

Shelby pouted with fake sympathy. "Aw, trouble in paradise already? I hate to say I told you so, but . . ."

"He said we're *busy*," Penny snapped. "Back off."

Ethan frowned, shooting Penny a look that had her irritation rising. Was he seriously going to defend Shelby right now?

"Looks like our table's ready!" Shelby leant down and kissed Ethan's cheek, holding eye contact with Penny as she did so and making Penny seethe at the crimson mark left in the place where her mouth had been. Ethan barely reacted. "See you around, doll. You know where I'll be."

The table was silent after Shelby's departure and Penny handed Ethan a napkin for his cheek as he pulled some notes out of his wallet to cover the bill, dessert forgotten.

"I'll send you Nicky's contact info. I think you should stay at your place tonight, I just—I need some space. Some time to think. OK?"

A prickle began in her eyes, welling up from her throat, and she nodded, glancing away so he wouldn't see the dampness of her eyes. She couldn't blame him for feeling this way, for not being entirely sure he could trust her. If he needed space, she could give him that. But she wasn't going anywhere, and she was going to prove it.

21

The following evening, Penny lay in her bed alone for the second night in a row. Up until he'd asked for space, she'd spent almost every night at Ethan's since the Halloween Orchard Fest. Now her bed felt too small and too empty at the same time. Her sheets were freshly laundered, the familiar smell of her mom's detergent making her well up before she firmly brushed the tears away.

She'd told her parents about her plan to stay in Magnolia Springs and open the restaurant that morning over breakfast. Just like Tasha, they'd been delighted that she was staying in town (she was sure that she'd seen a tear in her dad's eye) and since then they hadn't stopped telling her how proud they were that she was trying something new at every chance they got. She'd been so touched by how immediately supportive they were, and she loved them all the more for it. There was even a small part of her that felt relieved, knowing that they were going to be close by again.

When they'd asked if she'd told Ethan her plans yet, Penny had awkwardly explained their miscommunication and how he'd asked for some space. Her parents had clearly been able to hear the hurt behind her words, because Angie had offered her a consoling smile while Philip had gently patted her hand, reassuring her that these things always had a way of working themselves out.

To try and stay busy, she'd already been hard at work drafting potential menus with her mom's input which was exciting but also incredibly draining. All the decisions fell to her, something she'd never experienced in her time working in San Francisco. It was a little overwhelming but also empowering in a way, and more than anything she was really feeling the emphasis on the learning element of the process. More than anything, though, it made her think of Ethan. She wanted to ask his opinion of her meal choices, maybe to cook some of the dishes for him to get his feedback, but she knew that no matter how much she wanted to, she couldn't. He'd asked for space and she was trying to give him that.

She rolled onto her stomach, burying her head into the pillow as she resisted the urge to reach for her phone to see if Ethan had called or texted. She knew he wouldn't have in the five minutes since she'd last checked, but the hope brought her some comfort at least.

She still hadn't heard anything from him since he'd sent her Nicky's contact info the previous evening. It had only been a day without him, but his sudden absence from her life was painful, overshadowed by how amazing the last month with him had been. She was doing her best not to torture herself by worrying that keeping her plans a secret was actually going to drive them apart. Deep down, she knew she was doing the right thing. And even if Ethan decided he wanted their break to be permanent, she would still be staying in Magnolia Springs. At some point over the last couple of months the town had become *home* to her again. When she'd first got back, the ease she felt in the community had surprised her, but now she was going to be an active part of it with her restaurant. She still couldn't really believe it. Maybe she'd even have her own stall at next year's annual bonfire.

The buzz of her phone broke her chain of thought, immediately making her heart beat faster. *Ethan?*

Her heart dropped when she didn't find his name on her screen, but the sting was eased by the message she did find.

Nicky: Hey, Penny! Any friend of Ethan's is a friend of mine. I can be in town tomorrow afternoon if that works for you?

She read the message three times before it sank in. When she'd reached out to Nicky asking for his help, she'd only been expecting some advice, maybe a phone call at most. But he wanted to actually come here? Penny's mind immediately went into overdrive, worrying that she had nothing to show Nicky and he'd tell her she was too inexperienced to be running her own place. But she took a deep breath to calm herself, stopping the stream of worries as she took a moment to think.

The beginnings of a plan formed in her mind as she typed out an enthusiastic reply to Nicky and then headed to the internet to look up Ethan's company website and hit the button for *inquire*.

Nicky was coming to Magnolia Springs. She wouldn't be alone to make all of these big decisions. And, most importantly, she was going to fight to keep her man.

Penny fell asleep with a smile on her face.

Nicolo didn't look like she expected. She'd seen his face on his socials, but he was a lot taller than she'd thought he'd be for some reason. As soon as he spotted her inside Coffee Affair, his face lit up with a smile that was nearly as wide as his entire face.

She stood and held out a hand that was crushed as he swept her into an embrace.

"Sorry." He laughed. "I'm a hugger. Plus I've heard a lot about you from Ethan. He basically wouldn't shut up about you when we were at college."

"You have?" The idea struck her dumb as she fumbled for the seat behind her and Nicky sat down opposite her. Hearing Ethan's name and knowing he'd talked about her, even years ago, soothed something inside of her. This space and time apart was temporary, she knew that. She was determined to respect Ethan's wishes, even if she had to fight the urge to text him at least five times a day. But she could give him another week. Especially if it meant they'd have forever.

"Of course. The famous one who got away."

She could feel her cheeks reddening and hid her face behind her coffee cup. "Right."

"So you're opening a space here? Cafe? Restaurant? Bistro?"

"I, um . . ." She stuttered and bit her lip. "I'm still deciding. That's part of what I wanted your help with."

He nodded. "Well, it's really something only you can decide. What do you like to cook? What do you like to see in other food establishments? What feeling do you want to capture in your own place? Those will be your starting points." He held up a hand, chuckling at the wide-eyed look she was wearing. "You don't need to have answers to those questions right now. They're just helpful things to keep in mind as you begin the process. Do you want to show me the space?"

"Oh, yeah, of course, it's not too far from here. Just to warn you, though, it's nowhere near finished, I just got the keys this morning." Was she rambling? She stood too quickly and got an immediate head rush that made her sway even as she waved off Nicky's concern. "I'm fine. Sorry, just stressed." Penny headed for the door, leading Nicky out of the coffee shop and onto the sidewalk that led to her restaurant.

Her restaurant. The idea was still too immense for her to process.

"Is Ethan meeting us there?" Nicky asked as they walked alongside one another.

Penny couldn't ignore the pang in her chest at the mention of Ethan, at the fact that he was still hurting after their conversation a few days ago. But she pushed through it, certain that he would understand when he saw what she had been planning. "No, I'm hoping to surprise him at the end of the week."

To her relief, Nicky's eyes lit up. "I *love* surprises." When Penny halted in front of the large window, Nicky ran an assessing eye over the outside of the restaurant. She found herself waiting nervously for his judgment of the storefront. "Well, this looks promising. Let's open her up and see what we're working with."

It was Wednesday afternoon as Penny rushed back to the restaurant—*her* restaurant, she reminded herself—clutching three coffees in her hands. The weather had turned foul in the last couple of days, but Penny had been so busy cooped up in the store trying to get it ready for Friday that she'd hardly noticed. That was, until she'd stepped outside twenty minutes ago and been immediately drenched by the sheets of rain that were falling, while an icy wind had chased her all the way to, and back from, Coffee Affair.

The door slammed behind her, caught by a gust, and Tasha's head swiveled round in surprise from where she'd been on her hands and knees in the middle of the floor. If Penny wasn't mistaken, she was buffing the same patch of hardwood she'd been working on when Penny had left.

"Either you're really set on making that one spot shine, Tash, or you've been on your phone for the last twenty minutes while I was braving the weather, and you're now trying to play it off," Penny teased, as Tasha stood somewhat stiffly and gratefully accepted the cappuccino that Penny was offering her.

Tasha placed her hand over her chest in mock outrage. "Penny Larkin, I'm here helping you tidy this place up so you can win my brother back *out of the goodness of my own heart*, and all you can do is accuse me of slacking off?" Tasha retorted, her eyes sparkling with humor. "Nice to know you're appreciative of all my hard work."

The two of them dissolved into giggles as Nicky appeared at the back of the store, wiping his hands on his jeans.

"Oh, Penny, you superstar!" he said, beaming as he took his coffee from her. He took a long sip, before saying "I think I've finally managed to figure out what was wrong with that burner on the stove that wasn't working, but it might take me a bit longer to fix it. These are chef's hands, not engineer's, after all."

"Thank you so much, Nicky, I honestly wouldn't even know where to start with all of the electrics back there."

Penny had hardly known Nicky for four days and yet she could already tell that they were going to stay close for a long time after he headed back to New York. His can-do attitude had been invaluable as the three of them had worked tirelessly to clean the restaurant space up enough to make it presentable.

"No problem at all, Pen. Although, you might want to get a mop or broom under there when you get a chance." Penny looked up at Nicky, noticing a few bits of dust and dirt had caught in his hair. "Whoever was responsible for cleaning back there yesterday was clearly doing a rush job."

Both Penny and Nicky's eyes fell to Tasha, who held up her hands defensively. "Hey, don't look at me! These are librarian's hands, not cleaner's hands," she retorted, and all three of them broke into laughter again before falling silent, savoring their coffees and the break from their hard work. The rain pattering against the windows was the only sound as Penny took in the space.

It had already undergone a huge transformation since they'd started work on Sunday. Pretty much all of the dust that had coated every surface had been swept away, the cobwebs had been vacuumed up, the floors had been scrubbed and were now being polished, and every counter in the kitchen had been wiped down at least three times over. Now all they had left to do was give the walls a preliminary coat of paint, fix the burner in the back and—the one job that Penny was dreading the most—clean the industrial-sized oven that had clearly been left untouched when the old tenants had moved out. But even with a fairly long list left to check off by Friday morning, Penny was feeling hopeful.

The only thing she wasn't sure about was Ethan. The physical work of tidying up the restaurant had been effective at taking her mind off of him, but whenever she stopped for more than five minutes he quickly became her every other thought again. She missed him, the richness of his laugh and the gentle warmth that his eyes held as he looked at her, the safety she felt whenever he was around.

Penny honestly couldn't tell whether he'd appreciate the gesture and understand why she'd kept the whole thing a secret anymore. As his silence had stretched on she'd become more and more uncertain of her decision to try to surprise him with her plans. What if she'd taken it all a step too far? What if he felt like he really couldn't trust her again, after this? They were the same questions she'd been torturing herself with for days, but she was still no closer to answering them. As she looked around her, quietly sipping her pumpkin spice latte, she couldn't ignore the worry that gnawed at her insides.

"Hey, it'll be OK," Tasha said, gently resting her free hand on Penny's arm, having obviously noticed the concern on Penny's face. "If I know one thing about my brother, it's that he loves you more than life itself, Pen. There's no way he's going to want to end things, especially once he sees how much work you've put in here."

"Yeah, Tasha's right, Penny. Ethan would have to be an absolute idiot to not want to stay with you after he realizes why you were asking for my number," Nicky chimed in, and Penny was filled with a wave of gratitude for the two of them.

"And if he still wants to end things, I'll drive right over to his place and make it *abundantly* clear that he's making the wrong decision," Tasha added, grinning at Penny as she jokingly nudged her with her shoulder.

Penny couldn't help but chuckle at Tasha's threat, only half-certain her best friend was joking. "I just hope you guys are right."

22

By Friday morning, Penny was exhausted. It had been a long week and had taken more work than she'd expected to get everything in the store ready. She'd been there until one o'clock that morning with Nicky and Tasha painting the final wall so that the space would be finished in time.

Penny had spent much of Thursday convincing Tasha that she didn't need to chew her brother out for asking to take some space. He was entitled to whatever time he needed. She just hoped this would be enough to show him that she was serious, that she'd meant the things she'd said when they were talking about their future. Actions spoke louder than words, plus she was *literally* putting her money where her mouth was. And even if she could do this without him, she didn't want to.

As she stood in the kitchen at the back of the store, Penny still couldn't quite believe that this space was *hers*. But the keys were now securely on her chain and she was getting used to the idea, slowly but surely. It wasn't perfect, or even close to being ready, but it held hope. Possibility. She could only hope that Ethan saw it too.

"Hello?" a familiar voice called.

Penny's heart leapt at the sound, already feeling a bolt of electricity sparking through her at his proximity. She hadn't seen Ethan in the past week and his absence had been painful, like a bruise that was being pressed every time he crossed her mind. But she'd stayed firm, giving him the space he'd wanted. She took a deep breath to calm her jangling nerves, glancing at her reflection in the now-sparkling oven door. She'd gone for simple but cute today, an oversized rust-orange sweater and blue jeans hugging her curves, her trusty knock-off Uggs keeping her feet warm in the icy weather. She smoothed down her hair once more before she stepped out from the kitchen in the back.

"Hey."

Ethan looked at her, eyes widening. "Pen, what are you doing here? I'm supposed to be meeting a client." The words were soft, surprised, and she took that as a good sign as she stepped forward and nodded.

"Yep, that was me."

"You faked an inquiry to see me?"

She shook her head. "No." Her heart was thudding in her chest, anxious about how he'd respond to her next words. "I'm the client and this is the space." She gestured around as she said it and watched nervously as he took a second to respond, looking about in slight confusion until she saw the moment it clicked for him. The parting of his lips, the hope lighting up his eyes.

"This is your place?"

"Yep. Well, I mean, I'm renting it. Your dad actually helped me with the lease. Turns out Keith doesn't think I'm all bad anymore. But yes, technically it's mine. And I needed someone really good to help me design what it's going to look like—you know I'm not hugely visual."

He laughed and the sound echoed, bouncing off of the walls. "You're really—You want to stay?"

"I do. I'm sorry about what happened before when we were out at dinner. I definitely could've handled it better but I'd thought it would be a nice surprise for you. I hope you can forgive me?" She squeezed her hands together as she moved closer to him, savoring the fact that he was there, in front of her again. "So what do you think? Are you in?"

One second, she was a few steps away and the next she was in his arms as he picked her up and twirled her around. The feeling of him pressed into her, the warmth radiating from him and his familiar sandalwood scent were enough to make Penny feel giddy with happiness. She had missed him, more than she could've possibly realized.

"Of course I'm in! I'm so proud of you, Pen! This is incredible, I can't bel—Wait, hang on, if you're staying, why did you need Nicky's number?"

She grinned. "I just needed some advice from someone

with experience. He's waiting at Coffee Affair with Tasha right now. They helped me clear the space out this week, and he's going to keep helping me as I figure out my vision for what I want the restaurant to be."

There was wonder on his face as he set her down and rested his forehead against hers. "You never cease to surprise me."

"I hope that's a good thing."

"It is." He grinned again, and then in an almost awed whisper he murmured, "You're staying."

"Yes."

"You want me."

"Definitely."

"I love you."

She smiled, reaching up and pressing a soft kiss to his mouth. "I love you. Ready to make it official?"

His eyes flew wide again and she laughed, leading him over to the lone table at the back and handing him a small knife. The wood was in good condition, the only mark on its surface the freshly carved heart with her initials inside, waiting for the other half to be completed.

He took the knife from her and leant down to add his next to hers. She couldn't mask the smile spreading across her face.

"This way we'll always have a table reserved just for us," she murmured, moving to stand next to him so they could look down together at this addition.

PL + EB ∞

EPILOGUE

Penny squealed as water splattered onto her from the fountain's streams splashing into the pool and Ethan chuckled, tucking her into his side as they sipped their coffees.

The restaurant renovations had finally finished that week and she was hopeful that they would be able to open in the new year. In the end, she'd settled on a relaxed, family vibe for the venue and Ethan had been crucial in designing the space to be everything she'd imagined and more.

Magnolia Springs had embraced the holiday cheer with the annual Christmas market, which would be dismantled in the last week of December. Penny wanted to get her fill of the brown huts, dusted with real snow, for as long as she could. Once the restaurant opened, she would probably be busy for the foreseeable future. That was the hope, anyway.

It felt a lot longer than three months ago that she'd sat in this very same spot by herself and made her first wish in the fountain, but now here she was, back again with Ethan at her side. She turned a penny over in her free hand as she watched the streams of water catching the winter sun.

"What are you going to wish for?" There was a smile in his voice and she sipped her coffee, considering.

"Well, I can't tell you," she teased. "Otherwise it won't come true."

He laughed, the sound warm and making her heart swell as Ethan palmed his own coin. "I think I'll join you."

"OK. One, two, three!"

Their coins hit the water at the same time and Penny screwed her eyes shut as she concentrated on her wish: *Please let the restaurant be a success.*

When she opened her eyes everything looked the same, but a sense of peace had come over her, settling in her bones as she let the sound of the running water soothe her.

"Penny."

She blinked and looked to her left at Ethan. "Sorry, did you say something?"

"Will you move in with me?"

A smile broke out across her face and she didn't hesitate, throwing her arms around his neck and kissing him fiercely. "Yes. Absolutely." She practically lived at his place anyway at this point, something which Angie *loved* to point out with a twinkle in her eye at every opportunity.

Ethan grinned, kissing her thoroughly until a passerby whistled. Ethan's cheeks were pink when they separated and he smirked. "I guess wishes do come true."

Acknowledgements

Thank you so much for reading *Cozy Girl Fall*! Writing this book was such a whirlwind but I had the best time with Penny and Ethan and I can't wait for you guys to explore more of Magnolia Springs soon.

I'm beyond grateful to the team at Transworld who put this book together with such speed and ease, it was incredible to be a part of the process. Mega thanks to Cara, my editor, for her enthusiasm and encouragement while I was writing, as well as Judith, Jennifer, and Holly for their expertise and support.

This book would never have become what it is without my wonderful agent, Elizabeth, and the wider Northbank team who have supported me and this project from the get-go, thank you all.

My final shout-out is to my own high-school sweetheart, Connor, who supports me endlessly, and our two kitties, Socks and Biscuit, who kept me company while I wrote this book.

Lastly, thank you to all the cozy girls out there who picked up this book – I hope your blankets are extra soft and your bed is super cozy, snuggle up and watch the leaves fall.

Willow Hurst is an author of swoony romance books with plenty of heat and heart. When she's not cuddling her cats or writing, she enjoys walking in the rain while she drinks her coffee. Willow also writes steamy romance books under the name Jade Church.

Magnolia Springs is waiting for you in . . .

CLEAN GIRL SPRING

You never know where love might bloom . . .

April Jones needs a fresh start. Leaving behind a broken engagement and a dead-end job in New York, she returns to her hometown of Magnolia Springs with a plan: she'll renovate her late father's struggling dive bar and turn it into a flower shop, just like she and her mom always dreamed of.

As spring flowers start to bloom, April throws herself into the project, relishing the slower pace of life and finally beginning to mend her broken heart. But then her childhood rival Luke, now a successful real-estate developer, shows up with plans to tear down half of Main Street, including April's beloved flower shop.

April can't believe that the fate of her business now rests in Luke's annoyingly attractive hands, but she isn't ready to give up on her fresh start just yet. If only April could find a way to make Luke set aside his hard hat and follow his heart . . .

Coming spring 2026!

On a station platform, with nothing to read,
and a four-hour train journey stretching ahead of him...

That's where the story began for Penguin founder Allen Lane.
With only 'shabby reprints of shoddy novels' on offer,
he resolved to make better books for readers everywhere.

By the time his train pulled into London, the idea was formed.
He would bring the best writing, in stylish and affordable
formats, to everyone. His books would be sold in bookstores,
stationers and tobacconists, for no more than the price
of a ten-pack of cigarettes.

And on every book would be a Penguin, a bird with a certain
'dignified flippancy', and a friendly invitation to anyone who
wished to spend their time reading.

In 1935, the first ten Penguin paperbacks were published.
Just a year later, three million Penguins had made their
way onto our shelves.

Reading was changed forever.

—

A lot has changed since 1935, including Penguin, but in the
most important ways we're still the same. We still believe that
books and reading are for everyone. And we still believe that
whether you're seeking an afternoon's escape, a vigorous debate
or a soothing bedtime story, all possibilities open with a book.

Whoever you are, whatever you're looking for,
you can find it with Penguin.